Home Away From Home
Book 2: Abbott Island Series

Penny Frost McGinnis

M✝ Zion Ridge Press
Books Off the Beaten Path

Mt Zion Ridge Press LLC
295 Gum Springs Rd, NW
Georgetown, TN 37366
https://www.mtzionridgepress.com

ISBN 13: 978-1-955838-56-6
Published in the United States of America
Publication Date: April 1, 2023
Copyright: © Penny McGinnis 2023

Editor-In-Chief: Michelle Levigne
Executive Editor: Tamera Lynn Kraft

Cover art design by Tamera Lynn Kraft
Cover Art Copyright by Mt Zion Ridge Press LLC © 2023

Dedication

To my parents who encouraged me to be a reader and gave me opportunities to create.

To my sister, Bobbie, and brothers, Darryl and Ron, who cheer for me and read my books!

Acknowledgements

I'm so thankful to the folks who travel with me on my writing journey. Not just the characters who talk to me every day about their adventure, but the people in my life who encourage and help.

First and foremost, I thank God for His mercy and grace and for the opportunity and huge nudge He gave me that inspired me to write fiction. Through much prayer and preparation, God has helped me grow as a writer and a person. I'm so thankful for the hope I have in Him.

My husband Tim has loved, sacrificed, encouraged, brainstormed, and listened. Most of all, he has believed in me. I'm so grateful to take this daily journey with him.

Thank you to my wonderful children who encircle me with love and support, along with their spouses and my grandchildren. I so appreciate your encouragement.

This particular story reminded me what a joy it is to have siblings and to have known my parents. I want to give a special shout-out to my sister and brothers for being proud of their little sister and for reading my books.

A huge thank you goes to my publisher, Mt. Zion Ridge Press. Thank you, Tamera Kraft, for reading my story and giving me the opportunity to publish with you and for creating a beautiful cover. Thank you, Michelle Levigne, for your expert editing and making my story better. I appreciate the work you do to publish stories for God's kingdom.

Special thanks to my critique partner, Kathleen Friesen. Your editing and encouragement mean the world to me. Thank you to my beta reader and dear friend, Bev Cinnamon, for taking the time to read through *Home Away From Home* and giving me honest feedback. Thank you to my launch team, for taking the time to tell others about *Home Away From Home*.

A huge thank you to my readers. Without you, I wouldn't keep writing. I've met some wonderful folks along the way and so appreciate your encouragement and support. I hope I continue to write stories you want to read.

I believe God places people in my path to encourage and push me forward. I appreciate each and every one.

Books by Penny Frost McGinnis
Home Where She Belongs (Abbott Island book 1)
Home Away From Home (Abbott Island book 2)

Characters:
Sadie Stewart Grayson: *Moved to Abbott Island to live in her grandparents' home. Owner of Sadie's Rental Cottages and Joel's wife.*
Joel Grayson: *Abbott Island police officer who grew up on the island. Sadie's husband.*
Lucy Grayson: *Owner of The General Store and grew up on the island. Joel's sister.*
Marigold Hayes: *Owner of Kayak Rentals, entrepreneur. Thirty-year island resident.*
Johnny Papadakis: *Owner of Johnny's Place restaurant. Ten-year island resident.*
Alexa Papadakis: *Works at the Natural History Museum in Cleveland. Johnny's daughter.*
Levi Swenson: *Island police officer. Two-year island resident.*
Charlotte Mercer: *School teacher who spends summers on the island and works for Marigold.*
Henry Marin: *Johnny's sous chef. Six-year island resident.*
Emmett Grant: *Life-long resident lives as a bit of a hermit in the island woods.*
Miss Aggie, Miss Flossie, and Miss Hildy: *Abbott Island church ladies.*
Owen Bently: *local farmer.*

CHAPTER ONE

Marigold Hayes jabbed a spade in the soil. A flat of geraniums waved their scarlet heads as she lowered her fifty-four-year-old body onto a grassy spot. The joints in her knees popped and cracked, another reminder her fifty-fifth birthday loomed over her. Five years to sixty, but she had never lost hope of finding her father.

Forty years had passed since the accident, and the occasional nightmare still haunted her. Newspaper clippings, library research, yet not one morsel about her father. Mom had died, a fact Marigold learned the morning after the accident, and Dad vanished. Not a trace of him existed, except his keys in the ignition and a few man-sized footprints, after the crews towed the car from the wooded ravine.

She plunged the small shovel into the loamy soil she had worked for the last twenty years. Without fail, she planted annuals and nurtured the perennials plotted in the memorial garden she had created to honor her parents. Blooms of red geraniums and multi-colored zinnias would burst with radiance all summer. White daisies, the flowers Dad had gifted Mom with on anniversaries and birthdays, created a happy backdrop. Along the edge of the corner garden, she tucked in bright yellow marigolds, her namesake.

As she spoke her annual prayer, her heart pleaded and sought God's help to find her dad. After a murmured "Amen" soared to heaven, she tipped a geranium from its plastic container, loosened the bound roots, and plugged the plant into the earth. From a plastic jug, she sprinkled water into the hole, then scooped dirt in, and patted it around the stem. Soon, three red-headed flowers stood side by side. From the zinnia seed packet, she sprinkled the beginnings of a rainbow of color. Her steady work soon filled the flower bed with the promise of summer blossoms and her soul with restored hope. With an old, tattered dish towel, Marigold wiped the soil from her hands, then she rose from the ground and dusted dirt off her knees. She fingered a red bloom, and a pungent but pleasant fragrance filled the air.

Hands loaded with containers, gardening tools, and the water jug, Marigold trekked to the house.

Feet pounded on the nearby pavement, as Johnny Papadakis jogged from the street into her yard. His tall, slim, well-muscled form raised her pulse, even as she stilled. At fifty-eight, he kept himself in shape. She tipped her chin up.

1

"Hey, there."

"Hi, Mari." He stopped a few feet away, bent, and placed his hands on his thighs. After a few deep breaths, he raised to his full six-foot-three height. His brown eyes sparkled in the sun as he adjusted his baseball cap. Hands on his hips, he turned to the garden in the corner of her yard. "Working on your parents' flower bed?"

She moved to the porch and deposited her armload. "I finished a few minutes ago. You know, I wonder every year whether to continue. Dad would be eighty-three by now and may not be alive." All but a few memories of her dad and mom had faded with time. Whenever she found a worm in the garden, the squiggly creature between her fingers transported her to a happier time.

One autumn day, they had fished in Lake Erie right here on Abbott Island. She'd mustered the bravery, as only a child could, to bait her own hook. Mom had packed potato salad, apples, and a yellow cake with chocolate icing and Dad grilled the fish they caught, even the small one she had snagged, over a campfire. A full moon had shone and a cool breeze waved as she had cuddled between them in her safe place. Forty years had passed since she'd hugged her dad. Where had he gone?

Johnny rested his hand on her shoulder. "Giving up depends on whether the flowers bring you hope or make you sad." Without hesitation, he drew her into a hug.

Her head rested against his sweaty shirt, but she didn't care. This man, who had walked into her life ten years ago, empathized. Uncertain she deserved such a wonderful guy in her life, she stowed her emotions deep in her heart. Maybe afraid, perhaps set in her ways, or not sure how to respond to his affections, she valued his friendship and company without a deeper commitment.

He patted her back, then let go and reached for the jug and tools she had left on the floor. "Where do these go? I'm happy to put them away for you."

She grasped the jug's handle. "I appreciate your help, but I can do it." Her tall, handsome friend didn't budge. She released her hold and shook her head. "Thank you. They go in the shed out back."

With the gardening supplies firm in his arms, he trailed her to the backyard. "Your she shed, of course." A deep laugh escaped his chest.

Hand on her hip, she turned to him. "Do my paint choices make it a she shed? You know I love color, and chartreuse and periwinkle brightened the yard. Did you see my pink and red tulips when they bloomed and how they created a painting on the front? Besides, I love my little she shed."

She swung open the door to the building and the earthy odor of potting soil drifted to her nose. On the inside, an antique writing desk sat in the corner, covered with gardening books and journals. A shovel, rake, and several baskets lined the space behind the desk. A pale pink wall held life jackets, kayak paddles, and other lake life paraphernalia.

"Set them on the floor by the desk, and I'll put them away later. I want to spray out the buckets."

Johnny settled the load on the floor of the shed, then turned to face her. "You know you can ask for help, and I'm happy to do whatever I can." He wrapped her long silver braid around his hand. "I'm glad you don't dye your hair. The silver makes your blue eyes bluer."

Marigold stepped back and tugged her braid from him. "How about we sit on the porch and have tea?" She hurried out of the shed to the back door of her house, while he cut across the lawn and sauntered to the front porch.

From the porch swing, Johnny noted new growth sprouting across the road. Islanders had removed invasive species and added native plants to keep the pollinators in business. He and Mari spent several days helping neighbors and volunteers work with experts to make Abbott Island's habitat more natural.

The front door opened, and his favorite lady came out carrying two glasses of tea.

"Thank you. I worked up a thirst on my run."

She settled on the swing beside him. "Where's your water? You always carry some with you."

The royal blue swing swayed as he pumped his legs. "I left it on the counter at home. I'm a bit absentminded today." He ran his thumb across the moisture on the glass. "I want to show you something."

Her glass slipped from her hand and plunked on the side table. A few drops of tea splashed out. "What? Should I be worried?"

Johnny tugged a piece of paper from the pocket of his running shorts, then unfolded the sunflower yellow page. "Remember the flier the town council promised to print and display around the island?"

"I do."

"They made a mistake." He handed her the paper and pointed midway down on a list of island activities available to tourists. "The listing for your kayak rentals is on the wrong beach."

She held the sheet at arm's length to make out the print without her readers. "I've rented kayaks on the north side for close to thirty years. How did they get it wrong?" A deep sigh escaped her. "There's more competition every year, and without accurate advertising, I'll lose business."

He placed his hand over hers. "I know, and I found out yesterday a new food truck will be here this summer. They sell gyros and other Greek

3

food. I'm praying they don't take too much of my business, and although I'm happy to have new folks, I'm concerned. I've built the business at the restaurant over the last ten years, and I don't want to lose customers. If the food truck served a different cuisine than what I serve, it would help."

The wind chimes he had given her for last year's birthday tinkled in the breeze. "I don't want financial issues for either of us. We could get—"

"No, Johnny. I'm not ready to get married." Marigold stood and paced to the end of the porch. When she turned and faced the field, she crossed her arms and closed her eyes. "I know at fifty-four you'd think I'd be ready to settle. Part of me is, but finding a way to make peace with the past escapes me." She opened her eyes and turned to him. "We've known each other for several years and been friends for a while, but we only started dating eight months ago. Give me time, please. I care about you, but I've got to settle some things."

From the swing, he got up and crossed the wooden floor, then wrapped his arms around her. "I know you hope to settle the disappearance of your dad in your own mind. Without peace, you can't move on, and when you're ready, I'll be here." He let go and stepped back. "In the meantime, let's visit the town council and find out what to do about the flier."

~~~~~

A few days later, with the council's permission and a fat, black, permanent marker, Marigold sat at her kitchen table and corrected all the fliers. She hoped the bold lettering drew attention to her offerings. Last year, her kayak rentals dropped when another vendor opened his shop on the opposite side of the island. The cove where she rented from provided the best water for beginners and seasoned kayakers, but visitors spied the other rental from the road.

A giant foam board propped against her craft table garnered an idea. From a ceramic mug, she pulled the brightest markers. With the board and Sharpies, she hurried to the rear of the house and sat on the screened-in porch. With a flourish, she sketched the outline of a kayak with a person rowing along the water. The markers added color to draw awareness of her business. Displayed at the top of the hill, she'd catch the vacationers' attention, maybe.

In a few days, Memorial Day weekend opened the tourist trade. People swarmed the island until Labor Day, then the faithful few visited in the fall and spring. What other ways could she increase business? Poor Johnny. He'd worked hard to create a family atmosphere in his restaurant and win the trust of the islanders. Folks enjoyed his food, the mix of American and Greek. The taste of his burgers left patrons wanting more, and the cuisine from his grandparents' homeland outshined any she'd tasted. The homemade pitas and fresh hummus surpassed most, and the baklava was melt-in-your-mouth.

Marigold's heart overflowed with love for Johnny — she even loved his bald head, yet she hesitated to marry him. Too many years spent alone on the small island had left her too much time to herself to ponder her dad's whereabouts and her self-pity. If God answered her daily prayer, to find her dad and at least learn what happened, she'd have an answer and peace. Until then, she'd search.

From the porch, she studied the bluebirds. They flew to the island year after year and built nests in the boxes she had attached to the posts in the backyard. Their lives appeared simple. Create a home, eat, feed the babies, teach them to fly, nurture them, then travel south. Each year, she'd cheered the fledglings as they flapped fresh wings and fluttered from the nest to a neighboring branch, with Mom and Dad nearby.

At fourteen, she had lost her chance to fledge with her parents alongside her. By eighteen, she flew from her grandmother's nest in northeast Ohio to Abbott Island. Her stern grandmother, glad to get rid of her, handed her $500 and the keys to a VW Beetle she'd owned since the '70s. Forty years later, still lost in her questions, Marigold was determined to unearth answers about her dad, decide her feelings for Johnny, and figure out how to keep her business afloat.

CHAPTER TWO

Saturday of Memorial Day weekend, the waitstaff at Johnny's Place hustled from table to table. Johnny peered from the kitchen door and glimpsed Lucy and newlyweds, Joel and Sadie, as the hostess seated them. Any other day, Marigold might have joined them, but Johnny knew she waited on the beach to rent kayaks to folks on vacation. At least he hoped the visitors hung around once the morning rain stopped. Nothing like a gray day to begin the summer season. No doubt his own crowd resulted from the dampness.

The food truck parked two doors away didn't provide shelter. Maybe tomorrow he'd sample their fare and do a taste test for authentic Greek spices. If their offerings excited the palette and proved to be strong competition, he'd search for his *yaya*'s recipe for pastitsio, with layers of pasta, meat sauce, and bechamel to raise the competition. His stomach grumbled at the mention of his grandmother's rich comfort food. The island offered great eats and fun for people who stayed over or visited for the day. He prayed everyone benefited from the summer traffic. Otherwise, they'd all have to invent new ways to draw in customers.

"Order for table six." Johnny placed a sprig of parsley on a perch dish he'd adapted from a Greek recipe. With perch and walleye abundant in Lake Erie, he included the perch as his local signature dish. Frannie, who had been with him from the restaurant's beginning, lifted the tray to her shoulder.

Johnny called after her. "When table eight's food is ready, I'll take it out."

He piled plates with shoestring fries and cheeseburgers, the American dish most of the young people ordered, arranged them on a tray and carried them to Lucy's table. "Hello friends. So glad you squeezed in time to eat here." Johnny's smile stretched across his face.

"Hey." Joel stood to help distribute the platters. He smoothed the slacks of his police uniform before he sat. "This looks great and smells even better."

"Thanks, I try to do right for the island's finest." He placed a plate of pita bread and tzatziki dipping sauce in the center of the table. "I thought you'd enjoy this, too." He held the tray to his side. "How are you ladies? I haven't seen you for a few days. Do you have people renting your cabins, Sadie?"

Sadie unfolded her napkin and spread the fabric across her lap. "I do.

Both cabins are occupied. I added cots for a family of four, and a young couple is in the other one. I'm booked through the end of June. We took a break and came in for lunch. I grabbed Lucy from the General Store. It's hopping, too."

Johnny leaned on the table's empty chair. "Have any of you seen Marigold this morning? I'm afraid the rain may have detoured guests from the beaches."

Joel squirted ketchup onto his plate. "I saw her a while ago when I was making my rounds. A few people were out in kayaks. Since there's no lightning and the rain lightened, I think she had customers."

"Great." He glanced at the kitchen. "I better get to work. Henry's a great sous chef, but I don't want to leave him too long on a busy day."

"Later." Sadie and Lucy waved.

In the kitchen, Johnny chopped vegetables for his lemon chicken soup, a favorite on cool evenings. With each chop of carrots and celery, his mind wandered to Marigold. After work, he'd find her and see if she needed comfort or to share good news. Either way, he hoped to sneak a hug and kiss.

~~~~~

On the beach that morning, Marigold had scrubbed orange, blue, and green kayaks with soap and water, rinsed them and stacked them in the sand beside her building. Prepped for the day's business, she climbed on a stool, lifted her macrame chair to a low-hanging limb of a nearby oak tree, and secured the rope to a hook. She inhaled the refreshing scent of spring rain. Most days, she loved when the skies opened and doused her flowers, but today she prayed the sun shone through the clouds so vacationers would paddle in Lake Erie in the sturdy plastic boats.

Around noon the rain moved north to Canada and a few folks populated the sandy shore. Two teenagers had rented vessels for three hours. If the sun continued to shine, the afternoon traffic might increase. Campers pulled in and tents popped on the hillside campground above the beach, while vacationers milled around the porches of the yurts and cabins.

Marigold hoped the bright colors of the kayaks drew their attention and called them to paddle on the water, along with the sign she posted by the road. In the thirty years she'd rented canoes and kayaks, no one on the island had offered competition. Last summer, a new family purchased a home on the southeast side. They created a kayak rental on their private beach and opened an inn in the old house known as Abbott Manor. Last time she'd checked, they'd painted the house lavender with mint green and white trim. She admired their work and wished them well, but the competition had pushed her to seek publicity for her location. Her friend, Lucy, promised to help her create more of a web presence and advertise for her in the General Store. With Lucy's outgoing personality, she'd tell all her customers. Word of mouth still worked.

In the wooden box on her lap, Marigold sorted whistles, floating key chains, and lanyards for anyone who wanted to purchase the gadgets. Most customers grabbed a key chain with the island logo as an inexpensive souvenir. She had replenished the supply last month in hopes of a busy season.

The sun's rays pushed through the clouds and warmed her face as a couple of cars pulled into the lot. Eight young people climbed out of a van and hiked across the sand to the kayak stand. She smiled to the heavens and whispered a prayer of thanks. Day one showed promise, after all.

A young man, around twenty-two, approached the rentals. "Hello, ma'am. We're here to rent kayaks. Do you know how long it takes to paddle around the island?"

Not wanting to discourage the young man, she suppressed a laugh. "About eight or nine hours, if you include rest breaks. The circumference of the island is about fifteen miles." She swiped loose hair from her face. "Are you experienced kayakers?" A tour around the island proved a struggle for the inexperienced.

"I've been out several times, and my buddies have a few times." He nodded to his friends.

"Okay. Considering I require the boats in by six o'clock, you don't have time to circle the island today. Another day we could make special arrangements. I open at eleven each morning." She pushed her braid over her shoulder.

The young man approached his friends and chatted. When he returned to Marigold, he scratched his head. "We're gonna take them out for a couple of hours."

"Excellent idea. Have you been to the island before?" With a towel, she wiped off the plastic seats.

"Yeah. My dad brought me every summer for years. We stayed in my grandpa's old cabin."

"I thought I'd seen you before."

"Yeah, I remember you, too."

"How's your dad?" She lined up the kayaks for the fellas.

The blond-haired man shoved his foot into the sand. "He passed away in December."

Marigold stopped, raised herself to her height, and stared at the young man. "I'm so sorry. At least you know where he is, but I have no idea where mine is." She closed her eyes and took a calming breath. "I'm sorry. I shouldn't have mentioned my dad. He's been missing for forty years." She placed her hand over her mouth. Why couldn't she be quiet?

"Wow. That's a long time. I hope you find him." The boy fumbled with his paddle. "We'll be back in a couple of hours."

"Enjoy your trip." With her hand raised, she waved to the young men. Their rentals added to the monies for the day. Instead of a grateful heart for God's provision, she'd opened her mouth and sounded like an old fool. Those young men didn't want to know her problems. Seated in her macrame chair, she berated herself for laughing at them for thinking they'd paddle around the island, then putting her foot in her mouth. She prayed she'd behave the rest of the rental season and keep her lips zipped.

By 6:30 in the evening, she'd rented at least two kayaks per hour, if she averaged in the eight to the young men. Pleased with her take, she counted her cash, then locked the box she planned to carry home. With a metal rope and heavy-duty lock, she threaded the rope under the kayaks' seats then under their bellies, bolted them to her building, and locked the door.

Thank goodness for the golf cart, so much more convenient than driving her pale blue VW Beetle around the island. Somehow she'd kept the 1975 classic running.

After a busy day, her old legs refused to carry her home. Loaded with towels to wash, Marigold turned the key and zipped along home. Maybe Johnny would stop over after work. No, she'd grown to depend on him too much. She enjoyed his company, and he'd warmed her heart over the winter, but she wanted to find peace before she committed to a relationship. Her friend, yes, and he made her laugh, lifted her spirits, and gave the best hugs. He cared more than she allowed herself to show in return, at least for now.

She rounded the corner to her home, and as if her thoughts had beckoned him, Johnny waved from her porch swing. Her heart skipped a beat when he smiled his radiant smile. His grin warmed her soul, not for its brilliance, but because she understood he meant it for her alone. Until Johnny, no other man, except her dad, treated her like a princess. Perhaps she was better suited, at her age, to claim the title of queen. Marigold welcomed his presence, as long as he understood her desire to wait.

~~~~~

With a royal blue and scarlet woven shawl snugged around her, Marigold settled beside Johnny on the porch swing. The scent of his woodsy cologne wrapped around her like a comforting hug. Weary from a day on the beach, she rested her head on his shoulder and listened to the crickets sing a song of the approaching summer. Orange and light blue shades colored the sunset sky while the fragrance of Johnny's lemon chicken soup drifted from inside.

"I smell something delicious." Marigold raised her head and eyed her companion.

Johnny took her hand and kissed the knuckles. "Yes, you do. Let's celebrate the beginning of a busy season with a warm bowl of comfort."

Her gaze wandered to the hand he'd kissed, then to his face. "Sounds delicious."

As he stood, he held her hand and drew her from the swing. "Shall we?" He motioned to the door.

"Yes, of course."

"I'm glad you leave the spare key, so I can let myself in. I put the soup on to warm so you could eat when you got home." He took her shawl and draped it over a hook on a coat rack. "You sit at the table, and I'll bring you a bowl and homemade rolls."

With the chair pulled out for her, she settled at the small pine table she had refinished years ago. "You spoil me, Mr. Papadakis."

"I do my best." Steam rose from the handmade ceramic bowl, a remnant from her days of pottery making. The golden broth against the French blue bowl pleased her creative eye, and the citrus fragrance tempted her to gobble the soup. Instead, she waited and held Johnny's hand as he blessed the meal.

When she opened her eyes and watched the humble man across the table, her heart fluttered. She didn't deserve such an amazing man in her life. How could he care about her so much, when her own father hadn't cared enough to return home? She'd waited too many years to hear her dad's voice. Each night of her childhood, when she'd gone to bed, he'd called out to her, "Love you to the bottom of the sea, sweet pea." Then she'd reply, "Love you to the top of the old oak tree." Then she'd doze off into sweet dreams. Since he'd disappeared, sad dreams replaced pleasant ones with the occasional nightmare. With her fifty-fifth birthday in sight, she was determined to put her dad's absence to rest. But how?

CHAPTER THREE

Tuesday morning, Marigold stretched her arms over her head, then rolled over to check the time. Memorial Day weekend had skidded by with average rental income. Not a flagship time, but at least she made enough money to pay her bills.

At nine in the morning, she dangled her legs over the edge of the bed to rise and not shine, but caffeinate. She dressed, muddled around the kitchen, and rustled up breakfast. Bless Sadie's heart. She'd baked blueberry and cranberry muffins and shared them. With a swipe of cream cheese, Marigold lifted the treat to her lips. As she bit into the delightful flavor of fruit with a hint of cinnamon and crunch of pecans, she spied the family Bible she kept on the table.

Instead of a baby book, Mom had recorded memories on the blank pages at the end of the sacred word. With her elegant penmanship, she had written the date Marigold learned to walk, when her first tooth poked through, and the day she had started kindergarten. Mom had penned details of Marigold's first dance, days before she had died in the crash. She had promised to give the Bible to Marigold on her eighteenth birthday. Instead, she'd inherited the book too soon. In her middle school hand, she had penned the date of her mom's death and her dad's disappearance, August 22, 1981.

She swallowed a bite of muffin, took a sip of coffee, and opened the Bible to her mom's favorite verse, Romans 15:13, the one Marigold had clung to all these years. "May the God of hope fill you with all joy and peace as you trust in him, so that you may overflow with hope by the power of the Holy Spirit." Did she dare hope her dad might still be alive, and she might find him? She'd give herself the summer to search one more time, then if her search failed, she'd tuck the hope away and seek peace.

Coffee cup empty, she placed the dishes in the sink to wash later. She tied a knot in the hem of her flowy red and gold skirt, grabbed a jacket from the hall closet, and set out to the beach in the golf cart. Today, she planned to immerse Charlotte, the woman she hired for the summer, in the ins and outs of kayak rental. The young woman had visited the island with her family every summer since she turned four, often exploring the woods and water. She and Marigold had bonded as kindred spirits since, through the years, she taught Charlotte to crochet and draw. The young woman had finished her first year teaching first grade in Sandusky, and saved enough money to rent a small island house for the summer. When she had written to Marigold and asked about a part-time job, she replied with a heartfelt yes.

With the new competition and possible drop in income, Marigold would do without to pay Charlotte. In the meantime, she wracked her brain for ideas to increase cash flow. Lucy had worked on the website and asked her to stop by and go through the design with her. Instead of procrastinating one more day, she planned to call her tonight and set a time to finish. What did Marigold know about web design? As an artist, she appreciated color and graphics, but as far as selling points, she hoped Lucy would enlighten her. Maybe Charlotte should come too. As a twenty-something, current on computers, she might have excellent input.

Marigold slowed the golf cart and parked beside the kayak shed. Charlotte was bent over, digging in the sand at the edge of the beach.

"Good morning. You beat me here."

The young woman stood and lifted her hand in greeting. "Morning, I didn't want to be late on my first day. I've been searching for lake glass." She held out a smooth, frosted piece of green. "I rode the ferry over yesterday and got settled in my house. It's so cute, decorated in aqua and grassy green. This summer is going to be an adventure."

Smiling at Charlotte's enthusiasm, Marigold carried a box of papers from the shed. "I'm glad your new place is what you hoped. The summers here are magical, as you know."

Charlotte tucked the glass in her pocket. "Can I help you?"

"No, let me stack these over here." She lowered the box to a small picnic table beside the shed.

"The first thing I want to cover with you are waivers the renters have to sign. This box will be locked in the shed, so you can get a stack out each morning. We have to have proof from the patrons we aren't liable and they are responsible for their safety while on the water. Go over the list of safety recommendations and instructions on how to paddle and the need to wear the life jackets. We also offer helmets, if anyone wants one, but they aren't required. I'll collect the waivers at the end of the day. If I can't, I'll show you where to store them."

Charlotte studied the form. "I remember these from when we rented here with Mom and Dad. When I turned eighteen, I had to sign my own."

"Of course." Marigold handed Charlotte a set of keys. "You'll need these to get in the shed and to unlock the padlocks on the boats."

The young woman wrapped a hand around the metal roping that secured the kayaks to the shed. "These wire ropes are heavy duty."

Marigold nodded. "They have to be to keep vandals from taking them. So far, I've not had any trouble, and I don't want any."

By eleven o'clock, several families settled along the beach. Children ran into the chilly water, splashed, and raced to their towels. The children's laughter reached Marigold and Charlotte.

"They're having fun. Reminds me of recess with my class. Those kids could laugh louder than any I've heard." She nestled in the macrame chair, while her boss sat at the table. "I can't wait to have children. Of course, I'd need to have a husband first, which means meeting someone and dating." She laughed.

"That's the usual sequence." Marigold spied some children as they scooped water with their buckets and dug in the sand with plastic shovels. Dreams of her own children had drifted away over the years. In her twenties, she had dated a couple of guys who visited the island, but nothing long term. In her mind, she had compared them to her dad, then worried they might disappear too. Her silly ideas cost her relationships, but her dad's disappearance had eroded her trust—until Johnny. Something about him drew her in, maybe because they had explored friendship first. The man gave her no reason to doubt for the last nine years. Now, months into realizing she loved being with him, he stayed steady and did not push her into a commitment.

Charlotte stepped from the chair and stretched. "Have you ever been married?"

As the words spouted from the woman's mouth, two teenagers approached them. "We want to rent two kayaks for the afternoon."

"You've come to the right place." Marigold sighed with relief at not having to answer the question and walked Charlotte through the rental process. Now to keep the question about family life separate from work life. Not because she was ashamed or embarrassed, but because she didn't enjoy talking about herself. Though she appreciated Charlotte, she didn't know how much of her personal life she wanted to share.

~~~~~

In the afternoon, a line of people snaked along the sidewalk in front of the new Greek food truck. Johnny tugged the bill of his ballcap down to hide part of face and joined the group. A man in khaki shorts and a lake life t-shirt stood under a nearby tree. He unwrapped his food and bit into a gyro overloaded with meat. Juice dribbled onto his chin as he closed his eyes and licked his lips. Must be good. At Johnny's Place, business hopped all weekend. He'd served more than his target goal for opening tourist season, but Tuesday's lunch crowd left him short. The regulars showed and a few vacationers, but his bottom line suffered. From the satisfied expressions on the food truck patrons' faces, the gyro sandwich stole the customers.

In the lot's corner, Johnny spied one picnic table. Not enough to serve the patrons wrapped around the corner. The sidewalk around his building lacked the space for tables and chairs, but the courtyard behind his restaurant had the potential to hold four or five tables. With lights and potted plants, diners could experience an evening of Greek beauty. Johnny rubbed his temples. Money. Spend money to make money, his dad always said. A romantic spot for locals and couples visiting the island inspired him to dream. He'd advertise on the island's website and have a sign painted...

"Sir. Can I help you?"

Johnny craned his neck to find the voice. The window on the food truck framed a twenty-something man.

"How can I help you?"

"Um. I'll take the classic gyro and a honey walnut baklava." Johnny tipped his head to peer around the man and take a peek at the cook. A woman with a long dark ponytail managed the small kitchen.

"Good choice. Anything else?"

Johnny snapped his attention to the blond-haired man. "No, thanks. I'm good." He handed him cash and waited for change.

The young man smiled. "Here you go." He dropped a few coins into Johnny's palm. "It'll be a few minutes, you can stand to the side, and I'll hand it out."

He stepped to the other end of the window and peered at the line of customers. A few islanders had joined the long line of tourists. Johnny gave a slight wave to his friend Levi, who had joined the island's police force about a year ago. He had proved his worth when he helped Joel take down Sadie's stalker.

The young man ducked his head and straightened his cap. Was Levi embarrassed to be caught eating the competition's food? No shame there with Johnny hiding under his baseball cap. Levi raised his head, and Johnny gave him a thumbs up. A smile crossed the officer's face.

The blond from the food truck handed Johnny's food out the window. "Here you go. Thanks for stopping by."

Johnny grabbed the bag and trekked to his restaurant. Inside, he settled at his desk, in the backroom. As he unwrapped the gyro, the aroma of garlic, oregano, and the light scent of cucumbers escaped. He bit into the tender meat smothered with tzatziki sauce, lettuce, and tomatoes.

"Mmm..." The sandwich reminded him of the ones his *yaya* prepared with tender lamb meat. The delicious seasonings pleased his palate too much. Did he betray himself by enjoying the competition's food?

He shoved the rest of the sandwich aside, opened his bottom desk drawer, and pulled out *Yaya's* recipe box. He lifted the wrinkled, worn card with her scribbles sprawled across. She had written most of the ingredients and a few instructions for the gyro. Good thing Johnny had stood at her elbow and helped her cook. He'd learned more from her than his years in chef training. Seeing her handwriting left an ache in his heart. He'd love to hear her say again, "Eat! You need to eat something." She had commanded her kitchen, and no one dared to cross her when she wore her apron. He longed for her spunk and determination to infiltrate him and his kitchen, to help him take his restaurant up a notch.

"Johnny?" Henry stepped into the doorway and wiped his hands on a towel. "I need help, if you're available."

Johnny dropped the box into the drawer and pushed it closed. "Sure. I'll be right there."

Henry sniffed the air. "What do I smell?"

Before he saw the remnants of lunch, Johnny shoved them into the trash can.

"Spying on the competition? There's a Greek food truck wrapper in the can." Henry smirked.

"You value your job, right?" Johnny eyed his employee.

"I sure do. I won't tell a soul." He turned and marched to the kitchen.

Johnny trailed him, lifted his apron from a hook, pulled the cotton cloth over his head, and tied the strings in the back. Hands on his hips, he surveyed his kitchen. Clean, but messy in a food prep way. Cutting boards with fresh vegetables, pots of soup simmering on the stove, meat roasting in the oven, and servers loading trays with fragrant food for his customers. Would people enter the doors of Johnny's Place after they tasted the Greek food truck's offerings? As someone seasoned in the restaurant business, he encouraged competition, but he had built his business from nothing and refused to fail.

CHAPTER FOUR

On the first day of June, sisters Ivy, Violet, and Poppy opened boxes and suitcases in their dad's private apartment at a senior living facility in Mansfield, Ohio.

"Dad, I'm glad you didn't have to move any furniture, except your recliner. We all know how much you love it." The oldest daughter, Ivy, patted her dad's back, then carried a stack of clothes to the bedroom. A few minutes later, she waltzed back into the small living area with an empty container. "I put your undergarments in the top drawer with your socks."

"I'm not sure about you touching my personal stuff." Edward Downey rested in his recliner and watched his girls bustle around the new place. "I can get the rest of the clothes out of the suitcases and put them away after I rest. You all go home."

Ivy kissed her father on the forehead. "Are you sure we can't do anything else before we go?"

He lifted his hands. "We can pray."

At the whisper of his voice, Ivy nodded. Poppy, youngest of the three clutched her sisters' hands.

Violet sought out God as if she talked to Him like her best friend. "Please keep an eye on Dad and wrap those big arms of Yours around him."

Ivy peeked at her sisters. How could three siblings be so different?

In the parking lot, Violet stopped her sisters. "We have to figure out which day we're going to finish sorting out Mom and Dad's house."

Ivy and her sisters had donated most of Mom's belongings a year ago, after her death. The three of them had folded and boxed while their dad grieved. Most of the rooms in their childhood home echoed with emptiness, thanks to Poppy. She had moved from a furnished apartment to a small house and discovered her eclectic taste in furniture mirrored their mom's. Movers had loaded the breakfast nook table and chairs, an antique dresser, and a few other items into a truck and delivered them to Poppy's. The bedroom suites, couch, and a few other pieces went to an auction house.

Ivy crossed her arms and faced her sisters. "How about next Saturday, a week from today?" They dreaded digging into Mom's office. She had worked from home for years, as a realtor, and had piled files and boxes in every corner. "Once we dispose of the old documents and sort

19

through the rest, we can list the house to sell."

Poppy stuck out her lower lip. "I hate the idea of people tromping through our home."

"You could've bought it, you know. Instead of the tiny home you have out in a field at the park." Violet scowled.

She crinkled her nose. "I couldn't afford it on a teacher's salary."

Mom of twin girls and a boy, Violet challenged her sister. "How are the art classes going? Or is it crafts you teach? I never remember."

Poppy lifted her over-sized bag onto her shoulder. "You'd know if you ever let your kids come to the Y. I teach art and crafts to the after-school classes, and in the evenings, I teach adults and teens. Plus, I'm preparing for an art show at the gallery downtown."

"Good for you. Let us know when and where your show will be. You know the kids can't come during the school year. With church and sports, we keep too busy. Maybe this summer I'll send them to your art camp."

Poppy's face broke into a smile. "I'd love to have them in my classes."

"Sign them up. I'm sure Jess and Jenn would love being in Poppy's class, and Micah too." Ivy hugged each sister. "See you both Saturday at nine. I'll bring coffee and bagels." Ivy climbed into her SUV, Violet into her minivan, and Poppy into her well-used compact car. Ivy waved as they pulled out of the parking lot. "Lord, help us get along while we help Dad. And please keep him comfortable while he learns to live in the senior community."

~~~~~

A week into the summer season and Sunday morning's sunrise gave way to a brilliant blue sky. Puffy white clouds floated over Marigold as she hiked along the road to church. The welcoming committee, three white-haired ladies dressed in their Sunday best, waved to her as she climbed the steps to greet them.

"Good morning, Miss Aggie, Miss Flossie, and Miss Hildy. I hope you are all well today."

In unison, they nodded.

"Oh yes. Fine." Miss Aggie ogled the area behind Marigold. "Where's your young man this morning? You know, the tall, handsome fellow." The other two ladies snickered.

"If you mean Johnny, he'll be here soon. He checks in at the restaurant and makes sure everything is set, then he heads back to cook as soon as the service ends."

If they observed near as well as they gossiped, they would know his routine. Of course, at their age maybe they forgot. Marigold scolded herself for thinking unkind thoughts. She'd turn their age soon enough.

"You ladies have a good morning."

"We will, dear." All three cast a grin to her as if they'd practiced synchronized smiling.

Inside, she found Sadie, Joel, and Lucy. She slid into the pew next to Lucy. "Morning."

Lucy reached for Marigold's hand and squeezed it. "Morning to you. How are you? I haven't seen you all week. Have you been as swamped as I have?"

She patted her young friend's hand, then let go. "Not as busy as you, but steady. If business stays as it has this week, I think I'll be okay." As Marigold spoke, Charlotte stepped to the end of the pew. "Have you met my new employee?"

Lucy stood and shook Charlotte's hand. "Hi. I'm Lucy. Nice to meet you."

"Nice to meet you."

Marigold stepped out of the pew and motioned Charlotte in. "I'm saving a place for Johnny." Lucy and Sadie shared a knowing look. "Ladies, you can smirk, but we are simply friends. He happens to be a tall, dark, and handsome friend." Her face split into a smile. "Who I enjoy spending time with."

"Are you talking about me?" Johnny scooted into the seat beside her. She breathed in the scent of his woodsy aftershave, mixed with the smell of oregano, when he slid his arm around her shoulders.

"Been cooking already this morning?"

"Do you smell the spices on me?" He lifted his hand and sniffed.

She leaned her head on him. "Yes, but it smells good."

Piano notes filled the air with an opening hymn, and Marigold lifted her soprano to Johnny's tenor in perfect accord. After the singing ended, Marigold opened her Bible. Her mind wandered less when she wrote the pastor's words and Bible verses on her notepad, but the pad lay at home on her table. As the pastor spoke of God's grace, Marigold lifted her eyes to the stained-glass window of Jesus with the children. Her mom had displayed a painting, similar to the scene, in the house. An ache rose in her heart, as she longed to sit by her mom and dad in church again. They had attended every Sunday. She snuggled between them on a wooden pew and often fell asleep on her dad's lap. Where had her dad gone after the accident? Was he still alive, or had she spent the last forty years hoping for nothing? So many questions remained unanswered. Her sorrow overwhelmed her at times, and she drowned in her longing to find him. As the past swirled in her brain, her chest tightened. She tried to drag in a deep breath, but an invisible pressure stopped her, as her heart raced. Her arm ached and her mind fogged.

Johnny leaned into her. "Are you okay?"

She shook her head. "Not feeling so good."

"Do you want to go outside?"

She nodded. He stood and helped her move. "Let's go."

Her hand clutched his arm for fear she'd tumble over if she let go. Under the brain fog, she recognized the symptoms of a panic attack, but couldn't verbalize without crying. The crowd overwhelmed her as she followed Johnny to a quiet place.

He bent his head near her ear. "I'm calling the EMT team."

When they stepped out the church's doors, Marigold cleared her throat. "I think it's a panic attack. Did you drive?"

"I did."

"Can I sit in the car a minute?"

Johnny led her to his sedan. She climbed in the front seat and started counting the buttons on the radio. She touched the dashboard. Her breathing calmed. Her doctor once told her to ground herself if panic seized her. Find five things she could see, four she could feel, three she could hear, two to smell, and one to taste. Not able to do all five at times, she discovered two or three helped.

The EMTs pulled into the church lot and Johnny met them.

"Marigold is not feeling well, can you check her out?"

Two ladies and a man jogged to the car. One of the women leaned into the open door. "Can you sit on the edge of the seat?"

"Yes." Marigold swung her legs around and rested them on the ground.

The three worked to take vitals and ask questions. The young man wrapped the blood pressure cuff around her arm, inflated it and let it depress. He removed the cuff and folded it into a bag. "Your blood pressure is high. Have you had a panic attack before?"

Marigold rubbed her forehead. "Yes. I've had them before."

"Your heart sounds strong and your breathing is normal. You may want to rest today and come to the squad building tomorrow so I can check you again. Do you have a cuff at home?"

Marigold nodded. "I do. I'll check it later, too. I was pretty sure it was a panic attack. We shouldn't have bothered you."

"Better to be safe, Ma'am."

The EMT van drove away as the church doors opened. Lucy, Charlotte, Sadie, and Joel hurried to the car. The white-haired nosy ladies stood on the steps and eyeballed Marigold.

"Charlotte, do you mind running the kayak rentals today? I... um... want to rest." Independent to the core, Marigold hated relying on other people.

Her employee hovered over Marigold. "Are you okay? You know I'll do whatever you ask."

"I'll be fine. Thank you." She attempted a smile. "Johnny, I want to go home." She swung her legs into the car, gave a wave to her friends and closed the door.

Johnny slid behind the steering wheel. "I asked Joel to let Henry know I'd be in later. I want to make sure you're okay first."

Marigold closed her eyes and leaned on the headrest. "You're too good to me."

Johnny's kindness and care stirred emotion in Marigold's heart. She loved him. Why couldn't she admit it?

~~~~~

Johnny maneuvered the streets between the church and Marigold's house. He turned into her driveway, hopped out of the car, and opened her door. "Here we go. Let's get you in the house so you can rest."

Marigold wrapped her hand in his as they ascended the steps to her porch. "I can manage, you don't have to come in."

"I know you can, but I want to help." He pushed the door open and led her to the couch, where he sat and patted the cushion. "Let's sit here."

She lowered herself and scooted near Johnny. He reached his arm around her and pulled her close. His head leaned on hers as he wrapped his other arm around her. Marigold's shoulders shook.

"Hey, what can I do for you?" He cuddled her closer and prayed for God to pour His comfort and peace over his beautiful lady. She sobbed into his chest.

"I'm sorry, Johnny. I never cry in front of people. I look like an old fool." She wiped at her eyes.

"If you're an old fool, then what am I? I'm older, you know." He coaxed a smile out of her. "Do you want to talk about what happened?"

Hands folded in her lap she lifted her face to his. "Not particularly. Do you mind fixing iced tea? I need something to drink."

He rose and walked to the kitchen, then turned to her. "I'll fix the tea and make a couple of sandwiches. Okay?"

"Perfect. Thank you."

Johnny hummed while he layered turkey, cheese, and tomato slices on oat bread. She trusted him enough to take care of her. A step he had hesitated to hope for. He loved her so much, he'd do anything for her.

CHAPTER FIVE

After a few restful days, Marigold dragged a kayak across the sand on Tuesday morning and instructed her new customers. "Since you've never kayaked before, let me show you the easiest way to enter and exit the boat." She steadied the heavy plastic vessel as the water lapped around her knees. "You'll want the seat level with you, so this depth is good." After she bent her knees and sat on the seat, she lifted her legs and swung them onto the footrests.

"When you want to get out, paddle to this depth, swing your legs out and stand in the water." She dug the end of the paddle into the sand below the water's surface and leaned on it as she rose from the boat.

A woman with white hair, close to the length of Marigold's, nodded. "Thank you. This will be fun. I guess even over sixty, I can manage." She glanced at her husband, a man whose beard matched the color of her hair. "You ready?"

"Let's do this."

Marigold admired the couple as they paddled along the inlet. Newlyweds. They had shared with Marigold about their simple wedding and how they searched for a quiet place for a week-long honeymoon. Neither had married before due to busy careers. Now retired, they planned to travel and try new adventures.

How had fifty-four years of her life darted past her? Work, church, and the search for her dad filled most of her days. She had befriended Sadie's grandparents, who had since passed away, and now Sadie, Joel, Lucy, and of course Johnny. Thank God for good friends. Yet her heart ached for closure with her dad and the desire to have her own person, someone to spend her days with.

Marigold hiked back to the shed, ready to hang out a pity party banner.

"Excuse me, Ma'am."

Marigold spun around to find a young man and woman. Another happy couple, no doubt. "Hi. How can I help you?"

The twenty-something man folded the woman's hand into his. "Can you tell us if your prices are better than the kayak rental on the other side of the island?"

Marigold cleared her throat. "I'm not sure of their prices, but I can tell you mine." She rattled off the hourly rates.

His wife rolled her eyes. "I told you they're cheaper."

25

He hung his head. "Sorry to bother you." The young woman tugged his hand and pulled him away, leaving a strong floral scent in her path.

Levi rolled the police department's golf cart beside Marigold and cut the engine. "What's going on?"

She shook her head and laughed. "Two young people trying to save a penny."

Getting out of the cart, Levi surveyed the premises. "I'm doing my rounds, and I was hoping to meet your new employee. You know, so I know all the regulars on the island." He ground the toe of his shoe into the sand.

"Charlotte works this evening. She relieves me around four o'clock. Want to come back then?" Marigold lifted a paddle from the ground and carried it to the shed.

Levi followed her with three more. "Sounds good." A sheepish grin crossed his face.

"She's a beautiful young woman, a teacher. Did Joel and Sadie tell you about her?"

"Yes. They said they met her at church and she might be someone I'd want to meet." He stuck his hands into his pockets.

"Be here at four, and I'll be happy to introduce you."

"Thanks, Mari. I will. There aren't many people my age who hang around the island for long. Thought she might want to take a walk or something." He climbed into the cart.

Marigold flipped her braid behind her back. "You never know. It never hurts to make a new friend."

The older couple who went out in the morning returned about two o'clock. They slowed in the shallow water, flung their legs over the side of the kayaks, and stood beside them.

"We had so much fun." The older lady waded to shore with the kayak in tow. "I can't believe I've never kayaked before."

Her husband nodded. "It was sure relaxing."

"I'm glad you enjoyed yourselves. You were out about three hours, a long time for beginners." Marigold grabbed the handle on the end of the woman's kayak and pulled it into line with the others. The man followed and dropped his beside it.

"You got a tan while you were out."

The woman lifted her arms in front of her. "I sure did. I'm glad we used sunscreen, but the kiss the summer sun gave us makes me feel younger. What do you say, sweetie?"

"You're gorgeous, darlin'."

The endearing banter gave Marigold pause. She never called Johnny nicknames, although he sometimes spoke a sweet name to her. Did the lack of endearments mean she didn't love him? Of course not. Her parents didn't fling gooey names around, and they adored one another. At her age, she squashed the idea of "honey" and "dear." Obviously, the newlyweds found the practice fun, but her stomach turned a little at the thought. For her, Johnny was Johnny.

"Thanks for your business, folks. I'm glad you enjoyed your trip. I'd love for you to come back."

"We will. We'll be here a few more days. Right, snookums?" The woman wrapped her hand around her husband's arm and they trekked the rise of the hill.

A few minutes before four, Charlotte stashed her backpack in the storage shed. "Hey, Mari. How's today going?" She tucked her chin length hair behind her ear.

Marigold stood from cleaning and sanitizing the plastic seats. "It's been great for a Tuesday. We've had a steady flow and one couple who complained our prices were too high." She dropped her cleaning rag into the bucket of soapy water. "I suppose I should check the competition's prices and adjust mine, but I haven't suffered yet, so I'll wait. How about you? How was your day?"

"I've had better. When I woke this morning, my electricity was out, which meant a cold breakfast and no coffee. I walked downtown in search of a hot brew and tripped on a bump in the sidewalk. My shin is bruised but Catie's Cafe had electric, and at least I got my coffee. Best tasting cup I've had in a while. By the time I got home, the electric was on and I finished my chores and charged my phone." She took a breath.

Gravel crunched behind them. Marigold turned. "I think your day is about to get better." Right on time, Levi drove the golf cart down the incline.

He climbed out and sashayed across the grassy sand. "Good afternoon, ladies."

Marigold waved him over. "Charlotte, meet Levi. He's an officer on the island." She turned to her employee. "Levi, this is Charlotte. She's working for me this summer."

He reached his hand to her. "Nice to meet you."

"You, too." Charlotte took his hand.

A hint of a smile crossed Marigold's face as the young man held on longer than normal and Charlotte didn't let go. Young love, so sweet, yet so vulnerable. She prayed they might hit it off and at least be friends.

"Charlotte, I have all the kayaks ready for you. I'm hoping, you'll stay busy this evening, and Levi, maybe you'd bring Charlotte a bite to eat after you get off duty. If you aren't too busy."

"Oh, sure. Happy to." His cheeks pinked.

"You don't have to." Charlotte pressed her hands along her shorts, as if she ironed the creases out.

"It's no problem. I better finish my shift." He backed away and jumped into the seat of the cart. With a wave, he took off.

Marigold dumped the bucket of lemony smelling water behind the shed.

"You didn't have to set me up, Marigold." Charlotte folded her arms in front of herself. "But thanks. It might be nice to have someone my age to hang out with. Don't get me wrong. You act young for your age, but..."

Marigold stood straight and lifted her hand in front of her to signal her to stop. "I get it. Levi is a super nice guy. I hope the two of you will enjoy each other's company. I know I'm not young anymore, but I appreciate your kind words." If she let Charlotte ramble, she might never get to leave. "I'm heading home. Take care and have a good night."

"Okay. Bye for now."

~~~~~

Since the sun shined later on June evenings, Johnny invited Marigold for a quiet hike along the island's north shore. They could investigate the alvar system, a limestone plain with thin soil and unexpected plant growth. He found peace on the island's many trails, the alvar being the most unique.

Johnny toted sandwiches and drinks in his backpack for later. "Did you have a busy day?"

"I did. Business was steady for a Tuesday. I met interesting people and introduced Levi to Charlotte." They moved along the trail. "How is the restaurant business?"

Johnny shook his head. "I'm afraid folks are flocking to the food truck. When people are out and about, they tend to want to stay outside. I'm working on a plan to make the courtyard behind my place into an area where people want to spend time together. The ambience would entice diners to eat under the twinkle lights. Kind of a romantic setting. What do you think?"

She stopped and turned to him. "Brilliant idea. I'll help. Do you have tables and chairs? There's a store in Sandusky where they sell secondhand furniture, and I saw cute outdoor tables and chairs there. How about an eclectic and cozy arrangement?"

"You're a great partner for this project." More time with Marigold made his heart sing. "How about we have dinner tomorrow evening and brainstorm?"

She tilted her head. "I'd love to. I'll close the rentals at six and finish by 6:30. Where do you want to meet?" Her words teased.

"How about my restaurant?" They both laughed.

"I'll be there after work. Then we can measure the space and create a plan." Marigold straightened the strap on her camera.

"Sounds good. Are you ready to move on and take photos?"

"Yes." She pressed a button and the lens slid out of the camera's body. "You know I love the alvar. I'm fascinated by the plants and how they grow out of such thin soil on top of the limestone. They appear to grow right out of the rock." They hiked along the trail. "And it's time for the bog violets' pretty purple heads to pop and the gorgeous lakeside daisy."

He held a branch for her to step around. "They are beautiful. Almost as pretty as a marigold." He winked and watched her cheeks pink.

"You flatter me too much." A smile played on her lips. "I'm hoping to take a few photos to frame. If they're good, I'll use them to make greeting cards to sell at the craft shows."

"Great idea. You're so smart, and you plan ahead. Beauty and brains are a pretty special combination."

Large concrete ruins from the island's quarrying history rose from the ground. Johnny and Marigold stepped through one of the arched openings. "This fascinates me. The limestone industry brought life to the island so many years ago, then gave way to tourism. Funny how things change." He took her hand and led her to the trail. They descended the low cliffs to an opening where the water met the limestone. Marigold's hold tightened on his hand as she stepped down to the alvar.

Johnny said, "Careful, it's slippery."

Her feet landed on the rock, and she raised her head to the lake. "Takes my breath away."

Johnny soaked in her beauty as she took in the scene. He loved this gorgeous, intelligent, caring woman. If only she would accept the love he longed to give her. He'd never met someone like Marigold. Confident, able to care for others even as she grieved the loss of her folks. As the waves crashed along the shore, Johnny prayed for her. *God, help this amazing woman find peace.*

CHAPTER SIX

Thursday around seven, Marigold stepped inside Johnny's Place. Her maxi-length teal and white dress swooshed around her legs, and the beads dangling in her silver hoops tinkled. The patrons' voices and laughter swirled through the restaurant as she searched for Johnny. From a booth near the back, Sadie and Joel waved her over.

Joel stood and laid his napkin on the table. "Do you want to sit with us? The place is packed tonight."

Marigold leaned toward Sadie and hugged her, then gave Joel a side hug. "It's so good to see you, but not tonight. I'm meeting Johnny for dinner. Have you seen him?"

The corner of Joel's mouth raised. "A date with Johnny, huh?"

"Yes, Joel. You can wipe the smirk off your face." She scanned the room.

"We saw him go to the kitchen a few minutes ago." Joel nodded that direction. "I'm sure he won't mind you going back there."

"Thank you. He's probably in his office." She turned to find him.

Joel called after her. "Have fun."

In the kitchen, the fragrance of olives, cucumbers, and spiced meats greeted Marigold. Henry chopped vegetables and seared the meat on the stove. "Hi, Mari. Are you looking for the boss?"

"I am. From the number of the patrons in the dining room, you've been busy. Has business increased this week?" A tug of doubt pulled on Marigold. Johnny might not have time for dinner.

Henry pressed his knife into a stalk of celery. "Tonight has been busy. It's the first evening we've had a full house. I heard someone say the food truck is closed, which is good for us." He chopped a few more pieces of celery and tossed them into a stockpot. "Johnny's in his office. You can head on in. And by the way, I've got this under control. You go enjoy your date." With a wink, Henry cut another carrot in half.

"Thank you." She walked to the rear of the room and tapped on a half-open door.

"Come in."

Marigold pushed the door open and stepped inside. "Hi, there. I hope I'm not late." His brown eyes met hers and warmth crept into her middle.

Johnny rose from the desk. "You're right on time, and you're beautiful, as always." He lifted her hand and kissed it. "I have a surprise for you. Follow me."

31

He led her out the door into the courtyard. Strings of lights twinkled around two small cedar trees, and a round table for two, draped in a white cloth, sat in the middle of the brick-laid yard.

"This is lovely." She touched her hand to her mouth. "I picture people listening to a guitarist or other musicians playing in the corner on a small, raised stage. You have great potential here and it's... romantic." Her heart fluttered with delight. She had shied away from romance all her life, but Johnny's gesture warmed her. The candles on the table flickered, and the flowers released a sweet scent. The perfect setting for an evening with the man she cared about.

Never in her dreams had she pictured herself falling in love. Most of her life, she'd worked to keep herself fed and clothed while she searched for clues to her dad's disappearance. Of the few men she had dated, she never entertained the idea of a second date. She turned and found Johnny watching her. His eyes focused on her face, and the longing he showed gave her pause, while her pulse sped. This attractive, intelligent, kind man created this romantic dinner for her. No man had cared enough to listen to her and consider her ideas, let alone his vision, with her.

"I'm glad you like what I've done so far. I hired a young man to clean the area and get rid of grass between the bricks, then I strung a few lights. There's still much to do, but I wanted you to get an idea of what I had in mind." He moved to the table, pulled out a chair, and gestured for her to sit. "I'll be right back with our dinner."

Left alone, Marigold tried to view the space as a customer. She pictured a mural on the wall of the restaurant, fresh paint on the fence that enclosed the other three sides. Pots of ferns in the corner and an eclectic assortment of tables and chairs for two to four people. Candles on each table and the twinkling lights would add a soft ambiance.

Johnny carried two flat bowls filled with cherry tomatoes, peppers, cucumbers, fresh mint leaves, and feta cheese doused in olive oil-vinegarette dressing, with a loaf of crusty homemade bread. "Our starter for tonight. Enjoy." He sat across from her, placed his hand on hers, and blessed the food.

After a few bites, Marigold dabbed her lips with a napkin. "Delicious. You've outdone yourself."

"And that's just the salad. I'm eager for you to taste the moussaka."

"I've seen it on the menu, but I've never tried it."

Johnny placed his fork and napkin on the table. "I offer it about four times a year. It's fancy for the island, but I enjoy making it once in a while. I hope my Greek version of lasagna tickles your tastebuds." He chuckled.

"Sounds wonderful."

He gathered the salad bowls and headed to the building. As dusk turned to night, the stars came to life, and the full moon shone over the neighboring building, the tension Marigold carried in her shoulders eased. A sense of peace settled over her as she anticipated the rest of the meal. Johnny made the effort to enchant her with a fairytale setting and amazing meal. His kind ways enveloped her like a gentle hug.

The aroma of spices from the tray of food Johnny balanced on his arm enticed Marigold. At the table, he served the moussaka on white stoneware plates. The red sauce, lamb, and eggplant stacked in layers smelled incredible. After Johnny settled in his seat, Marigold dipped into the delectable meal.

"Oh my goodness, this is amazing."

"I'm glad you're enjoying it. My mom made it for us on Sundays, something she put together ahead of time and baked later. The taste brings back great memories of my loud family telling stories around the dinner table. Momma made meals special, but this one was the best."

Marigold laid her fork on the table and reached for his hand. She curled her fingers around his. "I'm honored you'd share your favorite meal with me. Thank you so much."

"I want to do whatever I can to..."

Henry rushed out the restaurant's door. "Johnny, kitchen fire!"

Marigold let go of Johnny's hand as he jumped from his chair, knocking it to the ground. "What?"

Henry bent over and held his knees, deep breaths dragged in and out. "I was cooking and must have turned the heat too high under the pan and flames mushroomed and caught the towel hanging overhead on fire." He waved his hands. "I tried to put it out with the fire extinguisher, but I couldn't get it all. The fire department is on the way. Joel cleared the patrons. The kitchen is burning as we speak." Flames glowed through the door.

"We better get out of here and meet the firefighters at the front." Johnny grabbed Marigold's hand and pulled her behind him, and Henry sprinted behind. Johnny shoved the fence gate open and ran along the sidewalk. They met the firetruck at the restaurant's entrance.

The volunteers hooked the hose to the plug and sprayed their way into the building.

Marigold stood in the middle of the street and watched Johnny pace the pavement. Helplessness depleted her emotions. How could she help this man who cared so much for his neighbors and for her? She sought God's ear and asked Him to pour peace and wisdom over Johnny. The tug at her heart for him transcended anything she had experienced for anyone else. She loved her friends, but the desire to protect and help him surpassed any she'd felt before. Was fifty-four too old to fall in love? Any other day, yes, but today her belief flip-flopped.

A hand on her shoulder pulled her from her rumination. "What am I going to do? So much for my big ideas. I'll be starting all over again."

"Oh Johnny, I'm so sorry. I'll do whatever I can to help. Maybe it will turn out to be a blessing and you can reinvent the restaurant." She turned and wrapped her arms around his waist.

He pulled her to him. "I hope you're right."

~~~~~~

Johnny kissed Marigold on the forehead, then spotted Henry on the curb in front of the restaurant, head in his hands. "I'm going to talk to Henry." He let go of her and approached his sous chef. He sank to the ground and placed a hand on Henry's arm. "This wasn't your fault. It was an accident, and unfortunately, they happen. I'm not blaming you. Got it?"

Henry raised his head. "How can you not blame me? It was my fault. I had too many irons in the fire, literally." He wrung his hands.

"If anyone is to blame—it's me. I left you on a busy night to impress Marigold. I should have postponed when I saw how full the place was. I'm sorry." He wrapped an arm around his friend.

Henry lifted his face to meet Johnny's. "I'm not fired?"

"Of course not." He squeezed his arm, then let go. "I'd be lost without you, man. And we've got a restaurant to rebuild."

Henry stood and offered his boss a hand up. "Thank you. I'm humbled by your kindness."

The firefighters exited the building, and the chief approached Johnny. "Most of the damage is in the kitchen. Henry said it started with a skillet fire which got out of control. Let me confirm and give you a timeline for when you can get in and evaluate the damage. I'll try to get my work done as fast as I can."

Johnny rubbed his hand over his bald head. "I appreciate your consideration. I'm hoping the insurance will be as quick."

When the fire truck drove off, Joel, Sadie, Marigold, and Henry stood beside Johnny and faced the building. Joel reached out his hand and took Johnny's in a firm grip. "Whatever we can do, you know Sadie and I will help. Say the word."

"Thanks. I'm going to call the insurance first thing in the morning, then I'll know my timeline. Until then, pray for guidance and wisdom. By the time I open again, tourist season will be close to the end. What if God's trying to tell me to forget my big ideas?"

Marigold stepped to his side. "God could be providing for those big ideas. Let's see what happens. I believe in you, Johnny, and I'm here for you."

He patted the hand she rested on his arm. "Thank you, that means a lot." Why burden her with his problems? After years with his family, then as an adult on his own, married with a child and divorced, he had hoped he'd found his paradise. One he could share with his daughter and now with a woman he cared about. Maybe God had other plans for him. What if God wanted him to return to Cleveland where his daughter, Alexa, lived? His little girl had grown into a responsible adult but kept her distance, sharing the occasional card or text. With the time off the fire would give him, maybe he should visit her. His stomach churned and anxiety swirled through his head. *Get it together.* He had been through tough situations before, and with God's help and his family and friends, he had survived and often thrived. Bad things happened, and he was determined not to let the fire depress him.

"I'm going to visit my daughter."

Marigold's eyes rounded. "What? Now?"

"Once the fire chief lets me know about the damage, and I settle with the insurance, I'm going to take a few days off, drive to Cleveland, and visit Alexa, if she'll have me." He breathed deep and let the breath out. "What do you think?"

With her hand wrapped around his arm, she turned him to her. "You've told me how much you miss Alexa. If you can work out the details, go see her. I'll miss you, but time with your daughter will be a blessing."

"Thank you." He drew Marigold into a hug. Her mere presence encouraged him. "I'll call her tomorrow. I hope she answers."

CHAPTER SEVEN

On the sidewalk in front of her parents' home, Ivy juggled paper boxes she'd gleaned from work. A few more steps and she dropped them on the stoop. With a plunk, they hit the cement. She drew her keys from her purse, inserted the gold metal and twisted. The colonial blue door swung open and the stale smell of lifelessness hit Ivy in the face. No aroma of spaghetti sauce and garlic bread or fresh-baked cookies wafted through the air. Not even the therapy candles Mom had burned for health reasons. Ivy choked back tears. Clearing out Mom's office would prove more difficult than she had imagined.

Tears of grief had filled her eyes for months. Now she urged herself to straighten her spine, lift the boxes, and go inside. As soon as the sisters purged the office, the realtor planned to stage their home for people to tromp through, while memories of Ivy and her sisters' laughter lingered in the corners. Life moved on, right? A new family might make lifelong memories, too. She pushed herself to let go and hand her former life over and relinquish the place she once called home.

Ivy stepped inside, closed the door, dropped the boxes, opened her hands, and raised them to the ceiling, as if to let go.

The door thudded behind her and bumped her shoulder. Poppy flew in, arms full of paper bags. "Happy Saturday, Sis. Oops. I didn't know you'd be standing in the doorway. I grabbed bags from the art store they were going to recycle. If we find anything we can recycle, I'll use these."

Ivy brushed her hands against each other as if to dust off the past and move forward. "Good idea. I've got more boxes in the car. Come help me get them?" Ivy led Poppy to the SUV and opened the hatch. "Here you go. I can get the rest. Have you heard from Violet?"

The two trekked into the house and stacked the boxes in the corner of the dining room. "You know she'll be late. She's probably waiting on Joseph. He said he'd take care of the kids, but he's always got something else to do first."

"I heard you." Violet stood in the open doorway, hands on hips.

Poppy put her hand over her mouth and closed her eyes. "Oops, sorry."

The middle sister walked in and closed the door. "You're forgiven, and you're right. Joseph had to finish mowing the yard this morning, then get a shower. I'm thankful he cares enough about us to take care of everything."

37

Poppy bowed her head to her sister. "You're right. He's a great guy. I've embarrassed myself now, so let's get started."

"Do we each take a corner, or do you want to sort together?" Ivy set two boxes and a large trash bag in the middle of the rusty red carpet. "Let's use a box for shredding, a box for keepsakes, if there are any, and a bag for trash. As we go along, we can figure out how many boxes and bags we'll use."

Her sisters perused the room. The corners overflowed with paper. Mom had kept notes on all her clients, the homes and businesses she sold and who knew what else. Dad had teased her about being a pack rat, but she had laughed him off with, "You never know what might come back to bite you."

Poppy sidled around an antique maple desk Mom used for office work. Since she had meetings with most of her clients at the Dreams Come True realty office, she kept her home office what some called messy, while she referred to it as relaxed.

From the desk chair, Poppy pulled open a drawer. "I can go through the desk, then we can use it to stack boxes on, if you want. I'm hoping it's more organized than the rest of the room."

Violet unfolded a wooden chair. "Good idea. I'll start with the file cabinet and the table next to it."

"Sounds good. I've got the boxes stacked in the corner, then." With a tug, Ivy pulled the lid from the top box and several papers fluttered to the floor. "Wow, this is going to test us, isn't it?"

Violet shoved her bangs from her face. "I think so, dear sister. Who knows, maybe we'll find money or a deep, dark secret. As if Mom had any."

The sisters chuckled and dug in to work.

~~~~~

An oversize dumpster blocked the sidewalk in front of Johnny's Place on Monday morning. Sweat poured down Johnny's back as he and Henry flung damaged equipment into the trash. The silence from his sous chef told Johnny Henry blamed himself. *Fires happen, and people make mistakes.* The young man's eyes glazed over more with each pan, broken plate, and twist of plastic they discarded. Before they piled another load into the wheelbarrow, Johnny stopped Henry and rested his hand on his shoulder.

"I don't blame you."

His protege wiped his face with a green bandana handkerchief, then stared at his dirty leather boots. "I'm so sorry." His dark ponytail swished side to side as he shook his head. "I should have been more careful."

"A fire can happen to anyone. We get busy, distracted, focused on the dish in front of us. If it's anyone's fault, it's mine. I left the kitchen on a busy night to court Marigold. I'm an old fool."

The corner of the young man's mouth lifted. "No, you aren't, Johnny. You're a man smitten by a beautiful lady. She's one of the good ones."

Johnny crossed his arms. "Smitten, huh?" He rubbed his bald head. "How about I admit I'm smitten, and we no longer blame ourselves for what Chief Larken recorded as an accident? Insurance will come through and we'll rebuild. I can use your help more than ever. I've got enough in my emergency fund to get by while we rebuild. You and the staff have unemployment, and I'll try to compensate some of the waitstaff's lost tip money. Plus, I'm paying you to help me clear out the mess. We'll figure this out." He tugged the bottom of his shirt out of his jeans. "Once we get the debris cleared, I'll have professionals come in and get the smoky smell cleared and everything cleaned. At least we didn't lose the furniture in the dining room. The big kitchen equipment is okay, and the generator is keeping the refrigerator and freezer running." He lifted the shirt tail and wiped his face. "I want us to both take a week off while the cleaning is going on. Although, I may have you check on the progress for me."

A spark lit in Henry's brown eyes. "You want me to check in with the cleaning crew? Are you leaving?"

"I am. I'm going to Cleveland to find my daughter, and I hope to have a visit." With a dustpan and broom, Johnny swept broken glass from the floor. "While I'm gone, make a list of what to replace in the kitchen. Throw in a few dream items, too. No promises on what we can do, but I plan to stretch the budget as much as I can." He set the broom against the wall. "You, young man, are the best sous chef I've ever worked with. Stick with me, okay?"

"You got it, boss." Henry whistled as he walked away.

~~~~~

Soft ripples washed tiny spiral-shaped shells along the sandy beach. Another Monday, slow and easy. Marigold and Charlotte carried buckets of sudsy water to the kayak shed. With robotic movements, Marigold unlocked the cord she used to keep the plastic boats from burglary and dragged them out to be washed. Her grandmother had designated Monday as wash day. A staunch, old-fashioned lady, she had employed a wringer washer for her chore. She never considered buying an automatic washing machine. In the summers, Marigold had cranked the antiquated machine to give her grandmother a break. After her grandmother passed and Marigold cleared her things, the washer stood on the porch and mocked her.

A few feet away, Charlotte scrubbed the seat of a red boat. "You're quiet this morning, Mari. Is everything okay?"

A breeze jostled the leaves on the nearby elm tree. "I'm sorry. I was thinking about the mess Johnny has to clean. Here I am wiping the kayaks, while he's got rubble in his kitchen. I asked if I could help, but he said he and Henry had it covered."

Water and soap dripped over the hard plastic of the boat Charlotte scrubbed. "You don't want to breathe in the smoky residue. I'd say he's got it under control. He's a smart guy."

Marigold poured clean water to rinse the suds away. "You're right. He's smart and knows what to do. I'd get in the way."

The ladies stacked the kayaks along the building, opened the shed, and prepared for business.

"Are you okay to man the rentals by yourself?" Marigold asked. "Mondays tend to be slow."

Charlotte unfolded a lawn chair, opened a book, sat, and crossed her legs. "Ready for business." She laughed and saluted her boss.

At home, Marigold unrolled the hose and watered her parents' memorial garden. Years ago, she had knelt on the ground beside her dad and dug in the dirt, applying the composted eggs, grass clippings, and coffee grounds he'd saved. In the fall, they planted tulip and crocus bulbs. When snow still covered the ground, the purple and yellow crocuses popped through and announced the hope of spring. She continued the tradition in a small flower bed by the she shed, dedicated to bulbed flowers. The sweet perfume of the hyacinth still tickled her memory. Maybe Dad found his way to a new life and planted flowers at a different home. If he had lost his memory, he could be anywhere. She'd read a book about a woman whose life memories disappeared after an injury, and she had to rebuild her life.

When Marigold had approached her grandmother with the story, seven or eight years after Dad disappeared, she'd called the idea hogwash. Grandmother may have been right, but what if she wasn't? What if Dad was still alive?

~~~~~

In the evening, after a shower and a bite to eat, Johnny reclined in his brown leather mission-style chair. His cell phone dared him to call. Before he changed his mind, he whispered a prayer for strength and direction, lifted the phone from the side table, and tapped in the number his daughter had sent him last year. Hope kept him from pushing the end button before the first ring. Three rings. Before the fourth one, he heard a click.

"Hello, this is Alexa."

His eyes closed at the sophisticated voice of his daughter. In her job at The Natural History Museum, she had polished her professional demeanor on her promotion to assistant researcher. As a child, Alexa had scampered along the Cuyahoga River with Johnny on hikes and exploration adventures. She spied a treasure at the water's edge, and he had held her hand while she stretched to wrap her fingers around a stone or piece of driftwood. On a blanket, she'd lay out every rock, then draw them in her field book or lay a piece of paper over them and rub them with a pencil to make an image of the texture. When she finished, she carried the rocks to the river and tossed them in with a splash. Her love of the natural world opened doors for her at Cleveland State University, as an adjunct, and at the museum. During the time she prepared for her life's work, Johnny opened his first restaurant—and lost his family. His ex-wife groomed Alexa for higher things, including a jam-packed education. His daughter's smarts paid the way as she climbed the ivory tower. A year ago, he had congratulated her on her new job. She thanked him and made an excuse to get off the phone. He prayed today she'd give him a chance.

Johnny straightened his posture and held the phone close to his ear. "Lexi, this is Dad."

CHAPTER EIGHT

The seconds ticked away on the glass-domed anniversary clock, a gift to Johnny from his *yaya*. He held the phone away from his ear as the sound of fingers clicking on a keyboard echoed. He tapped the speaker button. "Lexi, are you there?"

"I'm here, Dad."

He flipped the lever on his recliner so his feet touched the floor, then he rose and paced across the hardwood in his living room. "Thanks for answering. It's good to hear your voice."

A sound like rustling paper filled Johnny's ear. "Sorry, I have my phone on speaker. I'm trying to finish a project. Let me stack these files, then I'll have a minute to talk."

He rubbed his head, praying she'd want to chat with him. "Sure, I'm happy to wait." A few swishes and plunks later and the connection grew quiet.

"Dad?"

"I'm here. I hadn't talked to you in a while and I, well, I miss you." He dropped into the recliner and propped himself on the edge of the seat, as if he balanced on a tightwire. "How have you been?"

"Busy, as always." A light chuckle passed through the phone.

His forehead wrinkled. "You've always been a girl on a mission."

"How are you, Dad?"

A hint of actually caring in her question perked his spirit. "I'm good. An incident occurred at the restaurant last night, a fire in the kitchen, but no one was hurt, and I plan to rebuild. I called insurance, and I think everything will work out."

"Oh wow. I'm sorry." Alexa paused, and another voice sounded in the background. "Dad, I'm at work. I can't talk right now. How about another time?"

"Sure. I, um, I wanted to let you know I'd be in Cleveland next week and hoped to visit you."

"Yeah, stop by the museum. I'll be here from nine to six, unless I have a day I come in late. Ask for me when you get here. I have to go. Bye."

The call clicked off, and Johnny stared at his phone. What had gone wrong between him and his daughter? They had been buddies until she turned twelve, and his wife insisted Alexa enroll in enrichment classes, which left no time for outings with Dad. After the divorce, Alexa's teen years pulled her farther away, while Johnny worked to provide for her and create a brand in the restaurant business. He had worked too hard and spent too much time away. He loved his little girl and prayed he would get to know his adult daughter before too much time slipped away. If he visited the museum, she might be more comfortable on her own turf.

The doorbell interrupted his musings. "Coming." He lifted his button-down shirt from the back of the chair, slipped his arms through, then fastened the buttons. He hooked the last one through, then opened the door.

"Mari. Come in."

Dressed in a long lavender and green caftan, she carried a woven basket across the room and deposited it on the table. A smile crossed her face as her eyes twinkled. "I'd like to have a picnic in your backyard. I'm not the cook you are, but I can make pretty good sandwiches." She bowed to her humble offering.

Johnny closed the space between them and swept her into a bear hug. The spicy orange scent of her hair calmed his nerves, and peace settled over him. "Thank you. Being near you makes me feel better already. How about we take the food and sit on the patio?"

With the hamper in hand, they trekked outside. The concrete slab, bare except for a slatted table and two Adirondack chairs, faced a wooded area. The hum of bees hung over a clump of butterfly weed as the orange blooms waved in the breeze. A deer paused on the edge of the trees and stared at the movement on the patio.

"You sit and let me wait on you for a change." Marigold lifted paper plates, napkins, and bottles of water from the basket. "Good thing you have this big table by your chairs."

"I bought all this when I moved here. Sitting outside after a long run helps me cool down."

Marigold arranged the sandwiches on plates, the thick turkey and Swiss cheese draped over the edge of wheat bread. Chips and apple slices rounded out the meal. "Not fancy, but filling."

Johnny reached for her hand, bowed his head, and blessed the food. "I don't require fancy, and I'm hungrier than a buffalo." A rumble sounded from his stomach.

Laughter bubbled from Marigold. "Sounds like the buffalo are having a party." With a napkin in her lap, she perched on the chair and double fisted the sandwich. "Leave room for dessert. I don't cook much, but I enjoy baking. Pineapple upside down cake just for you."

He patted his belly. "I'll have to run extra tomorrow."

For the next ten minutes, he told her about his chat with his insurance agent and his plans to take a week off while he waited for the cleaning crew to finish.

Johnny swiped his mouth with his napkin. "I called Alexa today."

~~~~~

A heron swooped across the reddish pink sky, probably a traveler moving from the large pond on the other side of the road to the lake front. Oh, to fly away and forget everything.

Sandwich halfway to her mouth, Marigold stopped. "Really?" She placed the rest of her food on the plate, unscrewed her water bottle, and took a sip. Her napkin slipped off her lap. "Did she answer?"

A chip fell from Johnny's plate. "She did. I talked to her for about three minutes. Caught her at work."

Marigold picked up her stray napkin and twisted the paper between her hands. By the look on Johnny's face, the conversation hadn't opened any doors. "Does she want to see you?" A line of ants hustled to the discarded chip, marched under, and carried their dinner away.

"I'm not sure. I caught her at work and she sounded distracted. She told me to stop by the museum." He gulped a drink of water. "I don't want to bother her, but I sure want to talk to her."

Marigold lifted his hand and held on with both of hers. "She's your daughter, and I'm guessing she wants to see you. If I talked to her, she'd understand how precious having you in her life is. I'd give anything to be with my dad again. I've never gotten over losing him and my mom. My heart still hurts and longs to find my father."

Johnny wrapped his other hand around hers. "I can't imagine what you've gone through. To lose both parents at the same time."

"Grief is the price a person pays for love. When Sadie's grandma died, I mourned for months, even though Julia was in heaven. My mom, too. She loved God with all her heart. My dad, though, he could still be out there. Couldn't he?"

A doe on the edge of the woods nudged her spotted fawn into the trees, and a rabbit hopped across the yard.

"If he is, I pray you find him, and if I can do anything to help, say the word." Johnny let go of her hands and picked up his sandwich. "Want to take a walk after we finish eating? Sometimes it helps to clear my mind."

"I'd love to." A ramble through nature carried a peace she found only in God's creation.

Twenty minutes later, she embraced the hand he offered and stood beside him. Before they stepped off the patio, she wrapped her arms around him. "Thank you for understanding me."

He leaned in and kissed her forehead. "You're welcome. You are a special lady, and I'm thankful you're in my life."

At the edge of the woods, Johnny led her on a dirt path. The fragrance of honeysuckle drifted along the trail. She lifted the hem of her skirt and knotted it to keep it from dragging in the dirt. "I don't think I've hiked here before."

"This is private property. The owner told me to walk here anytime I wanted." He lifted a branch out of the way. "You know him. His name's Emmett. Says he's been here forever."

"I know Emmett. But he stays to himself. He stopped by one of the craft fairs one time, wanting a crocheted blanket. He said the one his wife made him had worn out. She'd passed away ten years earlier." Would she turn into a hermit like Emmett if she remained single? Her stomach twisted at the thought.

"He's an interesting fellow, for sure. Wasn't his grandson responsible for some of the trouble Sadie had last year?" Dead leaves crunched under their feet.

"He was. I'm so glad it all got figured out."

"Me, too."

His hand rested on Marigold's shoulder as they ducked beneath a tree limb. "When I go to Cleveland, I plan to secure some new equipment in a warehouse there. Then I'll try to visit Alexa, but I'm not sure if she'll take time to talk."

"I hope she does." A fallen tree blocked the path. "Want to turn around?"

"Yeah, Emmett put the log there, so I won't go any farther. He has a limit on how far in I can hike."

They turned and trekked to the house. Marigold gathered the picnic leftovers and tossed the garbage. "I'm putting the cake in the fridge for you to enjoy later."

He opened the door for her. "Sounds good."

The refrigerator hummed in the quiet kitchen. "Keep me posted on when you're leaving for Cleveland." Heartache swept through her at the thought of him leaving.

"I will. Do you want anything from any of the art stores? Any craft supplies?"

She shook her head. "No. I'm good. Thanks for asking. I'll be praying for you and your daughter. I hope you get a chance to connect." *And come home soon.*

"I appreciate your prayers. Henry and I will be clearing out and cleaning the last of what we can at the restaurant tomorrow. If the professional cleaners can come as soon as Wednesday, I'll leave for the city on Thursday. I'll call you." He pulled her to him and wove her into a comfortable hug.

~~~~~

Wednesday afternoon at the beach, Marigold demonstrated how to enter and exit a kayak for her customers. Muscle memory kicked in and she gave little thought to the movements. "Here's the easiest way to sit in the boat. Then when you come back, swing your legs out and stand. Make sure you are deep enough to stand and shallow enough not to fall in."

She steadied the kayak for the young girl, then held the end of another for the mom. "You two have fun and buckle those life jackets." They snapped the plastic grips and paddled into the lake. From the sand, Marigold soaked in the waves as the seagulls swooped and cried on the shore. The gray and white birds flocked wherever water met sand. Most days, the gulls minded their own business, but today they circled and a few flew inland. Dad had referred to seagulls as sensitive creatures. They sensed changes in the weather and big storms. More times than not, the wisdom proved true. She planned to check the weather tonight for any predictions the meteorologists forecasted.

At six in the evening, Marigold locked her shed and tied the kayaks together. The wind roared, and the waves grew. The seagulls proved accurate. By the time she opened her front door and carried her bags in, a torrent of rain fell. She flipped the switch on the lights, and nothing happened. No electric. Storms had knocked out the power so many times she had purchased a generator.

"It's somewhere in the basement." Down the steps and into the dark with the help of a flashlight, Marigold searched the corners. She lifted the machine and trudged upstairs. From the steps, her flashlight shined on an old trunk—her mom's earthly belongings, one of the few things she moved from her grandmother's home.

With the generator in place and a few lamps on, Marigold felt her way to the basement in the dim light. She hooked her hands on either side of the small trunk and lugged the box to the living room. Hesitant to dive into the contents, she ate a bowl of granola with blueberries and drank a glass of tea. Last time she had shuffled through the contents, she cried so hard, she'd had to stop and close the lid. The next day, she stashed the container in the basement, out of sight. Maybe this time she'd have the courage to rifle through all the contents.

CHAPTER NINE

Wind from the storm on Wednesday night had twisted and downed limbs from the old oak in the yard. The next morning, Johnny gathered the smaller branches and stashed them along the edge of the woods. One large limb lay under the tree, too big to tackle on his own. Eager to drive to Cleveland, he swiped debris from his hands, then headed inside.

From under the bed, he tugged a suitcase and tossed it on top of the covers. When he unzipped and opened the top, a card he had kept for years lay inside. A smile raised the corners of his mouth as he reached for the handmade construction paper Valentine. His precious Alexa had run into the house after school, jumped in his lap, and dug the special creation from her book bag. So proud of what she had made, she waved the red and pink artwork in front of his nose.

"Daddy, be my Valentine," her little six-year-old voice whispered to his heart.

"Of course I will, sweetheart, always and forever."

"I had wondered where this got to." The smell of school glue still clung to the paper. With care, Johnny propped the card against the lamp on the nightstand. *Back to your rightful place.* The reminder of his daughter's love fueled him with courage for the trip.

~~~~~

The same mother and daughter who had rented kayaks on Wednesday shuffled through the sand on Thursday morning. "We enjoyed the lake so much yesterday, we wanted to get out before noon and take a longer excursion." The woman waved her hands in the air as she spoke.

The lake roared and white caps spilled from the waves.

"I'm glad to be of help, but as much as I want to rent you boats today, I can't. I'm here checking for damage from the storm last night." Marigold turned to the lake. "Those waves could cause you problems. If you're still here tomorrow and the lake has calmed, I'll give you a ten percent discount."

The mom wrapped her arm around her daughter's shoulders. "I understand. What else could we do today?"

"Have you hiked the boardwalk? It's a nice trek through the woods on a raised walkway and ends at a beach. There's a pond and a couple of places to view wildlife. It's one of my favorites. Be careful of loose limbs or any branches on the trail." Marigold wrapped her braid around her hand.

Mom and daughter nodded at each other, then at Marigold. "Sounds like fun. Thanks." They waved and wandered off.

Marigold had missed out on so much in the last forty years. The affection between the mom and daughter increased the yearning in her to find her dad. Was her desire a pipedream or a possibility?

By the time Marigold cleared the area around her shed, her stomach growled for lunch. At home, she poured kibble into Cassatt's bowl, then warmed vegetable soup on the stove for herself. She carried a bowl to the table and knocked her foot into her mom's trunk.

Fearful of what she might find, she'd shoved it out of sight last night. Since she couldn't work at the beach today, she might take a peek inside. Digging into her mom's life might jostle her memory. What if she pieced together her father's disappearance from the clues in her mom's trunk, or would the things in there cause her heart to break all over again? In all these years, she'd not been able to sort through the contents. Every time she dove in, she stopped at the photo albums filled with pictures of her and her parents.

After a few bites of soup, a knock drew her to the living room, where she opened the door.

"Johnny, come in." An unexpected sizzle of electricity shot through her as she regarded his handsome face.

Dressed in dark blue jeans and a mint green polo shirt, he walked into her home. "I stopped to tell you I'm heading to Cleveland. Henry is overseeing the cleaning crew, and he'll organize what he can when they finish. I plan to settle into a hotel tonight, then check on replacements for what we lost in the kitchen tomorrow. I'm hoping Saturday to track down Alexa. She works on the weekend, so I know she'll be at the museum."

Excited for him, but sad for herself, she nodded.

Surprised the thought of him leaving left a hollow place inside her, she took a step back. They had spent time apart, but the idea of him reconnecting with his daughter gave her pause. Not one prone to jealousy, she shoved the thought aside and vowed to pray for them.

"I hope you get to see her." She pushed her hair behind her shoulder and kept a smile on her face. "Want something to eat or drink before you go? I have tea."

He shook his head. "No, I'm good. I'm going to get moving. Did you have damage from the storm? I noticed your flower beds survived."

"Other than debris on the beach and not being open for business today, I'm good. I'm hoping the rest of the week will be profitable." She caressed his hand, and a strong desire to hang on overwhelmed her. "You be careful. I'm praying all goes well for you with Alexa." She raised on her toes, and as she planted a kiss on his cheek, she soaked in the scent of his aftershave.

"Your kiss will carry me through." He smiled, hugged her, and left.

With a sigh, Marigold watched her dear friend drive away. Friend, or more? She loved him, but in what way? Enough to make a commitment? Perhaps enough to date and let other people know they were in a relationship. Enough to meet his daughter? Fifty-four-year-olds shouldn't be thinking about love, should they?

Before she allowed her brain and heart to battle, she dragged her mom's trunk across the floor. Seated on a low stool, she lifted the lid. A photo of her parents and her, at eight years old, smiled at her.

~~~~~

Poppy flopped on the chair behind her mother's desk. "I can't believe we had to come back to finish sorting all this junk."

Hands full of papers, Ivy nudged a box across the floor. "As if we had a choice. People are coming to view the house on Sunday, so we have to get it done. Thank goodness the rest of the house is ready." She dropped the papers on the floor and sank beside them. "I wanted to finish last Saturday, but Violet had to leave, and I ran out of steam."

Poppy twirled a pen with her fingers. "I know. I was here. Is Violet coming?"

With a shove, Ivy moved a stack of boxes to the side. "Yes, she'll be here as soon as she drops the kids off at their Thursday chess practice and math club. In the meantime, let's take the boxes for recycle to my car. I've got room. The extra space will give us room to finish." Her legs wobbled as she pushed herself from the floor. "The closet and the pile in the corner won't take long, once Violet gets here and helps."

A few minutes later, Ivy slid the nose plate of the dolly under the bottom box and tilted the stack. "Good thing Dad left a few tools in the garage. This makes the job so much easier."

Poppy led her out of the house, opening doors along the way. They lifted each box together and heaved them into the hatch.

"I hope someone is at the recycle center to help get these out," Ivy said.

"I can follow you and help." Poppy picked at her fingers. "I broke a nail, not sure how, since I keep them so short. But ouch." She shook her hand.

Ivy patted her on the back. "I think you'll be okay."

A blue minivan pulled into the driveway. The sisters waved at Violet as she opened the car door and got out. "Hi, girls." She raised a plastic container in the air. "I brought brownies."

With the dolly in front of her, Ivy rolled it along the sidewalk to the house. "Thanks, Sis. Come on in and bring them with you. I've got a thermos of coffee."

In Mom's office, the sisters tackled the stack of papers in the corner. "This is a pile of realty listings Mom kept from the local papers. Safe to say we can recycle those." Poppy filled three boxes with the aged papers.

"Now for the closet. Hard to tell what's in there. We've come across a ton of work-related paperwork. I'm not sure how much more there could be." Ivy blew a loose strand of hair out of her face. "How about we break for brownies?"

"Sounds good to me." Violet lifted the lid and served an extra-large square to each of her sisters, then sat cross-legged on the floor with a treat of her own. In to-go coffee cups, Ivy poured a decadent coffee roast with vanilla almond creamer.

After one bite, Poppy leaned her head on the wall. "These are amazing. Thank you, dear sister. The coffee is good too. This is worth all the work."

Ivy brushed crumbs from her Cleveland Guardians shirt, then opened the closet door. Neat shelves, with at least three boxes each, filled the space. "Looks like twelve boxes. Four apiece and we'll be done." Ivy stepped aside. "Take your pick." Each woman grabbed a box.

The first nine containers revealed more work papers. Most got pitched, a few shredded.

From the top shelf, Violet pulled a large box. "This is heavy." With a thud, the cardboard hit the ground and the lid popped off. Photographs tumbled to the floor. "What do we have here?"

"Dad, Mom, and us." Poppy lifted a large photo from the top. "I'm wearing a layette. Could be my first Sunday at church."

Ivy studied the photo over her sister's shoulder. "Is there anything on the other side?"

Poppy flipped the photo over. "Let me see." Faint pencil markings revealed a date and where the picture was taken. "This one is a month after my birth date and beside the church we attended." All three sisters examined the picture.

"Dad's expression seems sad. What if he didn't want me?"

"You know better, Poppy. Dad spoiled you and you know it." Hands on her hips, Violet gave Poppy a mom look.

"Yeah, he did, didn't he." A grin crossed Poppy's face.

The three of them shuffled through photos and divided the ones they wanted and re-boxed the ones they'd take to their dad. "He doesn't have much room in his new place. If you all don't care, I'll buy an album and make a memory book for him and store the rest in my attic." Ivy lifted the box and placed it on the desk.

Both sisters nodded in agreement.

"Two more containers." Violet peeked in one. "More newspapers." She opened the other one. "Clippings, letters, and more photos."

The box of newspapers proved to be more of their mom's realty sales with her face smiling in the ads. "Maybe we should each keep one of these and toss the rest." Ivy held an ad in her hand. "Mom worked hard all those years, while she raised us."

"She did. Between her work and Dad's landscaping business, they kept us well fed and clothed. Sometimes I wondered how they did it. Joseph and I struggle at times, and he has a decent paying job." She sighed and tucked an ad in her pile of photos.

"We're down to the last box, other than vacuuming and checking each room for any touch up work we have to do, then we're ready to sell." Ivy nudged the box with her foot. A pink paper poked out of the folded cardboard top. "What's this?" With a tug, she opened the box and pulled the paper out.

Her sisters crowded around her. "It's a letter in Mom's handwriting."

My Darling Daughters,

If you have found this box, I am gone from this world. No doubt you've had to help your dad clean out my office, perhaps the house, too. I'm sorry I left a mess, but by the time I realized I needed to clear things out, I was too sick. I'm also sorry you are making this discovery without me there to explain. I'm a coward, but I couldn't bear to tell you what a horrible person I was.

Don't get me wrong, I'd do what I did all over again. Yes, I have regrets, but you have to understand how much I love your father. He is my world. Please stand by him and help him. He's aging before my eyes, and I won't be there to take care of him.

After you go through the contents of this box, I hope you can forgive me. If I hadn't married your dad, you all wouldn't be here. I love each of you so very much. In the bottom of the box is a journal I hope explains what I did and a letter I want you to take to a woman I've kept track of for many years. Her location is on the envelope. Be gentle when you approach her. She has no idea of any of this. If you must, share this with your dad so he understands what happened.

I love you girls with all my heart. I'm sorry for the pain this will cause.

Love,
Mom

Ivy folded the letter. "What in the world?"

Dark shadowed the windows as Poppy and Violet stared at their sister.

"What did Mom do that was so bad?" The alarm on Ivy's watch

sounded as she stared at the letter. "It's getting late. I want to dig into this tonight, but we all have to get up early tomorrow. Can we tackle this on Sunday? Or I could take it home and go through it, then share with you?"

Hands on her hips, Poppy heaved a sigh. "No way are you finding out without us. We have to do this together. Either we do it now or wait until we can all go through the box."

"I agree with Poppy." Violet rubbed her temples.

The lone box taunted them from the closet floor. "Fine. Let's meet Sunday, after church. Until then, we better pray nothing too bad is coming at us."

CHAPTER TEN

Saturday morning, the beach buzzed with people. Charlotte shoved a kayak to Marigold, who pushed the green plastic boat to the water. Newlyweds, who married on the island and honeymooned in a cozy, secluded cabin in the woods, nabbed a double kayak and mooned about the fun they'd have on their excursion. Marigold wanted to roll her eyes but contained herself. The love of the young couple warmed her heart, but the gushing invoked her gag reflex. Had she allowed herself to be hardened to the flutters and beauty of two people who embraced their commitment?

Sorrow brushed a stroke across her heart. Most of her adult life, she had mourned her mom, searched for her dad, and worked to survive. If she opened herself to Johnny, did she give up on finding the truth about Dad? Years ago, her friend, Julia, had suggested she seek closure. *I miss Julia.* The wise woman spoke truth.

Charlotte tapped Marigold on the back. "Do you want me to ready the rest of the kayaks?"

She blinked as if to swipe the cobwebs out of her mind. "Yes. With it being Saturday and sunny, we'll be busy all day."

Her employee dragged the boats close to the shore, ready for launch. In the shed, Marigold arranged the life jackets by size and stacked the paddles against the outer wall. She checked the money box for change and carried towels from the golf cart to the shelves. Everything in place, Marigold perched on the macrame chair she had attached to the tree and listened to the water. The newlyweds glided along the edge of the bay in perfect sync. Charlotte instructed a couple of young men on how to get in and out and made sure they secured the life jackets. Too many people believed they could go out on the lake without a life preserver. Not on Marigold's kayaks.

"Did you have trouble convincing those two to wear the life jackets?"

Charlotte trudged through the sand. "I did. They said they were on the swim team and didn't need them. I told them they didn't have a choice. I hope they leave them on, since they plan to be out for hours."

"Thanks for sticking to the rules. We can't afford for anyone to get hurt." Marigold opened a bag with cotton yarn and a crochet hook.

"What are you making?" Charlotte fingered the yarn.

"Coffee rugs are what they call them now. Basically, they're oversized coasters." She handed her a finished granny square.

"Those are cute."

"They sell well at the festivals. Make nice stocking stuffers." Marigold worked the hook in and out of the yarn.

"How can you think about Christmas in June?" A laugh escaped Charlotte's lips.

Marigold shrugged. "I have to work ahead to be ready. Plus, there are a few festivals I attend in the summer."

A family of six approached the ladies. "We'd like to rent three kayaks for an hour. The two youngest are riding with us."

Charlotte and Marigold both jumped to help them. With a wave, Marigold led them to the shore. "Right over here. What brings you to the island?"

The mom smiled at the dad, then said, "Vacation. We live in Cleveland and wanted a weekend getaway. Island time is our remedy for our hectic week."

"Welcome, and I hope you enjoy your excursion. Let's get the lifejackets on and buckled." Marigold sent the two older children into the water, with a push on their kayak, followed by the parents and the two youngest.

The water rippled away from the vessels. Warm air wafted around Marigold as she stared after her customers. Johnny had traveled to Cleveland on Thursday. Other than a text that he had arrived and settled in, no word about Alexa or his search for equipment had pinged her phone. He planned to visit the museum today. *Lord, be with Johnny as he tries to open a door with his daughter.*

~~~~~

Inside Cleveland's Museum of Natural History, Johnny's eyes followed the Foucault Pendulum as it moved a smidge clockwise with each swing, emulating the earth's axis on its rotation. Each slight movement tipped a domino over and represented time slipping away. At least he imagined each second ticked away as he wasted more time apart from his daughter.

On his walk past the prehistoric exhibit, a shiver ran along his spine. So many dinosaurs' eyes pierced his back. He talked himself out of breaking into a run. Instead, Johnny sauntered through the gigantic creatures and found his way to the gallery where the gems and jewels sparkled. As a child, the shiny rocks and mysterious stones mesmerized Alexa. As an adult, this area turned into her professional playground.

A gray lump caught his attention. The lunar rock, pocked with holes, dull compared to the emeralds and diamonds in nearby cases. Yet this rock drew Johnny's attention. While he studied the lunar lava, footsteps sounded behind him.

"Dad?"

He turned to his daughter's voice. Dressed in a pale pink Oxford button-down shirt and a black pencil skirt, Alexa clicked across the floor in her dark gray pumps.

"Hi, Alexa."

"What are you doing here?" She crossed her arms over the pad of paper she held to her chest.

He rocked heel to toe with his hands shoved in his pockets. "I came to see you."

She stepped closer to him and hissed through her teeth, "You said you wanted to visit me, but I didn't think you'd hunt for me at work. I mean, I'm busy, you know, working."

He raised his hands as if to surrender. "I tried calling and your phone went to voice mail. When you didn't answer, I came by here and browsed the displays. You had mentioned I might catch you at work. Remember? I'd hoped, if I ran into you, we could plan to meet for dinner." His shoulders raised. "What do you think? Does dinner sound good? You always loved the restaurants in Little Italy. My treat."

What had he been thinking? He should have planned better and not raised her Greek ire. Like him at her age, she tangled with a quick walk to anger. For years, he had tamped down his temper until he controlled the temptation to bite the head off an employee. He prayed she might do the same.

The tension eased from her face. "I can do dinner. How about Trattoria on the Hill? I haven't had the lobster ravioli in ages." A smile lifted the corners of her mouth.

Johnny nodded. "Sounds good. I haven't been there in years. Thinking about linguine and clams makes my mouth water. Can I pick you up after work?"

Soft classical music drifted from the ceiling speakers as she pursed her lips. After a moment, she flipped the page on the pad of paper she'd been holding and scribbled her address. "Call when you get there, and I'll be out. It's a walk-up flat, and the parking is terrible."

When she handed him the paper, he clasped her hand and gave it a squeeze.

Her hand wrapped around his for a few seconds. "It'll be good to visit with you. And Dad, thanks for coming."

~~~~~

At 6:30, Johnny pulled his car to the curb in front of a high school built in the early 1900s, renovated into apartments. The contractors had refreshed the white trim around the red brick entryway and retained the charm of the original construction. He drummed his fingers against the steering wheel and watched the door. His beautiful daughter, wearing a red sun dress flowered with daisies, exited the building. A toot from the horn captured her attention. With grace, she stepped to the curb.

Johnny hopped out of the car, moved to the passenger side, and opened the door. "My sweet girl, you are beautiful."

"Thanks, Dad. It's nice to change from my work clothes." Once in the seat, she smoothed the fabric across her lap, and he closed the door.

Settled in the driver's seat, Johnny pulled into the Saturday evening traffic. "I checked the GPS, and we aren't too far from Little Italy." As his phone mapped the way, the sound of silence filled every crevice of the car. Perhaps music might lighten the mood. "Do you have a favorite radio station?"

Her dark brown eyes stared straight ahead. "The quiet is nice. I spent the morning teaching a group of homeschoolers about the fossils and minerals found in Ohio. They behaved, but they asked a ton of questions. As a matter of fact, they scheduled a tour with me on your island. They want to study the glacial grooves and the big rock with the inscriptions marked on it."

He glanced over at her. "So you're coming to Abbott Island?"

"I am. In a couple of weeks. We have to firm the details." She ran her hands over her dress again.

Johnny cleared his throat. "I'd love to have you stay with me. I have an extra bedroom with plenty of space."

She traced a flower on the cotton fabric. "I'll think about it." She turned her head and stared out the window.

Behind Trattoria on the Hill, he pulled into a parking space in their lot. She opened her door before he got around the car.

"You know it's okay to let a man open your door, even your old dad."

Alexa stopped and glared at him. "I know, Dad. If you'd treated Mom the same way, you might still be together." She stomped her feet as she plowed to the entrance.

After a deep breath, in and out, Johnny followed his daughter. Before they entered, he stood to the side of the building. "Alexa, can we talk before we go inside?"

Her brown eyes darkened. "I'm sorry I sounded off and acted rude."

"Let's get this straight. I don't know what your mom has told you, but I was always a gentleman to her. If I wasn't, my mother would have had my hide. Yes, your mom and I had our differences, but they never involved you. We both love you. Although I haven't told you enough. Now let's go in and enjoy the food and try to have an adult conversation."

Her head bowed, she nodded and climbed the steps under the brick archway. The fragrance of Italian spices mingled with garlic lingered in the air.

"Table for two, please." Johnny placed his hand on his daughter's elbow and followed the server to a table by the window. "This place is so full of heritage. I love restaurants that embrace the authentic foods of their culture."

"You do, don't you? I remember tasting food for you when you had your restaurant here. A ten-year-old running around in your kitchen had to drive you crazy." She unfolded her napkin and placed it on her lap, then opened the menu.

"You never bothered me. I loved having you in the kitchen with me. Remember, I had the stool with your name carved into the seat. You'd sit there and do your homework or help with little tasks. Then you got too busy."

His daughter's lips morphed from smile to frown in seconds. Her chin dropped, and she stared at the menu. Before he stopped himself, Johnny reached for her hand. She pulled away.

"I'm so sorry, honey. I meant you joined extracurriculars and had more homework.

She raised her head, and her brown eyes shined with tears. "I'm sorry, too. I wanted to be with you instead of all those meetings and activities, but Mom said I had to do the extra stuff if I wanted to go to college on scholarship."

This time Alexa embraced her dad's hand. "Can we start over? I mean our dinner. I'd like us to have a nice memory from tonight."

"Me too. Let's create many more pleasant memories from this point on." He had missed his daughter and thanked heaven for a second chance at growing their relationship. "What do you say? Want to spend more time with your old dad?"

CHAPTER ELEVEN

Sunday afternoon at their dad's house, the bright sun glared through the slatted blinds, and Ivy brooded. Poppy lifted the ominous box from their mom's closet and placed it in the middle of the carpet.

As if they required an opening ceremony before they continued, the three sisters stood and stared at the cardboard container.

"We may as well get this over with." Violet bent to sit on the floor. "You going to join me?"

Poppy and Ivy settled on the floor as Violet pulled the battered box to her.

"Let's take one thing at a time and see what this is all about. I haven't slept well since we read the letter, and I want to know what happened." Flaps on the box hung over the sides and revealed the letter they'd read on Thursday. "Let's put this aside and read it again after we sort everything else."

Mom had gloried in organization, but this box was a jumbled mess, kind of like her office and unlike the rest of the house. Papers stuck out from notebooks and newspaper clippings appeared to be ripped from the page instead of trimmed with scissors. Faded newsprint hung from Poppy's grip.

"How about we sort all the clippings and put them together, then make a pile for the loose papers and anything else we come across?"

"Good idea. At least we'll get a feel for what's in here." Violet unfolded and smoothed a sheet of paper. "Here's a yes and no list, like you make when you're trying to decide something."

"Let me see it." Ivy snatched the lined notebook paper from her sister. "Try to find out who Edward is or let him think he belongs here. Take him to a psychologist for evaluation or see how he does on his own. Use homeopathic remedies to try to help or seek a doctor's advice. What is this? What does she mean, find out who Dad is? He's our dad." She dropped the paper to the floor as if the words burned her fingers.

"What else is in here?" Poppy tugged a small nondescript photo album from the pile. Loose photos fluttered to the floor. "These look old. Is this Dad? He's bruised and pale." She passed the picture to her sisters.

Ivy studied the image. "This is Dad all right. He's got a purple mark on his face and a couple of cuts, and he's asleep on a couch. Why did Mom have a photo of him sleeping?"

Poppy pointed to the other side of the photo. "What's scribbled on the back?"

Ivy flipped it over. "Nineteen-eighty something. Edward, after I found him." Her brow scrunched, and she shook her head. "Found him, as in, oh I found a person I love or found him as in, I picked him up along the road? What on earth does she mean?"

"Here's a book about memory loss. Mom or somebody dog-eared a bunch of pages and made notes in the margins." Violet flipped through and stopped at a bookmark. A chapter titled *Retrograde Amnesia* stared at her. "Listen to this. 'Uncommon, in most cases, retrograde amnesia causes the person to lose all or most recollection of their previous life. They retain skills and often remember things like how to brush their teeth and prepare food, but do not recollect their previous life.' We'd better keep digging."

Poppy unearthed a flowered diary from under clippings and photos and waved it in the air. "I'm guessing this has the answers to our questions. Anybody find a key while we cleaned the other day?"

From her pocket, Ivy pulled a set of keys. "House key, car key, not sure what this is to, and this little bitty key. Might work." Poppy poked the gold key into the lock and turned. "Mom made locating the key easy on purpose, now I'm not sure I want to open the book."

"Then give it to me." Violet took the journal and flipped the cover open. She tossed the keys to Ivy. "Before we read this, let's pray. God knows what's in here and we don't. We need His help." Both sisters nodded, and Violet asked God to give them understanding hearts and minds. "Okay, here we go."

~~~~~

In Cleveland, Johnny waited for Alexa at a local sandwich shop. After dinner on Saturday, they had promised to meet for lunch and say goodbye. Last night, Alexa chuckled at funny stories from her childhood and a few of his crazy restaurant tales. A laugh with his girl encouraged him to reach out more.

In khaki capris and a short-sleeved lavender top, Alexa passed by the window, then entered the shop. "Hey, Dad. Sorry I'm late."

"No problem, but my stomach is complaining." Johnny pulled Alexa's chair out for her, then sat in his seat. "I've been watching them make the sandwiches, all fresh ingredients. What would you like?" His stomach rumbled as the smell of Italian dressing tickled his nose.

At the counter, as Johnny ordered the food, a soft breeze blew in the door as folks entered. Behind him, a voice he recognized called to his daughter. No. He longed to chat with Alexa and make plans for her visit to the island. He didn't want to talk to his ex-wife. As far as their relationship, they managed to get along, but he had hoped for a quiet lunch, with no interruptions.

He gathered the food and drinks and marched to the table. "Robin, how are you?"

Three-inch heels added to her five-foot-ten height as she stood. "I'm great. And you?"

"Doing well." He lowered to the chair she'd left warm.

"I don't want to disturb you, and Alexa said you're leaving soon. So nice of you to take the time to visit your daughter." She glared down her angular nose. Her haughty stare betrayed her somewhat kind words.

His hands gripped both sides of the turkey on wheat, then he drew it to his mouth, and savored a bite of avocado spread. Best not to answer. He nodded and chewed while he counted to ten. Nothing would please him more than for them to get along better, yet with each encounter, no bridge crossed the difficult divide as hurt feelings stretched between them. *Be polite and kind,* he repeated as he swallowed.

"Yes, I'm delighted to visit with Alexa." He shoved another bite in his mouth and found sympathy in his daughter's eyes. A first for her to show empathy toward her dad.

Robin left them, ordered a salad, then waltzed out of the shop.

"I'm sorry, Dad, I had no idea she'd show. I told her last night what we were doing today. I figured she'd be at her home, across town. By the way, she's worked her way into the loan officer position at the bank." Her voice reverberated with pride. "She makes a good salary, and I think she's dating someone."

"Good for her." Johnny ripped open a bag and crunched on a salt and vinegar potato chip.

Near the end of their meal, the noise level in the deli rose when four young men entered, dressed in business suits. One flashed a smile their way. "Hey Alexa, how's it going?"

Johnny raised his eyebrows in curious dad fashion. "You know them?"

"Yes, Dad. The one who said 'hi' goes to my church." She wadded the sandwich wrapper and tossed it in the can behind him.

Johnny did the same, sipped the rest of his tea, then tossed the cup and chip bag. "I haven't asked, and maybe it's not my business. Are you dating anyone?"

"You're right, it's not your business." A laugh followed. Alexa joking with him was a first, too. She hadn't laughed much since she entered high school.

He stood and pushed his chair in. "A dad has to try."

Alexa stood and Johnny appreciated the beauty she'd grown into. No more braids and braces. Stunning was what he'd call her. Happy to hear the tidbit that she still attended church, he left his questions for when she arrived on the island.

"I'll have your room ready. Please let me know when to meet you at the ferry. The restaurant will be under construction for a few weeks. The contractor starts tomorrow morning."

"As soon as I discuss the date with the home school group, I'll let you know. I'm hoping they either want a Monday or Friday, so I can spend the weekend. This has been good, Dad. I'm glad we talked some things out yesterday. Helps me understand you better. Thanks." She tagged behind him to his car and wrapped him in a hug he would hold on to for a long while. As he drove away, he checked the rearview mirror. His little girl, who had grown up, stood on the sidewalk and waved goodbye.

~~~~~

A cacophony of weeds waved in the raised garden behind Marigold's house. The vegetables had sprouted, too. Pepper stalks shot to the sky while the tomato vines embraced their stakes. Cloth gloves decorated with tiny rakes, shovels, and spades covered Marigold's weathered hands. Nothing better than playing in the dirt to help clear a person's mind.

Earlier, on her way home from church, she had dropped by the restaurant to see if Johnny had returned from Cleveland. Disappointment met her instead of her handsome friend. A text yesterday told her he had planned to come home on Sunday. She had swung past his house, but no car sat in the driveway. Perhaps he and his daughter reconciled and enjoyed a great weekend, or he wanted to hang around to try to get closer to her.

The little garden sighed with relief as she mounded weeds into the utility basket. Marigold removed a glove and swiped her forehead. Fifty-four and still able to kneel on the ground felt pretty good for a lady of a mature age.

When her grandmother was in her fifties, she had worked circles around Marigold. In the spring, after a day of high school, she had come home to find her grandmother preparing a quarter-acre garden with a horse and a common walking plow. Her neighbors offered to use their tractors, but she refused. After Grandpa passed, a few months before Mom, Grandma took over all the chores. Said she preferred the outdoor work, which left Marigold to tend to the house. Not such a bad thing, except she still used a wringer washer. At least they had electricity and running water.

Living with Grandma, she had learned her dad and grandma stood at odds most of the time. She had opposed the marriage, because she wanted more for her daughter than to marry young and raise a family. When Mom had declared her love for him, Grandma threw her hands in the air and said, "It's your life. Don't run to me when you have trouble." Mom held her own and enjoyed her part-time job at the local craft store and loved on her family.

The day Mom had arrived home from the hospital with Marigold,

Grandma had stood on her daughter's doorstep with a bag filled with groceries and a box with two casseroles, homemade biscuits, and a crocheted baby sweater. Grandma ignored Dad, but Marigold's birth had mended the fence between mother and daughter. At least that was the story Mom had shared.

That had to be why Grandma refused to search for Dad. Marigold had begged her to call the hospitals, the police and anyone else who might help, but Grandma's stubborn streak held. "Your dad used this as an excuse to leave." The words hurt, but deep in her heart, she refused to believe her grandmother's angry words.

Marigold stood and brushed dirt off the hem of her skirt. Still enough time in the day to sit on the porch and crochet. Thank goodness Charlotte worked the kayak rentals this afternoon. She had found a gem in her employee. An inquiry to her friend Jo, who sat on the school board, about a possible teaching position might be warranted. Convincing younger people to stay on the island added life to the long winters.

So did snuggling with Johnny on a snowy day.

Hurry home, please.

CHAPTER TWELVE

Quiet blanketed the house Sunday afternoon as the sisters read through newspaper clippings and notes. Ivy set aside the book explaining memory loss and lifted another photo from the bottom of the box. A woman with a long white braid stood on the shore of a beach. Her back to the camera, she wore a long, purple paisley skirt with a yellow peasant blouse. Ivy had considered buying an outfit like it for Poppy in a vintage shop once, but the skirt would have wrapped around her petite body twice.

"Why did Mom have a picture of a hippie on a beach?"

Poppy snatched the photo and Violet hung over her shoulder. "Could be a friend or acquaintance of her or Dad. She might be the woman Mom talked about in the letter." Violet tapped her finger against her mouth, then tore the picture from Poppy's hand. "I don't recognize the beach. Do you?" She squinted at the woman, then handed the picture to Ivy, who held it out in front of her, as if the photo told a story.

"The newspaper clippings we found refer to a wreck about five miles from here. A woman named Louise Hayes was killed and the husband, Nick, was never found. Why did Mom care? Do you think they were old friends?" Poppy shuffled through the pile of pictures. "Most of the photos are of Dad or Mom before we were born. Check this out. They had a convertible for a while. Mom's sure wearing a big smile, but Dad looks like a lost little boy. Do you want to add any of these to the album you're putting together, Ivy?"

"I'll look through them. Dad might have good memories of the convertible."

Poppy lifted a pile of newspaper clippings from the floor, where she sat with her legs crisscrossed. "These are stories about kids at a school pretty far north of here. Honor roll lists and school plays. Did Mom or Dad have cousins on the Lake? Want to toss these?"

"Not yet. Let's read the journal first, then we'll figure out if they're something Dad wants to keep." Violet gathered a paper box to put the keepsakes in. "There are a few things we can pitch, like the realty ads we found, but let's keep anything we don't know about until we figure out why Mom had them. Do you agree?"

Ivy and Poppy nodded.

"Let's go through the journal. I'm guessing it will tie this mess together." Ivy opened to the first page.

~~~~~

Sunday evening, in her living room, Marigold tugged her mom's trunk across the floor until it rested in front of the couch. Seated beside the leather and wood box, she opened the lid and wrinkled her nose as a musty odor, of years past, spritzed the air.

She ran her hand across the stitches on an old handmade quilt. Beneath the flowered cloth, she discovered a white cardboard box. Under the lid, her fingers touched fabric softened by time. With trembling hands, Marigold lifted ivory colored lace that covered a silk bodice. Years ago, her mom had modeled the delicate dress for her and twirled around the bedroom. The silk fabric of her mom's wedding dress hung from her hands. She had sewn the fabric herself and had recounted the story of Grandma and how she refused to look at the dress, but then when she saw it, she burst into tears and hugged her daughter. Regardless of how Grandma acted, Mom loved her.

Marigold's hands, freckled with sun spots, smoothed her mother's dress. She held the fabric to herself and eyed her reflection in the mirror. Years ago, the ankle-length, slim-waisted dress may have fit her, but not now, not with the years of enjoying island food. With gentle hands, she folded the gown, wrapped the fabric with the thin wrinkled tissue paper, and nestled it in the box.

Beneath the dress box, more wrinkled and yellowed tissue paper covered another surprise. The fragile paper crumbled as she lifted the edges and uncovered a pink crocheted baby cap and sweater. Marigold fingered the yarn and looked at Cassatt. "Mom made this for me. I remember her showing them to me when I was a girl." They had dressed one of Marigold's baby dolls and set out a tea party. Her heart still ached for her mom and for the opportunities she had lost over the years. By now, if she had had children of her own, she might be a grandmother, but she didn't regret her choice to stay single.

In the bottom of the trunk, a stack of letters her dad and mom penned to each other waited. She'd read them another time. Enough nostalgia pierced her heart for one day. As she closed the trunk and scooted it to a corner of the room, a knock drew her mind away from the discoveries.

A small cloud of dust escaped her dress as she shook it out on her way to the door. Through the window, she spied Johnny, and a bolt of excitement soared through her. She hurried to open the door.

"Come in."

"Hello, sweet lady." He pressed a kiss on her cheek, then trailed her to the couch.

"Have a seat. Would you like tea or water?"

"No, I'm good, but thank you. Sit with me. I want to tell you about Alexa." He patted the flowered cushion.

Marigold settled beside Johnny, pulled a crocheted afghan around her shoulders, and leaned in to listen. "Tell me about your trip. Was it good?"

Johnny took her hand and held tight. "I found the kitchen equipment I needed and am having it delivered next week. A higher grade of plates and silverware was on sale."

"Good to hear." She patted his arm. "I saw Henry on Saturday, and he said things are coming along."

"I got a text from him saying the same." Johnny released Marigold's hand and scooted closer. "I surprised Alexa at work, then had dinner with her. She's going to come to the island for a homeschool group who wants her to lecture about the glacial grooves and other interesting geology. She's going to stay with me. I'm not sure of the dates yet, but soon."

"Great. I bet you're excited." A twinge of nervousness flitted through Marigold's mind. She had never met Alexa. Being Johnny's only child, she might scrutinize his relationship with Marigold. Not one to worry too much about what others thought, meeting Alexa gave her pause. The young woman might be protective of her dad and wonder why he chose her to be his friend.

Johnny patted Marigold's hand. "She's going to love you. We can take her kayaking or out to the alvar. She's been there when she studied in college, but a personal tour might be fun."

Visions of falling off the kayak or tumbling on the rocks trickled through Marigold's mind. What if she left a poor impression? Alexa might see her as an old hippie with her claws in her dad's bank account.

"Hey, don't get nervous about meeting my daughter. She's going to see you the way I do, a kind, caring person." His arm wrapped around her shoulders.

With a tentative smile, she lifted her face to his. "How did you know what I was thinking?"

"I know you pretty well." He touched his finger to her chin. "No worries, okay?"

"All right." *At least she'd try.*

~~~~~

Photos and newspaper articles lay strewn across the floor. Eight-thirty Sunday evening, Ivy, Violet, and Poppy stared at their mother's office wall. No one voiced a word. The journal rested in the middle of them on the carpet, with pages flipped open. Ivy cleared her throat. "Do you want me to keep reading?" She eyed her sisters as if to ask them to say no. "I'm not sure how much more I can take and it's getting late."

A palm on each temple, Poppy shook her head. "No more tonight."

Violet raised her hand. "I want to go home. I can't take anymore."

"We should at least talk about what we've read." Ivy raised from the floor and stretched her arms out to her sides.

Her sisters stood and the three of them joined hands. Ivy nodded at Violet. In a solemn voice, the middle sister prayed. "Lord, we ask for wisdom and understanding. Finding out life isn't what we believed has punched us in the gut. Can You please help us?"

"Thanks, sis." Ivy lifted the journal from the floor, placed a paper in it to mark where they left off, and closed the cover. "From what Mom wrote in here, we don't know who our father is and neither does he."

"Yeah. She found him in the woods behind her house one night. Her car wouldn't start, so she didn't take him to the hospital." Poppy pushed a loose strand of hair behind her ear. "Why didn't she call the police?"

Violet wrung her hands, then rubbed her arms. "Wasn't Mom an EMT then? She talked about the runs she went on. She had a friend, Becky, who taught her homeopathic medicine, she may have tried to treat him with some herbal remedy. Obviously, she didn't feel threatened or she wouldn't have taken him home." The three sisters paced around the room.

Ivy placed the box with the journal on the top shelf of the closet. "On the last page we read, she said she took him to the doctor, but by then she'd given him a new identity. Did she steal someone else's social security number? People do after someone has been dead for a while. That journal is full of secrets, but I can't take in anymore tonight." She placed her hand on the knob and pressed the closet door closed. "We can't say anything to Dad. He may not know. What did she call it? Retrograde amnesia. So he must have gone to a doctor at some point.

"We're about a fourth of the way into the story. Let's take time to let it sink in. I want to do research, too. I'm guessing the journal, newspaper pieces, and photos are all connected. Must be why Mom kept this closet locked. I remember coming in here one day looking for a notebook, and she blew a gasket when I tried to open the door. She ran me out and found a notebook in the kitchen desk." Ivy lifted an empty folder from the recycle box, sorted a few articles and photos and tucked them in. "I'm taking these home to do some more research. Do you mind?"

Violet shook her head. "No, not at all."

Her sisters gathered their purses. "Please share what you discover."

Arms wrapped around the folder as if it contained gold, Ivy nodded. "Of course I will. When can you guys meet me back here?"

Poppy tugged a calendar from her bag. "How about Monday, late afternoon? I don't have any classes then."

"Sounds good to me." Violet checked her phone app. "The kids have a meeting after school for band, but Joseph can pick them up."

The three of them left the house. Ivy locked the door, stashed the folder on the passenger seat, then walked around the car, opened the door, and settled into the driver's seat. Hands on each side of the steering wheel, she rested her head on the top and closed her eyes. "Mom, what have you done?"

A peck on the window jolted her. When she raised her head, she stared into the greenest eyes she had ever seen, a shade of jade, and she caught herself staring. Before she embarrassed herself further, she turned on the ignition and rolled down the window. "Hi."

The man with the enchanting eyes leaned in. "I'm sorry to bother you, but I'm trying to find Edward Downey."

"Can I ask why?" She wrinkled her brow.

His hair, longer on the top, flopped over his forehead. "I have questions for him. I'm Christopher Downey, and I want to know why he's posing as my grandfather."

CHAPTER THIRTEEN

The visit with Alexa and a good night's rest left Johnny energized. After a run Monday morning, he loaded the car with the paperwork and computer he'd taken from the office after the fire. Henry called and assured him the cleaning crew had finished scouring the restaurant and the smoky smell had dissipated.

At the restaurant, he raised the lid on his laptop and logged in. Thankful the localized damage to the kitchen allowed him to open his office and work from his desk, Johnny emailed his employees with progress and an estimated reopening date. In two to three weeks, he hoped to have all the work completed and the outdoor space ready. If he could tie his idea into the reopening, he'd grab the tourists' attention.

A knock reverberated from the office door. "Hey, Johnny. How was your trip?" Henry leaned on the doorjamb.

Johnny stood and motioned to a chair across from the desk. "The trip was great. I got to spend time with Alexa and order the appliances and dishes for the kitchen, with a few upgrades. I think you'll be pleased." He and Henry settled into their seats.

"Awesome, but I still feel bad..."

Johnny lifted his hand as if to say stop. "Don't. We're looking for the silver lining. Thankfully, I invested in good insurance. I think if we search out bargains, we can eke out a few things for the outdoor space I want. I got a nice discount on the stove and dishwasher. Since the burnt wiring shorted both out, they have to be replaced." He rubbed his hand over his bald head. "At least the fridge and freezer survived and ran on the generator, so we didn't lose too much food. And the other things we lost are small compared to those. So, no, don't worry. Let's face forward and pull this place together."

"Has anyone ever told you, you're the best boss ever?"

"No, I don't think so, but with the employees I have here, it's easy to be a good boss." He reached out his hand and shook Henry's. "We can do this. We can make Johnny's Place the best on the island. What do you say?"

Henry nodded and grinned. "Let's do it."

~~~~~

In the afternoon, squatting beside her raised garden beds in the backyard, Marigold pulled weeds and dug out roots with her trowel. "Do you multiply overnight?" The wild annoyances, much like worry, sprouted and grew faster than any of the vegetables in her garden.

Somehow the crabgrass jumped the wooden planks surrounding her gardens and rooted themselves deep. Not one to use weedkiller, she preferred to pull them by hand. Time in the garden gave her a chance to ponder life and pray.

With fifty-five around the corner, she counted back to the last time she had celebrated her birthday. Her dear friend and Sadie's grandmother, Julia, had made a Victorian sponge cake. Her aunts had taught her to make the delicious light cake before she married Ben and moved from England to Ohio. Julia had split the cake and added a butter cream filling and a layer of her homemade berry jam.

Several years had passed since the day they celebrated. After Marigold's mother died, no one else gave her cake and gifts, including her staunch grandmother. How had her mother turned out to be so caring and kind after growing up with Grandma? Reality smacked Marigold on the forehead. Her grandmother had mourned the loss of her daughter as much as she had mourned the loss of her mom. As a self-centered teen, she had dismissed the tears her grandmother cried at night. The sniffling and muted sounds of mourning echoed through the house, but Marigold had shoved them aside.

God, forgive me for being selfish.

All these years later and she still struggled with selfish desires. She had pushed and pulled Johnny like a seesaw. One day, she adored him, and the next, she emotionally shoved him away. Loving another person opened the door to vulnerability and loss. The realization stunned her. Her trowel dropped to the ground. She sprawled on her back, in the grass, and raised her face to the heavens. Cumulus clouds in cauliflower shapes floated across a blue sky, and a sense of awe filled Marigold.

"What do you see up there?" Johnny's voice startled her from her daydream.

"I don't know, could be a lamb or dog."

He walked to where she lay and dropped beside her. His long legs stretched in front of him as he leaned back. "I see a dinosaur and a reindeer. Different clouds, of course."

She smiled at him. "I love your imagination."

"Anything else you love about me?" He turned to her, and his eyes sparkled with mischief.

Her lip twitched, and she bit on one side. "Too soon to tell." As she flirted in her own shy way, her heart pounded with joy because this man chose to spend time with her. Once she settled her angst over her dad and let the past go, she planned to tell this handsome, kind man her heart's desire. Until then, she prayed his patience with her lasted. Funny how she vocalized her beliefs and encouraged others to go after what they wanted, but when it came to matters of the heart, she curled in her shell like a snail.

Johnny lifted himself from the ground and brushed off the seat of his khaki shorts. "Want to take the kayaks out this evening?" He offered his hand, and Marigold gripped it to help her stand.

On her feet, she picked up her trowel, then stood beside Johnny. She rested her free hand on his arm. "I'd love to. What time?"

His hand covered hers. "I'm on my way home to grab a few files I left there this morning. I plan to go to the restaurant and work for a few more hours. How about seven o'clock? Eat a snack before, and I'll whip up something when we get back."

The warmth of his hand warmed Marigold's heart. "Seven sounds good. Did you get to go to the office today?"

"I did. The restaurant smells better and all the soot was removed. Now I'm waiting on the electrician and contractor. They come tomorrow to assess and go over schedules with me. I can't wait to get in the kitchen."

"Many people are anxious for you to get into the kitchen. They don't have the privilege of having you as a personal chef." Her cheeks heated. More flirting, not her style, but she lo... liked Johnny more than most.

The two walked to the she shed, and Marigold left her little shovel on the garden bench. "Do you want to bring your truck by before seven and load the 1960s tandem Folbot?"

"You like saying 1960s Folbot, don't you." Johnny chuckled. "I remember how excited you were when you bought it."

"I do love to let Folbot roll off my tongue. She's a beauty."

"I'd love to paddle with you in your vintage kayak."

Before she contemplated too much, she planted a kiss on his cheek.

Johnny's eyebrows raised, then a grin split his face. "Why, thank you sweet lady." He nodded, turned, and walked away.

"See you later." Anticipation of an enjoyable evening propelled her to the house to pick what she might wear. *I'm acting like a teenager. A fifty-four-year-old teenager.*

~~~~~

At 6:45, Johnny drove his cherry-red, 1957 Ford F-100 into Marigold's driveway. He downshifted and pulled alongside the house to load the kayak. Eyes on the rearview mirror, he rubbed a smudge of grease off his forehead, then hopped out of the cab. Must have gotten oil on himself when he checked the engine. Around the back of the house, Marigold toted two paddles and two orange life jackets.

"Hey. Let me help you." He jogged to her and lifted the equipment from her arms.

"Thank you." As he headed to the truck, she trailed behind. "The kayak is in back of the shed. It'll take two of us to carry it over."

The paddles and jackets rested in the truck bed. "No problem."

With his hand on Marigold's back, he led her behind the shed. "You know, if I were a teenager, I might try to sneak a kiss."

She swatted at him. "Good thing we aren't teens anymore." A smile curved her lips as she reached for one end of the plastic vessel.

He lifted the other end. "Yep. Good thing." Too bad he didn't have the gumption he had as a young man, but some things were worth waiting for.

With the kayak loaded in the truck, Johnny drove to the beach. "It's a perfect time to be on the water."

"I love this time of day. The quietness of the island envelops me, and I can relax." She stroked the dash of the classic truck. "This is the first time I've ridden in Gertrude. I don't see her out much."

"I didn't realize you hadn't ridden in her. Sorry." He patted the steering wheel. "I don't drive her much, and I want to preserve her as long as I can. Dad was so proud of this truck. He bought her after he saved enough money to pay outright. Before the truck, we had a station wagon he used to deliver food from the deli he ran. Of course, all of us kids piled in the car for road trips, but Dad dreamed of a truck and got one. Now she's mine, and I try to take good care of old Gertrude."

"She's a beauty." Her hand swept across the seat. "This leather upholstery feels so soft and the camel color is perfect."

Johnny pulled into the beach's parking lot. "Thank you. I had a mechanic go over her a few years ago and had the interior updated." He got out, walked around the truck, and opened Marigold's door. "Ready for an adventure?"

"I am."

When Marigold turned to him, her eyes twinkled and his heart thumped faster than usual.

~~~~~

Their mom's journal glared at the sisters from the middle of Violet's kitchen table. "Thanks for agreeing to get together tonight. I know Mondays aren't the best for you, Poppy, but I'm glad you had an opening. And Violet, thanks for letting us crash here." Ivy fingered the hand-quilted placemat. "I can't believe Christopher Downey is accusing Dad of stealing his grandfather's identity. No way would Dad steal someone's social security number. You hear about people who do, but not our dad."

Poppy placed her hand on Ivy's. "Um... Mom said she gave Dad a new identity. Do you think she found an obituary and gave Dad the name? If he had the type of amnesia that made him forget his past, then he may not have realized what she did. He probably accepted whatever she told him."

Hands flat on the table, Ivy glared at the journal. "I'm afraid to find out any more of what's in Mom's book. I mean, I'm afraid, but I'm also curious." Nothing rattled Ivy like this. An unexpected mystery shrouded her parents. One bound to have an unhappy or at least unsettling ending. Cramps formed in her stomach as acid rose in her throat. "I think I'm going to be sick." Before her sisters answered her, she bolted for the bathroom.

Fifteen minutes later, with a washcloth to her lips, she padded to the table. "I'm sorry. I've never been this upset about anything."

In unison, Poppy and Violet nodded. "We know."

Her ponytail swung as Violet lifted the journal from the center of the table. "I say we dive in and read whatever is in here. It's going to take a while to get through all of it, so let's at least get past the beginning. Mom found Dad, nursed the scrapes and bruises he had, and gave him a new identity. Let's see if she writes about Dad's reaction." She paused and looked from one sister to another. "You know, once we figure this out, we have to talk to Dad."

Ivy closed her eyes and put her head in her hands.

Poppy rubbed Ivy's back. "It'll be all right. We'll stick together, figure this out, and hope the answers aren't as bad as we think."

"Right, sure. We'll go with that." Violet opened the journal.

As Violet read the next passage, Ivy rose from her chair. "I'm sorry. I can't do this tonight. Can we wait until Wednesday? My stomach is churning, and I've got to go home."

Her sisters moved to stand beside Ivy. Poppy handed her a tissue. "Sure. We can wait. Right, Violet?"

The dark-haired sister nodded. "Of course. No problem." The wince on her face spoke otherwise.

"I'm sorry." With her purse and coat in her arms, Ivy escaped out the door.

CHAPTER FOURTEEN

Tuesday morning, Marigold dipped her toes in the lake. Johnny had splashed her with the cold water yesterday evening as they paddled on the water. Excited for his reconnection with Alexa, he had chatted about her most of the trip. She sounded like someone Marigold wanted to get to know, but she had no desire to take time away from their father-daughter bonding.

When she turned to walk back to the kayaks, she paused to watch a dad pour lake water from a purple bucket into a hole for his curly-headed little girl. She dipped her hands into the sand, stirred the water in, and molded the base of a sandcastle. Had Marigold's father played on the beach with her? Those memories remained distant, no matter how hard she tried to remember the details. A giggle breezed through the air as the little girl chased her dad and splashed a bucket of water on him. Marigold prayed the curly-head would create many years of memories with her daddy.

Out past the dad and daughter, a few teenagers gathered in the water and took turns sliding under and holding their breaths. Marigold shook her head. Oh, to be young again. A light wind carried the hint of campfire from the nearby state park campground, and a blue sky invited tourists to the lake on this perfect Tuesday morning.

The hum of a golf cart sounded behind her. "Hey, Mari." She turned and waved to her friend Sadie and Sadie's golden retriever, Rosie.

A basket covered with a blue and white checked cloth hung over Sadie's arm. "I brought you muffins from my new recipe, lemon poppy seed and blueberry. Joel and I picked the berries on Owen's farm, across the island yesterday. My renters enjoyed them, and I thought you would too."

Marigold lifted the towel and breathed in the sweet berry and lemon fragrance. "These smell amazing. I didn't bring my lunch today, so I think I'll have a muffin or two." She carried the basket to the picnic table. "Want to visit until I get some business?"

Sadie slid onto the bench seat, and Rosie nudged Marigold's hand for a pet. "You must love working by the water all summer."

Marigold rubbed her hand over the golden's back. "I do. I love to hear the children play and see the families enjoying the sunshine." A little girl with ringlets and a pink swimsuit toddled along the surf. "Reminds me of when Mom and Dad took me to the water. We went at least two or three times a summer. The memory is fuzzy, but we had fun."

Sadie patted Marigold's hand. "Of course you did. Good memories are a treasure, and your dad's disappearance has been hard on you. I can't imagine how the lack of closure hurts your heart."

The older lady's hand clasped Sadie's. "What a perfect way to say it. My heart hurts from the not knowing. But I think it's time I let it go. Put Dad to rest, regardless of where he is. He may be dead and buried, or could be walking around as a different person. I'm so weary from wondering."

"Not to mention how you fuss over me, Joel, and Lucy." A smile crossed Sadie's lips. "By the way, I came for more than the muffins. I have news I hope might brighten your day."

Marigold's full attention darted to Sadie. "What's going on?"

"I wanted Joel and I to tell you together, but he had to work, and I couldn't wait." The news blurted from Sadie's mouth. "We're expecting."

The picnic bench tumbled as Marigold jumped and hurried around the table. "I'm so happy for you." She squeezed her in a momma bear hug, and Rosie yipped.

"Thank you." A giggle escaped Sadie. "We weren't planning to have a baby this soon, but aren't there verses about God's timing being the best timing?"

"Yes, there are." Marigold nodded and placed her hands on the expectant mom's shoulders. "How far along are you?"

Sadie patted her belly. "About two months. The doctor says I'm due in January. Not sure how delivery will go with winter here. I may have to stay with Joel's parents on the mainland the last month, or depend on the airplane for transport. Of course, we have EMTs here too. I can't start thinking about the difficulties yet. At least I'm due between rental seasons." A laugh rumbled from her.

"I'm so happy for you."

"Thank you. Now I better get to work. The cabins won't clean themselves."

"You take care of yourself. I'll talk to you soon." She waved as Sadie pulled the cart over the hill.

Sadie's Grammy Julia and Grandpa Ben would have been thrilled to meet Sadie's little one. She could stand in for them, a surrogate grandmother. Birthing babies of her own had passed her by long ago, but she had never expected to be a mom. Sure, when she was younger the thought of her own children intrigued her, but she had no regrets. She loved the people in her life and now planned to be a surrogate grandma to Joel and Sadie's little one, if they didn't mind. Crochet patterns for baby blankets and sweaters flitted through her mind. The Craft Shack in town carried the perfect aqua blue baby yarn. The owner kept a decent stock of yarn and thread for the islanders and tourists. She'd take a jaunt there tomorrow while Charlotte worked the rentals for her.

The circle of life continued whether she moved forward or not. If she dug her heels in and stayed stuck, she'd miss out on so much. *Lord, help me let go.*

~~~~~

In the office of his restaurant, Johnny's cell phone chimed. He had finished orders for replacement pots, pans, and dishtowels in the morning. This afternoon he searched for bargains on outdoor seating options. The site he searched listed a few faux wooden tables and chairs, but they didn't fit the atmosphere he hoped to create.

"Hello, this is Johnny."

A familiar voice came through the phone. "Hi, Dad."

He leaned back in his desk chair and twirled his pen. "Alexa. Hi. How are you?"

"I'm fine, busy, but fine." A pause crept over the line. "I called to tell you the homeschoolers want to come this weekend to see the glacial grooves. The weather is supposed to be nice, and a majority of the children can come. This is kind of last minute, but can I stay with you?"

The pen fell from his hand. "Sure. I'll have your room ready." His chest expanded and his lips curled into a grin. Alexa wanted to come and stay with him. "When will you be here?"

"I'm coming on Thursday, if you don't mind. I plan to explore on Friday, have the session on Saturday, then head home on Sunday afternoon."

He stood beside his desk then paced across the room in ten steps. "Sounds great. I can meet you at the ferry. Please text me the time."

"Will do." The phone clicked, and the call ended.

Less than two days to get a room ready for Alexa. Phone tucked in his pocket, he walked to the kitchen. "Henry, my girl is coming. Can you take care of things tomorrow? I'm going to have to clean and make sure I have sheets fit for her to sleep on."

His sous chef turned from the cabinet where he was taking inventory. "Sure. Sounds like you have a lot to do. If I had someone coming to stay with me, I'd take a week to prepare. We bachelors aren't great housekeepers."

"I spend so much time here, I tend to neglect the house." He grabbed a pad of paper and pencil from the counter. "I'll jot a list of things for you to do. Thanks, man."

"No problem. By the way, I've seen your daughter's photo on your desk. Is she single?" Every tooth showed from his teasing grin.

"I don't know, and you don't need to know either. Keep your eyes to yourself."

Henry's laughter followed Johnny to his office.

~~~~~

Wednesday morning, Johnny perused his extra bedroom. What a mess. He carried a stack of cooking magazines and a pile of clipped recipes from the extra bedroom to the kitchen. His two-bedroom, two-bath bungalow left little room for extras. The living room, dining area, and kitchen opened into one another, with a pantry and small laundry room off the kitchen. Perfect for a man alone, but not for a family.

No sheets or blankets covered the bed, and he could inscribe his autograph in the dust on the nightstand and dresser. With a microfiber cleaning cloth, he lifted the grime, then collected a lamp from the living room and plugged it into the wall. From the closet, he pulled blankets, two pillows, and a bedspread, but no sheets. He hoped Lucy had sheets at the General Store.

He secured his wallet from the kitchen table, grabbed his truck keys, and ventured to town.

Most of the parking spots filled by eleven. He maneuvered the old Ford in behind his restaurant. Tourists milled in and out of the specialty shops, and the smell of gyros from the food truck met his nose. Johnny's Place stood on the corner with the doors locked. At least with the place closed, he had time to spend with Alexa.

The door to Lucy's swung open and a boy, maybe eight years old, held the door for him and then his own parents. "Thank you, young man. Much appreciated." Johnny nodded to the boy's parents, then stepped inside.

"I love polite kids, don't you?" Marigold laid her hand on Johnny's shoulder.

"Me too." He side-hugged her. "What are you doing today?"

They scooted away from the door. "I've been to the craft shop to buy yarn, and I stopped in here for the cleaner I use on the kayaks." A reusable shopping bag hung from her arm. "How about you?"

"Alexa's coming to visit, and I don't have sheets for the bed in my extra room."

She shifted the bag from one arm to the other. "When is she coming?"

He fingered the keys in his pocket. "Tomorrow evening. She's teaching a group about the geology of the island, then leaving Sunday. I want you to meet her, so I plan to fix dinner Friday and want you to join us."

With her free hand, Marigold pulled her braid over her shoulder. "Are you sure you want me to meet her? Don't you want time with the two of you?"

A frown crossed his face. "Don't you want to meet her?"

Marigold gave him the did-you-really-say-those-words glare. "Of course I want to meet her."

"Then it's settled. Friday for dinner at my place."

Lucy bounded over to them. "Hey guys. Can I help you with anything?"

"Hey, lady." Marigold lifted the bag. "Thanks for keeping this cleaner in stock, especially in the summer." She waved to Johnny and Lucy. "I've got to get home and get my chores finished. I'll see you both later."

"Friday, if not before," Johnny said.

Lucy's attention shifted to Johnny. "What can I help you find?"

He sighed. "Do you carry sheets for a full size bed?"

"Sure do. I keep a couple sets for each size bed. They're light blue. Hope that's okay." She led him to the shelves in the household section.

"Perfect." He grabbed a pack with a flat, a fitted sheet, and two pillow cases.

Lucy stopped in the middle of the aisle and whirled around to face Johnny. "Do you have pillows?"

Her abrupt stop brought him to a halt. "Yeah. I have two new ones. When I moved, I bought extras, but forgot to get sheets. The pillows were in the closet and the bed has been bare."

With a nod, Lucy moved to the front of the store. "Any particular reason you're sprucing up the place?"

Johnny piled his items on the counter. "My daughter's coming for a visit."

"You have a daughter?" She scanned the barcodes and bagged the sales.

"Yes." He handed her a debit card. "My one and only. She lives in Cleveland and works at the Natural History Museum. She's coming to teach a class on Saturday." He took the bag.

"Cool. Hope your visit goes well." She waved and sauntered off.

Lucy wasn't alone in hoping for a pleasant visit.

Johnny loaded the purchases into the truck and drove home. Had he pressured Marigold into meeting his daughter? Alexa might not feel comfortable eating dinner with her dad's girlfriend. Should he introduce her as his girlfriend or his friend? He and Marigold never discussed what to call their relationship.

By the time he parked in the driveway, Johnny's stomach knotted and his chest tightened. *Get a grip, Papadakis.* One dinner would not make or break a relationship. Not with Marigold or Alexa. He understood why young people dated and not oldsters like him.

He scooped his packages from the truck's seat and trekked to the house. *Lord, help me be my best self as I reconnect with my daughter.*

The calming act of tucking the flat sheet over the fitted and covering the pillows settled him. From the rocking chair he had kept from his grandparents, he snatched a floral quilt his *yaya* had sewn. She had stitched the blocks from the pieces she had salvaged from worn out dresses and shirts, then tied the layers together with yarn. Perhaps Alexa might appreciate the sentiment. Johnny fluffed the pillows, then sat on the edge of the bed. A vase of fresh flowers might brighten the room.

Tomorrow morning, he'd phone Marigold and find out if she had any ready to pick, then he would raid the freezer at the restaurant for ingredients to recreate one of his mama's dishes. Running a restaurant and planning a meal proved easy compared to bringing his daughter and lady friend together. With a sigh, he fell back on the quilted bedspread and closed his eyes. Would his two favorite women connect, or would the dinner be a mistake?

CHAPTER FIFTEEN

A breeze lifted Ivy's long bob off her neck as she knocked on Violet's door. Monday, when her stomach revolted against the contents of the diary, had slammed into Wednesday with lightning speed. Tuesday, Ivy had poured herself into a marketing campaign at the local television station where she worked. She had secured local authors for a panel on the morning show, then had lunch with the producer, Mavis. She had promised Ivy a raise if the next few months brought in more revenue than projected. After work, Ivy shoved her workload aside to focus on her mom's journal and the secrets she kept.

Joseph greeted Ivy. "Come in. Violet is in the dining room. I'm taking the kids to my parent's house for a while. Poppy is already here." He pointed down the hallway.

"Thanks. I'll see you later." Ivy trudged to the end of the hall. Her sisters' laughter met her halfway. How could they be so jovial? Could she tweak her attitude so she could laugh, too? She stepped around the corner.

"Hi, girls."

Poppy wrapped her in a tight hug. "Thought you might need some love."

Ivy nodded. "I do. Thanks. I'm hoping I can get through this without freaking out again. Sorry about the other night." She dropped her purse in a chair and sat next to Violet.

"Not a problem. I think it was all coming at us too fast." Violet poured her a cup of decaf and handed her a plate of cookies. "The kids made these today. I told them Aunt Ivy needed a bit of sweetening.

"They look delicious. What kind are they?" She nibbled on one and the powdered sugar sprinkled her cotton shirt.

Violet gave her a napkin. "Mexican wedding cookies. They're messy, but they are so good." She popped one in her mouth.

Ivy bit into another cookie, closed her eyes, and savored the sweet sugar, pecans, and vanilla. "These are heavenly. Thank the kids for me." She sipped her coffee, then brushed the powdered sugar off her hands. "Ready to get started?"

Hands folded together, Poppy pushed them out in front of her, and stretched as if she was preparing for an athletic event. "I'm ready."

The journal, with an envelope holding their place, lay in front of them, page turned to where they left off. "Do you want me to read?" Violet reached for the book. "I promise to stop for a break."

"Sure, go for it," Poppy blurted, and leaned her head on the chair. Her red curls cascaded along her back.

Violet cleared her throat and read her mom's writing. "I'm convinced this man I found is my soul mate. Even though he doesn't remember his name, he knows he enjoys flowers and gardening, reading, and traveling. All pluses for me. I sure need help in all the flower beds I've planted. If he sticks around, he could work in landscaping or something. Trouble is, what identity can he use? Without a Social Security card and ID, he won't get hired. What to do? A call to the police may complicate my plans, because I don't want to let him go."

"Oh, Mom, how could you?" A sniffle came from Ivy.

Poppy leaned on the table and folded her arms. "Maybe she experienced love at first sight. It happens. Or so they say."

Her sisters glared at her. Ivy gave her the mom stare, which had stopped her in her tracks as a kid.

"I'm trying to be openminded, okay? I hate this as much as you do, but it happened, and we are stuck figuring out what to do with this... this unbelievable situation." Poppy waved her hand in the air.

A sigh sounded from Violet's side of the table. "You're right. Mom stuck us with this. The situation makes me mad and sad all at the same time."

"Me too, Vi." Ivy touched her sister's arm. "Want to keep reading?"

After several pages of day-to-day activities, Violet turned a page and a photo ID fell out. The man in the photo appeared about forty-five. "Check this out." Violet clamped the card between her fingers. "Edward Vincent Downey. Dad's name, or at least what we knew as Dad's name." She handed the card to Ivy and continued reading the journal. "I did it. I found an identity of a man who has passed away, a tragedy in a barn fire. He resembles my mystery man enough to pass with the ID. My friend Harry, the only one I've told, said he'd help me create an identity. I can't believe I'm doing this, but love makes you do crazy things."

Violet dropped the journal on the table and lowered her head to rest in her hands. After a minute, she stared at her sisters. "Earlier in the journal, Mom mentioned she gave him a name, but I can't believe our mom stole a real person's identity. I had no idea she was crazy."

"Hey, don't call Mom crazy. She did something ridiculous, yes, but I don't think she was crazy." Poppy poured more coffee into her mug.

"Then what do you call it, besides unlawful and awful?" Ivy pushed her chair from the table. "Christopher Downey was right. He said Dad stole his grandfather's identity, but he was wrong, too. Mom stole it and Dad doesn't have any idea." She paced across the room. "The grandfather has been gone for about forty years. Recently, the family decided to sell some property he had owned. When they started the process, Christopher discovered his grandpa's social security number was compromised. Did I tell you Christopher is a lawyer?"

"No, you didn't. I hope he doesn't cause Dad trouble." Violet tapped a pen on the table. "Mom was weird about their savings. Dad's boss didn't pay in to social security, so she set up a 501k. That's what Dad lives on, plus the sale of their house, which was mortgage-free. I check his finances weekly."

"This is overwhelming." Poppy sighed and fingered the envelope sticking out of the journal. "Do we dare open this letter with the name Marigold Hayes scribbled across it? Or is that another mess we have to wade through?"

Violet stood and cleared the dishes from the table. "How about we call it a night? Joseph will be home with the kids, and I want to tuck them in before they go to sleep. Besides, if we don't digest what we've read, we won't want to dive in again in a few days."

"Sounds good to me." Ivy carried the cookie tray to the kitchen.

"Me too." Poppy followed with the coffee carafe.

Violet stored the leftover sweets in a plastic container and poured what little coffee was left in the sink. "How about Sunday after church? The kids are going to a friend's house and Joseph is playing golf. I can fix lunch."

"Sounds good. I can bring a salad." Ivy hugged her sisters.

Poppy lifted her sweater from the chair. "I'll bring a cheesecake from the farmer's market. I'll be there on Saturday and Mel makes the best there is."

"Perfect. I'll see you Sunday."

~~~~~

Before seven on Thursday morning, Marigold wrestled her blankets until she tossed them from the bed to the floor. The wind howled, and the rain poured. A summer storm had hit the island. She squinted as she listened to waves crash the shore. The water roared louder than usual for her to hear it from her house. Her hands ached from the knots she had tied on her macrame project last night. She closed her eyes as another pain shot through her, an unexpected heartache from the early morning dream.

In her hometown, she had run door to door. All the neighbors who knew her mom's mother told her to stop looking. Her grandmother stood behind her yelling, "He's gone! Leave it alone." By the time she opened her eyes, sorrow draped over her.

Cassatt, her calico, climbed on top of Marigold and licked her arm. "Good morning, girl. I haven't seen you for a few days. Have you been hiding under the bed again?" She lifted the cat and scooted her to the floor, then sat up and swung her legs over the side. Cassatt wove in and out of Marigold's ankles and sauntered off.

The rain slowed and light dawned through the wet morning. After breakfast, Marigold peered outside. No point opening the kayak rental until the storm passed and the water calmed, which might be tomorrow. Instead, she lifted the lid on her mom's trunk and snagged the bundle of letters she had left on top the last time she shuffled through the treasures.

On the couch, she snugged into the corner and untied the ribbon her mom had used to bind the letters. The top one in a pale blue envelope bore the name and address of her mom, Louise.

> *Dear Louise,*
>
> *I hope you don't mind me writing. After meeting you at the county fair, I couldn't stop thinking about you. I just live one town over, but between work and helping my dad in his shop, I don't have much time. I want to know what you think about me making the time to come see you. You sure are a beauty inside and out, and this guy wants to get to spend time with you. If you want to see me again, please answer my post and tell me when and where. I'll be there.*
>
> *Yours Truly,*
> *Nick Hayes*

Marigold had forgotten they met at the county fair. Her mom mentioned the story a few times, how her friends set them up to ride the Ferris wheel together, and she trembled most of the ride. Dad misunderstood why she shook, not because of him, but because she feared heights. When he realized her fear, he held her hand and prayed for her. Mom had left the fair with a crush on Dad.

She placed the letters on her coffee table and brewed Darjeeling tea. With a cup in hand, she settled on the couch again. A peach-colored envelope caught her attention.

> *Dear Nick,*
>
> *How sweet of you to write. I've been thinking about you, too. I work at the telephone company, and I'm off on the weekends. Could we meet on Saturday at the soda fountain, here in town, then take in a movie? I should probably have you meet my mom, but I'm not ready. How about four o'clock for a soda, then a movie? We can go Dutch, if you want.*
>
> *Sincerely Yours,*
> *Louise*

Mom had dreaded for Dad to meet her mother. Once Grandma had met him, she never treated him with respect. Mom said she wouldn't have respected anyone she brought home. After all, Grandma made no secret of the disdain she carried for her deceased husband. They had married young, and when he moved her to Ohio she had suffered from acute homesickness.

The corners of Marigold's mouth perked into a smile. Mom had kept secrets from Grandma.

She opened the next letter as her phone chirped. She picked it up. "Hello."

"Hey Mari. I'm hoping you can help me out." Johnny's voice flowed through the cell.

The timbre of his voice soothed her, as she pressed speaker on her phone and placed the device on her coffee table. "In what way?" She bundled the letters with the ribbon and tucked them into the drawer of a small oak end table.

"I'm hoping the rain has slowed enough for me to pick a few flowers for Alexa's room, to brighten the place. I don't have much in there and it's pathetically bare."

She carried the phone to the window and peeked out. "It's a slight drizzle. Come on over, or do you want me to pick them and bring them to you?"

"Do you mind bringing them here? I've got so much to do. I'm trying to clean the place." A sigh murmured from the speaker.

"Give me about an hour, and I'll be there."

"Thanks. See you in a bit."

The phone clicked off, and Marigold tucked hers in her pocket. On the back porch, she pulled on her rain boots and sloshed across the yard to her shed. The clippers lay by the door with a bucket to collect flowers. Near the shed, she snipped blooms and stems from the day lilies in yellow, pink, and orange, a few tufts from the oakleaf hydrangeas, pink and purple coneflowers, and a bunch of daisies. Happy with her selection, she carried the bucket to the shed and found a clear glass vase. With care, Marigold arranged the flowers into a summer bouquet. She planned to add water once she arrived at Johnny's.

On the drive over, she realized she hadn't looked in the mirror since before breakfast. On his doorstep, she smoothed her hair with her left hand and held the flowers with her right. Before she knocked, Johnny opened his front door.

"Come in."

He took hold of the vase and carried it to his kitchen table. "Beautiful — you and the flowers. Thank you so much."

Marigold clicked the door closed and joined him. "You're welcome. I'm sure it's unnerving having your daughter as a guest. I hope the flowers add comfort and a welcome air to her room." The vase of flowers in hand, she moved to the kitchen. "Let me fill the vase with water, then we'll take them in there."

Once she filled the vase, she trailed him along a short hallway into a small bedroom. A pile of clothes covered the bed, and a vacuum cleaner stood in the middle of the floor.

"I finished dusting and wiping the woodwork, now to sweep and put these clothes away. Then all I have to do is tidy the rest of the house." He wiped a bead of sweat off his forehead.

Marigold perused the room. "How about I vacuum, while you take care of the clothes and clean the rest of your place?"

"I can't ask you to vacuum." A lopsided grin crossed his face. "It sure would help, though. I meet Alexa at the ferry around six."

"No problem. With the storm I can't open my business, and I'm caught up on my crafts." She plugged in the sweeper and shooed him out of the room.

Today she vacuumed and tomorrow she would sit across the table from Alexa, on display as Johnny's girlfriend. Her tummy felt like rocks going through a tumbler.

CHAPTER SIXTEEN

At the dock, Johnny shoved his hands in his pockets and swallowed the lump in his throat as the ferry sped across the choppy lake, then settled into the slip. Clouds shadowed the evening and cooled the air as Johnny waited for the vehicles to drive off the ferry's ramp onto the road. Once people ascended the steps from the top deck, he ribboned his way from the truck to the pavilion to wait on Alexa. He thanked the Lord his daughter wanted to visit, even as his nerves jangled with excitement and fear.

When he spotted her, the joy of spending time with her wrestled with concern she might never want to see him again. What if, after spending a few days with him, she decided to keep her distance?

Dressed in jeans and a paisley tunic, Alexa waved at him and made her way through the crowd. "Dad."

Johnny jogged over and retrieved her suitcase. "Hi. Wow, this case is heavy. What did you pack? Rocks?"

"As a matter of fact, I did. Remember, I'm teaching a class on geology." A laugh bubbled from her.

With the suitcase in the truck's bed, he held the door open on the passenger side. His little girl had grown into a beautiful woman. One he didn't know anymore. *Lord, help me love my daughter well.*

"I love this old truck. I remember Papa driving me to school. He let me sit on his lap a few times." She climbed in and buckled her seatbelt.

In the driver's seat, Johnny started the engine and moved into gear. "Of course he did. He had a soft spot for you and your cousins. He'd have never let one of his own kids drive. I'm glad Gertrude is still running." He patted the dash. "I think she has a few more years in her."

At the house, he showed Alexa to her room. "Nothing fancy, but it's nice and clean."

"The flowers are gorgeous. Did you grow them?" She leaned in and sniffed the blooms.

"No. My friend Marigold grew them and brought them over this morning. If you're okay with it, I want to have her over tomorrow for dinner so you could meet her." He stood with his hands in his pockets.

She sat on the edge of the bed. "Sure, fine with me. How close of a friend is she, Dad?" Her eyes twinkled with mischief.

He twisted his mouth before he spoke. "She's a good friend I've known for several years, and let's say we're getting better acquainted."

"It's about time. I want you to have a special lady in your life. After Mom left and took me with her, all I've ever wanted was for you to be happy." She stood and walked to her dad and hugged him around the neck.

"Thank you." Johnny embraced her, then let her go. Ready to move on from his love life, he walked to the door, then turned. "I have cold cuts and pretzel buns for sandwiches. Tomorrow night I'm fixing one of Mom's dishes. Are sandwiches okay?"

"Perfect. I'll be out in a few minutes."

In the kitchen, Johnny let out the breath he had been holding for days. He had never dreamed Alexa would approve of him dating.

~~~~~

In her office at the television station, Ivy checked the clock. She'd start the weekend at noon. Thank goodness for Friday. After she had left Violet's on Wednesday, she hadn't slept more than a couple of hours each night. The bags under her eyes resembled bulk mailbags from the post office. The coffee she poured down her throat revved her brain, but then made her trot to the restroom too often. A nap sounded enticing but had to wait until after she walked through her parents' home one more time to make sure they had not forgotten anything and to ensure all the finishing touches were complete. Thrilled her friend with a cleaning company agreed to tidy the place, Ivy planned to buy a box of chocolate and a thank you note to give her. If the place passed Ivy's final inspection, she'd contact the realtor and confirm the showing.

Mom's professional realty photo flashed through her mind. A beautiful bottle brunette, hair curled under at the chin, big brown eyes and a captivating smile had filled a space on benches and posters all over town. How did such a caring person dupe a man into marrying her and building a life? Of course, Dad had no idea or memory. The book she read about retrograde amnesia revealed the person affected might never regain memories of his or her previous life. Basic skills like eating, walking, and even gardening should continue, but specifics were buried. If Dad had this whole other life, how would his past affect her and her sisters? Did they have other siblings they didn't know about? The obituary for Louise Hayes mentioned a daughter, who survived. From the clippings and journal, she and her sisters assumed Louise was Dad's first wife.

The phone on Ivy's desk rang. "North East Television, Ivy Downey. How can I help you?"

"For starters, you can change your last name. This is Christopher Downey. Have you found out anything about why your dad took my grandpa's name and identity? We have to get this settled." A huff blew through the line.

Ivy took a breath. "First, Mr. Downey, don't call me at work. Second, we are still going through papers and information, trying to find out what may have happened. Third, my dad is not aware of any of this. When I have an answer, I will call you on the number you gave me. Now wait for my call." She placed the receiver on the cradle and leaned her head into her hands. *Mom, how could you?*

~~~~~

The sun shined on Abbott Island Friday morning as Johnny and Alexa hiked the alvar trail to the water and searched for interesting rock formations to photograph. With camera, notepad, and phone recorder, Alexa marveled at the layers of rock along the face of the low cliffs.

Johnny reached for his daughter's hand as she descended the slippery terrain where the land met the lake. "Marigold and I come here to enjoy the quiet."

Alexa turned away from the water and studied the surrounding low ridges. "Dad, look at the strata. The layers of the limestone tell so many stories." She snapped photos and jotted notes on her paper. "Limestone is sedimentary rock, rich in fossil history. It's fascinating."

As Alexa rambled on about rocks, Johnny's heart grew with pride. His little girl, who had collected as many stones and shells as she could find, had turned her passion into a career. "You must enjoy your job."

"I do, Dad, but sometimes I want to be on the Lake Erie beaches scouring for lake glass and pebbles." The waves washed over the rocky terrain. "I miss the days we spent together, and I want to recapture the fun times we had. Being on the island is so satisfying. I love field trips and exploring with the home school and elementary school children. In Cleveland, I get to visit the schools once a year and share information about Ohio's geology, but most of the time I'm at the museum in my office, preparing programs."

Johnny wrapped his arm around her shoulders. "I miss those days, too. We had so much fun. Cleveland isn't too far from Huntington Beach. We could meet there from time to time. How about once a month?"

"My schedule is all over the place, depending on the programming, but I'll try." She moved away and knelt on the limestone. "What's this?" A tiny purple flower bobbed its head.

"A northern bog violet, and they're about finished blooming by this time. They're one of the rare plants growing on the alvar." Johnny lifted Alexa's camera from her hand. "Let me take a picture of you with it." She smiled at him as she knelt beside the purple bloom.

The picture taken, she stood and brushed dirt from her knees. "How did you learn so much about the nature on the island, Dad? As I recall, you took me out, but you didn't love it as much as I did."

His face warmed at the memories of all the hikes he'd shared with Marigold. "You know my friend Marigold? We take hikes often, and she's

93

knowledgeable about the nature on the island. She can tell you every species of tree, flower, and weed on the island." He ran a hand over his bald head. "I guess I'm a good listener."

"I bet you are." She winked and laughed.

~~~~~

The day had dragged. Friday rentals were on the uptick, but discouragement and doubt played badminton in Marigold's brain. The uncertainty of dinner with Johnny and Alexa pestered her all day. Thank goodness Charlotte took over at four o'clock and relieved her of her duties. Now in front of the mirror, Marigold stared at herself. What does one wear when meeting your boyfriend's daughter? No idea.

A knock sounded on the front door and drew her away from her anxiety over clothes. She had not one time in her life worried about what to wear. Even the Bible told her not to think about her clothing, good grief, God dressed the flowers, so why think about what skirt and blouse to take out of the closet?

Whispers and giggles floated from the porch. When Marigold opened the door, Lucy and Sadie greeted her with smiles. "What are you two up to?"

"Can we come in?" Sadie swung a bag from her hand.

With a step back, she let them in the house. "What's in the bag?"

Her friends made their way into the living room and sat on the blue flowered couch. "We've come to help you get ready for your big night. We figured you were nervous about meeting Johnny's daughter. I mean, I would be if I were you. I need to keep my mouth shut." Lucy twisted her hand as if she locked her lips.

Hands on hips, Marigold stared at the two of them. "I'm not sure how you plan to help me. I can dress myself." Although a few minutes ago, she waffled about what to wear.

Sadie opened the bag she had carried. "I have a product to enhance your hair. Your white locks are gorgeous, but this stuff smooths the frizzies and leaves a nice shine." From the bag, she placed a bottle on the table. "And I have a subtle perfume I hope you'll try."

Marigold plopped in the red chair across from them. "So you think you can help me get ready?"

They chimed at the same time. "We do."

"Okay, the hair stuff, but not the perfume. I prefer the honey infused lotion I use. Johnny said he likes my smell." Her hand covered her mouth. "I said that out loud, didn't I?"

"You sure did." Lucy chuckled and hopped from the couch. "Do you mind if we peruse your closet?" A grin spread across her face and her eyes twinkled.

"I realize I'm old, but I'm not incapable." With her arms crossed,

Marigold moved to the doorway of her bedroom.

With a pout on her lips and her hands clasped, Lucy begged. "Please, we'd love to help. It will be fun."

A sigh released from Marigold's lungs. "Fine. You can help me. Did you use your pout on your parents, Lucy?"

"No way. They would have never let me get away with it."

"Of course." Marigold led them into her room. "I've picked a couple of outfits and laid them on the bed. Or you can check the closet."

Sadie pointed to the stool in front of the old-fashioned vanity. "Please, sit while I treat your hair, and Lucy can check your wardrobe." She set out the supplies. "This is a beautiful vanity set. The oval mirror is almost full length."

Marigold ran her hand over the surface. "It's one of the few things I have of my mom's. After my grandmother died, I had to clean out her things, and this is one I kept. I have memories of my mom brushing my hair on this stool when I was young." Her eyes burned with unshed tears. "Mom's the reason I keep my hair long. She often told me how much she loved my hair. Silly, but it's something to hang on to."

"Not at all. I cherish the things I have left from my grandparents. They bring me comfort." Sadie rubbed the oil into her hands. "When Joel and I married and he moved in, I was pretty specific about what I wanted to keep, and he didn't mind. Thank goodness." With a light touch, Sadie smoothed Marigold's long white tresses with the oil. "Are you nervous about meeting Alexa?"

Visions of her stumbling over her words or putting her foot in her mouth tumbled through Marigold's mind. "A little. I'm afraid I'll appear a silly old woman."

"You aren't old, and you're one of the coolest people I've met. Stop worrying. Didn't you tell me to be myself when I dated Joel?"

"Touche, I did. I'll pray before I go and let God take the lead."

"Good idea." With Marigold's hair in a fishtail braid, Sadie handed her a small mirror to check the back. "What do you think?"

She turned and held the mirror. "It looks good, shiny and smooth. Thank you."

"Ta-da." A long navy maxi dress dotted with periwinkle paisley danced from a hanger. "This is perfect. The colors set off your hair and tan. What do you think?"

Sadie held out the bottom of the dress. "This crocheted trim is pretty. You made it, didn't you?"

"Yes. I sewed the dress and added trim. I'm not sure I want to wear one of my homemade dresses." When she had tried it on earlier, the word dowdy crossed her mind.

Lucy slipped it off the hanger and handed the creation to her. "Put it on and let us decide."

"Fine. Step out and I'll tell you when I'm ready."

A few minutes later, she summoned her friends.

Lucy's hands flew to her mouth. "Beautiful. Turn around."

She kept her balance as she spun.

"I love it on you. The dress has flattering lines and fits you so well." Sadie touched the sleeve. "And it's so soft."

"It is comfortable." Marigold held out the skirt and checked the mirror. "Not bad."

"Are you sure you don't want a little make-up?" Lucy waved a brush for blush.

Marigold blinked. "No, no make-up. I want to be myself and not give Alexa a false impression."

"Understood." Lucy placed the brush in Sadie's bag. "Are you ready for a fun evening?"

"Thanks to you girls, I think I am." *Unless Alexa doesn't like me.*

CHAPTER SEVENTEEN

Lamb, soaked in a marinade flavored with garlic, peppers, and onions, scented Johnny's kitchen. Two hours earlier, he had wrapped the concoction along with Graviera cheese, potatoes, and tomatoes in parchment paper and baked it. As he lifted the meat out and allowed it to rest, he popped the vegetables in the oven to brown. Alexa watched from the small kitchen island.

"You are so skilled in the kitchen. You're making an elaborate meal prep easy. How come I didn't get your talent? I can cook, but not like you." She twirled a spoon on the island's top.

Johnny's eyes locked with his daughter's. She had been inquisitive since the moment she spoke her first words. Who, what, when, where, and why were her main vocabulary. "I'm not sure. You had more interest in playing outside than you did in the kitchen. If you darted out the door without us stopping you, then you were happy." He stirred the rice pilaf. "My years working with Papa in his restaurant instilled a love for cooking, similar to how you love identifying rocks."

"Makes sense." She climbed from the stool, placed the spoon in the sink, then carried the plates, silverware, and cloth napkins to the drop leaf table in the dining area and laid them out. "The linen tablecloth is fancy."

"I grabbed it from the restaurant." He raised his hands in the air. "The entire table setting is from there. I keep little here at the house, since I eat most of my meals at work." He dished the rice into a serving bowl and carried it to the table, along with a basket of homemade bread and butter.

The sound of tires on gravel crunched through the open window. Alexa peered out. "Marigold is here, Dad. In a golf cart."

"Golf carts are common on the island. Most people who live here year-round drive them." He placed the main dish on the table and answered the door. Before he opened it, he turned to his daughter. "How did you know who was here?"

"Simple. We were expecting her, and you display a photo of an attractive lady on your nightstand." A grin split her face.

"Pretty observant, eh." His guest had her hand raised to knock when he pulled the door open. "Come in."

"Thank you." The skirt of Marigold's dress swished as she walked into the living space. "Wow, something smells amazing."

Johnny's daughter approached and reached out her hand. "Hi, I'm Alexa."

"Hello. It's so nice to meet you." Marigold's bracelets jangled as she shook the young woman's hand.

"Dad has prepared an amazing dinner." She turned and walked to the table. "Sit wherever you'd like."

~~~~~

At the table, Marigold reached for Johnny's hand, and he prayed over the meal. Then he lifted the lids off the dishes. A delicious aroma rose from the bowls.

"This smells amazing, and so colorful with all the vegetables."

Johnny handed Marigold the rice, then the main course. "Guests first."

"Thank you. I assume it's a Greek dish." She spooned a portion of each on her plate, passed the bowls to Alexa, and took the bread basket.

"Yes, it was one of my papa's favorites. They call it lamb kleftiko. Legend says the Klephts, Greeks who retreated to the mountains during the Ottoman Empire, had stolen lambs from farmers and cooked them in underground ovens they dug, so the farmers wouldn't smell their feast and catch them. As time passed, their secrets for cooking the lamb surfaced, so we have a great dish and an enchanting tale to tell."

"Dad, are you telling the truth?" Alexa stabbed a piece of meat and a potato.

Johnny buttered his bread. "I read it on the internet, so it must be." He laughed out loud. "No, Papa shared the story with us every time we ate it."

The seasoned potatoes and peppers left a pleasant taste on Marigold's tongue. "This is delicious. The meat is so tender." As good as the food tasted, couldn't she think of something else to talk about? What had Johnny told her about his daughter?

Alexa cleared her throat. "Dad tells me you enjoy nature and have taken him on several hikes."

A breath of relief left her lungs, finally a topic to expound upon. "The trails are one thing I love about the island. I'm much happier outside than in the house. Did your dad tell you I run a kayak business?"

"He did." She patted her mouth with a napkin. "We have a bit in common. As a child, I was outdoors any chance I got, and I wish I could be outside more now. Dad took me to the alvar. If I'd realized it was in his backyard, I'd have visited sooner."

Hand lifted as if making a pledge, Marigold nodded. "I love going to the rock ledges. It's the quietest place on Abbott Island. The only sound you hear is the water washing along the shore. I'm still amazed at the plants. They grow in scant soil. God has sure invented amazing things." She realized she babbled on about what she enjoyed instead of asking Alexa about herself. Marigold attempted to turn the conversation around.

"You work at the Natural History Museum?"

"Yes. I'm in the geology area, but I'm hoping to find another job. One where I'm involved in more field work. I saw a few job listings in Colorado, but we shall see. " She stacked her silverware on her plate.

Marigold chewed her last bite as tension stretched across the table. Johnny stared at Alexa, as if he was unaware of her decision to find a new job until that moment. Oh no, had she pricked the surface of a topic they hadn't discussed? His features softened as he piled the plates on one another and carried them to the kitchen.

"I didn't mean to bring up a prickly subject." Marigold sipped her water.

Alexa shook her head. "No worries. I shouldn't have said anything about going out of state. It may not be a possibility. I'm planning to apply for my PhD, and I'm not sure where I want to go. Dad and I are on a page again, so I don't want to rush off too fast."

Why was Alexa confiding in her? Perhaps the young lady wanted a neutral listening ear.

"Ladies, how about baklava and coffee? Henry baked dessert for us. I think he's getting anxious to return to the restaurant's kitchen." A tray of layered dessert rested on Johnny's hand. He placed the treat on the table with white porcelain plates and delicate forks. "Let me grab the coffee."

Alexa dished the baklava on the plates and passed one to their guest. "I don't think I've eaten this since I was a girl."

"Doesn't your dad make it for you?" Marigold studied the pecans and thin layers of filo dough.

Johnny delivered cups of coffee and a bowl of sugar and a pitcher of creamer. "Alexa and I haven't had the opportunity to spend much time together. Whenever we were together, we were out tromping in the woods." He squeezed his daughter's shoulder.

"We'll get out and hike again, Dad. I've missed being with you." She lowered her head and poured cream into her coffee.

Awkward. Marigold pursed her lips and nodded. A few positive words might help. "Since you aren't sure when or if you might move, maybe the two of you can get together more often."

With her fork raised to her mouth, Alexa mumbled, "That's possible."

"Sounds good to me." Johnny glanced from woman to woman and shoved the dessert in his mouth.

"How about the two of you join me after your class tomorrow and go kayaking?"

Johnny put his fork on his plate, leaned his elbows on the table, and tented his fingers. "Sounds fun to me."

"Sure, I'd love to. I won't finish until five o'clock. What time is too late?"

Marigold chewed the last bite of dessert and swallowed harder than she meant to. "Six is perfect. The rental closes then, so we'd have access to the boats. Charlotte can close for me."

"We'll meet you there." Johnny patted her hand.

For the rest of the evening, Marigold listened as her hosts reminisced about trips to the New England states and visits to the ocean. Her heart longed for the experiences Alexa and Johnny shared. Even though they didn't visit each other as often as they had wanted, they had spent many days together, when Alexa was young. Marigold missed the special times she had shared with her parents. Even as she thanked God Johnny and Alexa got along, Marigold guarded herself against jealousy. The green-eyed monster, as her grandmother called it, could wreck her relationship with Johnny.

~~~~~

Lips pressed against her cheek, Johnny wished her a good night. She climbed into the golf cart and waved goodbye. Marigold admired the sky as stars glimmered and a full moon lit her path. Another pleasant evening on Abbott Island, except... Marigold frowned, rubbed her forehead, and fingered the worry lines. She cared about Johnny, loved him even, but agreeing to marry a man with a grown child sat sideways with her. Alexa presented herself as a kind and intelligent young woman, but an undertone of uneasiness created stress. Johnny had told her he had not spent enough time with his daughter since he moved to the island ten years ago. Should she step away and give them space to reconnect? Or should she try to draw them together?

On the way home, Sadie and Joel's light shined through the window and drew her to them. She parked the cart and walked to the house. After she tapped on the door, the porch light flashed on and Sadie peered out.

The door opened. "Hi, Mari, come in." Sadie motioned to the huge red couch sprawled across the room. "Please, sit."

"Thank you." Sadie's golden retriever nudged Marigold's leg. "You still have Grandpa Ben's couch." Marigold perched on a cushion and patted Rosie's soft fur.

Beside her, Sadie pushed a pillow behind her. "I can't get rid of this couch. It's a behemoth, but I have so many memories of time with Grandpa and Grammy here."

More family memories. Had Marigold buried hers so she couldn't conjure them anymore? The harder she tried, the less she remembered about Dad. Plenty surfaced about Mom, but the recollections she had of her dad seemed to disintegrate.

Sadie placed a hand on Marigold's arm. "Are you okay? Did dinner go well?"

"I'm good." She squeezed Sadie's hand. "Is Joel around?"

"He's on duty. Can I get you something to eat or drink? Tea, water?"

Marigold shook her head. "No, thank you. Johnny prepared a Greek feast. I'm so full I think I may not eat tomorrow."

Sadie gave an excited squeal. "Did you enjoy meeting Alexa?"

"I did."

"You don't sound enthused." Sadie leaned into the couch.

"Don't get me wrong, she's a friendly person and sweet, but I'm thinking I should give her and Johnny space. They've had little time together, and this was a reconnect for them. I don't want to get in the way." She wrapped her braid through her hands. "I don't want to use my age as an excuse, but it's different when you're older. We both carry more baggage and have lived more life. You and Joel had tough things to overcome, but I can't decide if I'm ready for a permanent commitment. Meeting Alexa made me a little nervous, like meeting the family. A closer step to commitment, I guess."

Her young friend stood and walked across the room, then turned to face her. "I hear you, and I'm sure love is different for different ages, but if you love Johnny, and he loves you, and if Alexa approves of her dad being in a relationship, I don't see what's holding you back." She put a hand on each hip. "Alexa is on board, right?"

Marigold patted the couch. "Please sit, and yes, Alexa appears to be on board."

"Then what's the issue? A lot of kids wouldn't be supportive." Rosie climbed on the couch and curled into a ball beside her owner.

"I want them to take their time to reconnect without me getting in their way." She shoved her braid behind her back.

Sadie bit her lower lip and nodded. "How about we pray about it? I'll bend God's ear for you and you do the same. I bet you'll find your answer."

"Good thing you are a dear friend, or I'd be upset you gave me the same advice I gave you last winter." A chuckle escaped Marigold as she stood. "Thanks for listening. By the way, how are you doing?"

Sadie patted her stomach. "I'm wonderful. Excited about this little one."

After they hugged, Marigold climbed in the cart and steered to her home. "Thank You for friends, God. Now about the issue with Johnny..."

CHAPTER EIGHTEEN

Rain pattered on the over-sized, red umbrella as the sun played hide and seek with the clouds. Outside the assisted living facility, Ivy balanced the umbrella as she tugged her car's back door open. She looped her free hand through several plastic grocery bags on the back seat, then bumped the door closed. On the sidewalk, her foot landed in a puddle.

"Ugh. Why did it have to rain on a Saturday morning when I have errands to run?" The water in her tennis shoe squished with each step to her dad's apartment.

Inside, the pale yellow hallway connected several private residences. A bouquet of summer flowers stood on an oak table and added a splash of color to the otherwise dull space. Ivy dropped the bags next to the table, folded her umbrella, and propped it in the corner. She shook rain off her coat, lifted the bags, and headed to her dad's door, where she pressed the doorbell and waited.

"Hello." Dad's voice called through the door.

"It's Ivy, Dad. Can you let me in?" The door swung open, and her father balanced behind his walker.

A smile split his face. "Come in, sweet girl." He motioned with his hand for her to enter.

Once inside, she carried the groceries to the kitchenette, unpacked them, and shelved them in the cabinets and refrigerator. "There you go, Dad. Those will keep you stocked for another week."

"Did you buy my favorite cookies? Those ones with the stripes of chocolate?" He wiggled his eyebrows.

"Of course I did. You won't have a good day without those cookies." Her laughter filled the air.

"Can you stay awhile?" He shifted his feet as he turned to walk to the living room.

Ivy followed him. "Yes. I can stay for a bit." Her dad reclined in his comfortable chair and she sat on the couch. "It's supposed to rain off and on all day. I can't do any yard work." She untied her wet shoe and removed it, along with her sock.

"Did you step in that confounded puddle? I wish they'd fill it with concrete or something. I've dipped my foot in a couple of times when it's rained. And by the way, when are you going to get married? Then you'd have someone to share your work."

He never failed to ask her about her singleness. "Dad, I doubt I'll find anyone who wants to put up with me." No one wanted a workaholic wife who preferred to sit at her computer and sort numbers than stand at a stove and cook. "I'm content, and I enjoy yard work. My plot is so small I can finish with the push mower in about thirty minutes. And it's good exercise."

"Who's mowing my yard?" He rubbed his hand over his stubbled chin.

Thank goodness he got away from the marriage questions. "Remember, we hired a company to take care of it until it sells."

"Yes, right. Did you girls get the rest of your mom's stuff out of her office?" His eyes sparkled with unshed tears. Her heart hurt for him because he missed Mom so much.

Guilt stabbed her. How much should she reveal to him about what they had found? She wanted to wait on her sisters and speak to him together, but if she broached the subject and peppered him with a few questions, she'd prepare him for the shock.

Ivy limped to the kitchen and found a roll of paper towels under the sink. She carried them to the couch, sat, and attempted to dry the water from her shoe. "We carried everything out and finished cleaning. The realtor has the sign in the yard and has set a couple of appointments."

"Did ya find anything interesting?"

With the paper towel, Ivy focused on drying her foot to buy time before she answered. "Most of what we found were old realty ads and paperwork. We discovered one box of personal papers and photos. As a matter of fact, Violet, Poppy, and I will sort through the stuff and bring it by as soon as we finish."

He smacked his hand on the chair's arm. "I want to go through it with you. If it's personal, don't you think I should be the one to check it?" His voice cracked, and he started coughing.

"I'll get you a drink." Ivy headed to the kitchen and filled a glass with water. She carried it to him. "Here, this might help."

After he had suffered from a stroke, the sisters handled him as if he might break. He grumbled at them and declared he had regained his strength.

He sipped the lukewarm water and nodded. "The water helps, but a glass of sweet tea might be better."

"Fine, I'll pour you tea." Tired of limping in one shoe, she kicked the other one off.

Tea in hand, she served her dad, then sat with her own glass. "You still make the best tea in the north."

"Thanks, dear. It's not as sweet as the southern version, but I like it this way." He raised his glass, then lowered the drink to his lips.

"Dad, I wanted to ask you something. I know you've had memory issues, but when did they start?" She shifted in her seat. "I don't want to pry, but if you'd be willing to share, I'd love to listen."

He set the etched glass on his mahogany side table, then rubbed his chin. "From what I understand, I lost part of my memory when I was in an accident. Your mom said I never talked about my years before she met me. I'm not sure if they were so bad, I blocked them out or if I couldn't remember. Renee said it didn't matter, and to move on, which I did, but I've always wondered what happened." He flipped the recliner's foot down and dropped his feet to the floor. "Once in a while, I get a memory of a little girl, most of the time in my dreams. Her name dances in front of me, then slips away. Could be one of you, but she seems familiar in a different way."

"Mom told us you met when she found you in the woods behind her house. She made it sound romantic. Was it?" Was she poking too far into her dad's life? Everyone deserved privacy, but after finding the box in Mom's closet, the sisters wanted answers.

Dad flipped the recliner foot up. "I reckon your mom did spin the whole thing into a lovey-dovey story, but all I remember is she nursed a head wound and bruises and scrapes. I wasn't much on doctors and didn't want to go to the hospital. After a week of her caring for me, I stayed. She had a small cabin on the property she had inherited from her dad. We fixed and cleaned the place, and I stayed there. Once I healed, Renee helped me find a job with the landscape company I retired from. About a year later, we married." He rubbed his hands together. "I loved working in the flowers and creating gardens for folks. That's why I named you girls after plants. They're the best thing God created."

Ivy's head spun. The fake ID Mom had secured must have worked to get Dad a job. Did she keep him hidden until he healed? Back then, they lived in the woods on a gravel road, away from the world. After Violet was born, Mom had sold land to a developer, and they removed the cabin. By the time Poppy was born, neighbors surrounded the property.

Dad coughed again. She had prodded enough for one day.

~~~~~

Sun shined through the restaurant windows at Johnny's Place. Henry and Johnny wielded paint rollers as they layered the last coat on the kitchen walls.

"I plan to open by next weekend. I want to make it an event to draw in customers." Johnny stepped aside and admired their handiwork, then patted his employee's back. "You've been a blessing. Thanks for putting in the labor. I know this isn't your favorite thing to do. Mine either. We both prefer cooking to painting."

Perspiration glistened on Henry's forehead. "Yeah, I'm not much with a paintbrush. I can't wait to get to chopping carrots and celery." He pulled a handkerchief from his pocket and wiped his face. "Sure looks good in here, though."

Together, the men shoved the stove in place.

"I can't wait to try out the new appliances. You chose well, boss."

A tap on the front door drew Johnny to the dining room. Joel, Lucy, and Sadie had spent evenings painting the walls where the customers dined a pale blue-gray. The Italian artwork he had collected dazzled against the neutral walls. Far better than the yellow he had from the previous owner. When he had bought the place ten years ago, he had given the walls a fresh coat of the same color. All those years he'd stored the art in a closet at home, except for two or three he had on display. The new color added class to the place, and the paintings added splashes of color. Maybe the fire turned out to be a blessing after all.

At the door, Johnny turned the latch and let Alexa in. "Hey. How did your class go?" He wanted to hug his daughter, but she spun in like a hurricane.

"Oh my goodness, Dad. I had a blast. The kids asked great questions and the parents let me take the lead. We explored the glacial grooves, then hiked to the alvar. Thanks for all the info on the flora here." Her arms waved as she spoke. "The weather was perfect for a June day. I can't wait to tell the museum director how successful a field trip can be. He may let me do more, since I have a place to stay on the island." She took a breath.

His daughter wanted to come to the island and stay with him. Thankful she experienced success, he stood straight and his chest puffed. More important, his little girl wanted to see him again. Sure, work drew her here, but at least she felt comfortable staying with him.

"Johnny." Henry ambled into the room. "I'm about to leave. Can I do anything else?" The young man paused in front of Alexa. "Hello, I'm Henry."

Johnny scrubbed a hand over his face as Alexa tugged her t-shirt hem and Henry pushed a hand through his thick black hair. A smile crossed both of their faces. Whoa, did he catch sparks between them? No, not happening. A relationship between his daughter and his sous chef might cause complications at work or for daughter and father.

"Alexa, this is Henry, my sous chef. We've been painting the kitchen, preparing to open next weekend." Johnny nodded at his friend.

She reached a hand to Henry. "Nice to meet you." They held the handshake longer than Johnny deemed appropriate. "I may have to come for the reopening."

"Great. I hope you can." He wrapped his arm around his daughter. "Henry, weren't you leaving?"

"Yeah, I gotta go. I'm heading to the mainland to run errands." Henry's gaze caught Alexa's. "I hope to see you soon." He hiked a bag over his shoulder and left.

Did the man use whitener on those sparkling teeth? Johnny shook his head, then guided his daughter to the office. "Let me finish a few things, then we can get ready to kayak."

"So Dad, is your sous chef single?"

Johnny shuffled papers on his desk. "I think so. He's never mentioned a girlfriend. Why?"

"Why do you think? He's cute and you speak highly of him." She blinked her big brown eyes. "Of course, he lives here, and I live in Cleveland. It would be silly to start anything."

"You met him five minutes ago."

She leaned on the door frame. "True. Never mind."

Maybe she'd visit more often, if... *No, don't go there.* "Let's go meet Marigold."

CHAPTER NINETEEN

Lake water slapped against the kayak's hard shell. In rhythm, Marigold, Johnny, and Alexa paddled across the inlet from Marigold's rental business. The voices of children playing on the beach faded as the trio made their way to the open water. Once they passed the fishing pier and glided into the deeper area, they rested the paddles across their laps and floated.

"Have you kayaked much, Alexa?" Marigold tugged a hair clip from her pocket, wound her braid into a bun and secured it.

"A couple of my friends and I have gone on the Cuyahoga River and along the shore of Cleveland. I love the skyline, but I also enjoy the swiftness of the river. How long have you owned your business?"

A double-crested cormorant glided across the water, ducked under, and emerged a few feet from its submersion point. "I've lived on the island since I was eighteen. I'd been here about ten years before I opened the rental. Canoes were all the rage, then kayaks became more popular, so I switched to those. The business has provided, along with my sales at craft fairs. I've learned to live a frugal lifestyle, but I wouldn't change how my life turned out, except for..." Her eyes closed at the thought of her dad. This young woman didn't want to hear her woes. "How did your class go today?"

The kayaks bobbed as they drifted farther from shore. "Class was great. I was telling Dad I hope the director will approve more field trips. If I could come and stay here for a few days at a time and teach once every couple of months, I'd shake the claustrophobia I've been experiencing in my office. I never dreamed I'd enjoy showing kids the geology of the island, but turns out, it's fun. By the way, I'm hoping to come next weekend for the reopening of Dad's restaurant."

"The reopening is next week?" Marigold turned to Johnny.

His hand dangled in the cool water. "I decided today we'd have the place together in time to open on Saturday, right before July fourth. Henry and I finished painting, and some of the money I saved doing the work ourselves can be used to buy outdoor tables and chairs. Want to come with me on Monday? I plan to scour the thrift shops in Sandusky. I'll buy lunch."

"Yes. Can we stop at the craft store?"

Johnny tossed her a smile. "Sure can and we'll stop for dinner, too."

"Sounds wonderful." Her insides quivered at the thought of time alone with him.

Before she got too carried away, she dipped her paddle in the lake. "Ready to head back?"

The trio pushed the paddles through the water. The swish of the gentle waves against the paddles and the act of moving the boat through water by hand gave Marigold a sense of satisfaction. Most days, she kayaked alone, but today she appreciated the company of this young woman and Johnny. She welcomed Alexa's enthusiasm and interest, but she hesitated to be too intimate in her conversation. No point burdening her with the story of her missing dad. Besides, she vowed not to interfere with Johnny and Alexa's relationship. Should she talk to Johnny and tell him to focus on his daughter instead of her? Monday, while they shopped, might be a good day to chat with him about it.

~~~~~

The scent of lavender mixed with lemon thyme stirred in the air as a soft breeze crossed Violet's patio. On Sunday afternoon her herb garden, filled with fragrant plants, served two purposes—flavoring food and visual beauty.

"Dad helped you plant your herbs, didn't he?" Ivy touched the leaves of the rosemary. "The smells out here calm me." She took a slow, purposeful breath. "I'd be out here all the time."

With a tray of lemonade and cookies in hand, Violet set it on the metal, glass-topped table. "I love to wander through my garden. After the kids go to bed, Joseph and I relax out here. I rub the lavender between my fingers and breath in the fragrance. Lavender aids in sleep. I've made sachets and placed them under my pillow."

"Why am I hearing about this now?" Poppy stepped onto the stones Joseph had dragged from a creek bed and laid in an attractive pattern. "I need help sleeping."

"Hey, Poppy, I'll make each of you one when I harvest the buds and dry them." Violet handed her sisters a drink. "Help yourself to the macarons. I bought them at the new bakery in town. They're delicious."

Ivy lifted one of the light pink treats from the plate. "Don't you mean macaroons? Actually, this looks nothing like a macaroon." She bit into the sweetness. "But, wow, does it taste delicious. Am I getting an almond flavor?"

"You are. Macarons are baked with almond flour, and macaroons with coconut. They're both yummy, but I love the crispiness and flavor of these." Violet popped the rest of her cookie in her mouth."

Poppy nibbled on a green one. "Doesn't matter to me what they're called when they're this good."

The sisters settled in the wicker porch chairs and sipped lemonade. Ivy cleared her throat. "So, I went to visit Dad yesterday. Took him groceries."

"I haven't stopped in for two weeks." Poppy had mentioned her art classes had doubled over the last few weeks. "How was he?"

Ivy placed her glass on the side table. "He coughed a lot, and the doctor says he's regaining his strength after the stroke. The cough may be from allergies or a dry throat. He scheduled an appointment next week with his general practitioner, so I'll have to make sure Dad tells him how he's feeling." She tapped her red fingernails against the arm of the chair. "I confess, I probed some while I was with Dad. He asked if we had cleared Mom's office. I asked a few questions about his memory loss, and he said he has dreams of a little girl he's familiar with but can't place. Did he have a daughter before he met Mom?"

A soft breeze waved across the patio and carried the fragrance of lavender. "We found those newspaper articles. If he was the man from the car wreck who disappeared, he did. If the obituary we found was his first wife, he left a daughter behind. She'd be in her fifties by now. Imagine your dad vanishes and you have no clue where he is." Poppy bit into another cookie and spoke with her mouth full. "If I were her, I'd want to know what happened." A choking sound came from her throat. "If our dad is her dad, we have a half-sister."

"If we have a half-sister, do we want to tell her what happened?" Ivy looked from Poppy to Violet.

With legs crossed, Violet swung her foot in rapid succession. "Let's finish the journal."

Two hours later, the sun lowered in the sky and the three sisters stared at the horizon. Ivy stood and paced in front of the other two. "Mom gave Dad a new identity, married him, kept track of Dad's first daughter, Marigold, had us, and lived happily ever after. I'm struggling to wrap my head around this. Mom was always different, some might say paranoid, but good grief, after all this, it makes sense. Poor Dad has no idea." She sunk into her chair.

A bluebird flitted across the garden. "The part about our trips to Abbott Island to attend church camp makes sense now."

Violet gathered the glasses and moved them to a tray. "What do you mean?"

"From the journal, it appears Mom kept tabs on Marigold when she took us to camp." The rising full moon's light cast an eeriness over the patio. "I always wondered why Dad never went with us to drop us off. Mom said he was busy, but in reality, she didn't want him to run into this woman. Not to mention, she's named after a flower."

"You're right. Mom took us, but never Dad. I wonder if this woman is still there? We haven't been to camp in so many years, and we have no other references, except the photo on the beach of the hippie woman. It's of her backside, but could be a clue. Her name fits Dad's love of plants." Violet cleared the napkins and saucers from the side tables and added them to the tray. With a cloth, she wiped a few crumbs off the furniture. "I don't know about you, but my head hurts."

With a broom, Ivy swept crumbs from the stones. "The articles I took home confirm the story of the accident and the time of Mom and Dad's meeting. I can't figure out how Dad got there, though. He was several miles away. Do you think Mom found him along the road and made up the part about discovering him in the woods to throw people off?" She set the broom in the corner. "With her home in the woods, she may have pulled it off. I wish Dad could remember."

"The next thing we have to figure out is if we leave this alone or we try to contact this Marigold woman. What will this do to Dad with his fragile health?"

"I agree, Violet. I'm concerned for Dad. My heart hurts for the woman, but more so for Dad. And what about Christopher Downey? Shouldn't we tell him, too?" Ivy slipped into the brown wicker, placed her elbows on her knees, and rested her head in her hands.

Poppy leaned on the back of a chair. "I say we scope out Marigold before we tell Dad. She may not be around anymore." She placed her hands on the small of her back and stretched. "We need to find out if she still goes by Hayes or if she's married."

"Easy enough to find out." With her phone, Ivy typed in Marigold Hayes, Abbott Island, Ohio. "No social media about her, but there is a kayak site with the address on a beach on Abbott Island. The site looks unfinished, but it could be a lead."

"Why would somebody post a half-finished website?" Violet frowned.

Leaning over her sister's shoulder, Poppy tapped on Ivy's phone screen with her fingernail. "If they aren't a professional designer, they may be working on it a little at a time. Not the best practice, but it happens."

Ivy shook her phone at her sisters. "Does the unfinished site matter? Good grief, can you two focus?"

"Sorry, Ivy," the two chimed together.

"When can we go? Do we all go?" Ivy opened her calendar. "I'm free Saturday."

Poppy checked her planner. "Me, too."

"Not me. The kids have a swim meet. I'm not sure this is a good idea. Meeting this lady may cause a whole new set of problems, and what about Dad?"

"I'll pick you up at nine, Saturday morning, Poppy. We can catch the ferry and snoop around. I don't want to ask too many questions until we know if this lady is who we think she is or until we decide if she's a decent person."

"Maybe you better reconsider. It sounds like trouble to me." Violet crossed her arms.

~~~~~

Vacationers milled around Lucy's General Store on Monday morning. A gray-haired gentleman held the door for Marigold to enter.

"There you go, young lady." His crow's feet and mouth creases wrinkled as he smiled.

She nodded thanks as her spirit plummeted. If Dad was alive, he'd be the same age as the tourist who held the door for her. She shoved her thoughts aside, even though her stomach quivered, and walked along the front of the store. To the left, college students and locals off school for the summer waited on customers. Lucy's blond head rose above the shirt rack.

"Hey, Lucy."

"Marigold. Good to see you. I was straightening the racks. We were so busy yesterday, no one had time to straighten the displays." She adjusted the collar on a polo shirt. "I'm glad you stopped. I've about finished your website, but I need a few photos. I made it live so people can at least find you, but I want to add the pics." Lucy trooped to her office at the back of the store, and Marigold followed. "Sit here and I'll bring the laptop over."

Marigold settled into a faded, flowered chair. "This has seen some days."

Lucy snorted a laugh. "Yep. I got the old thing from Sadie's grandma. It's the comfiest chair I've owned. I've made the mistake of sitting in it during the workday, and my employees have found me snoring. Not cool." She propped her behind on the chair's arm. "Here we go. Tell me if you approve, and please check the info for accuracy."

The laptop rested on Marigold's knees. She ran her finger across the screen as she read each detail. "Everything is correct. I like how I scroll, and a scene from the lake shows in the background. I'd like a photo of people on the water."

"Sure, and I want a photo of you and one of your shed with your macrame chair hanging from the tree, to add local flavor." Lucy retrieved the computer and closed the top. "When can I shoot those? I know Charlotte's working for you today. How about tomorrow? I want to get this finished."

"I don't enjoy having my picture taken. How about me helping a kayaker?"

"Perfect. Charlotte could pose as a customer?"

"Sounds good. I'll talk to her later today." She stood up from the cozy chair. "I'm off to meet Johnny. I promised I'd help him today."

"Johnny, huh? You two sure spend a lot of time together. When are

113

you going to get serious?" Lucy covered her mouth with her hand. "I'm sorry. I'm trying not to be so nosy, but it's a struggle."

"No worries. I'm still trying to figure out what I want. He's the kindest man I've ever met, and he cares about me, but his daughter was here, and I don't want to take him away from her."

A frown crossed Lucy's face. "Shouldn't you ask Johnny whether he feels pulled from his daughter? Assumptions are never a good idea."

"I'll consider talking to him. In the meantime, keep this conversation between us, please." She leaned in and hugged Lucy. "Thanks for all your hard work." As she left the store, a memory of her dad played on the fringe of her thoughts.

She and Dad walked out of a store and into the street. A car screeched around the corner and her dad wrapped his arms around her and carried her to the sidewalk. He checked to see if she was okay, then confronted the driver, who had come to a stop about a foot from where she had stood. Dad didn't yell, at least not until he demanded the driver get out of the car. Then he put a hand on each shoulder of the man as his voice raised.

"You could have killed my daughter. Slow down before you hurt someone." His hands dropped, and he turned, walked to her, and swept her up in his arms. From the day he saved her, she had declared him her hero.

No surprise she had trouble giving her heart to Johnny. She had placed her dad on a pedestal no other man could attain.

CHAPTER TWENTY

The cherry-red paint on Johnny's 1957 Ford F-100 gleamed as the morning sun shone. As Johnny and Marigold stood along the railing of the ferry, he tucked her hand in his. The lake water crashed against the sides and the breeze blew strands of Marigold's hair away from her face.

Intent on the woman beside him, Johnny reached a hand to her cheek. "You are the most beautiful woman I've ever known. Your kind heart and the way you live your life make me want you to be part of mine."

Marigold lifted her chin. "I'm not sure this is the time or place to spout our feelings for each other." A blush colored her cheeks.

"I can't help myself. We haven't had a minute alone for a while, and I want to assure you I still care." He moved behind her and wrapped his arms around her waist.

As they cruised to the mainland shore, Marblehead Lighthouse grew closer. Johnny nodded at the small peninsula. "I'd like to take a break one day and explore the lighthouse. I stopped there about five years ago, and it's a beautiful place. Peaceful, even with all the visitors."

"I'd like to go again. It's been a long time since I've stopped there, too." She leaned her head against him. "We'd better get in the truck, since we're docking soon."

A chill shivered through Johnny when she pulled away. In moments, he missed her nearness and her sweet, honey fragrance. At their age, he longed to hurry their relationship, even though he understood Marigold wasn't ready. He prayed she'd find peace and lay the search for her father at God's feet, or did he dare pray would she find him? Either way, he wanted to marry her.

Inside the truck's cab, Johnny started the engine and soon joined the line of cars and drove off the ferry. "Is there anywhere you'd recommend we shop first?"

She turned to him. "How about the Nifty Thrift Shop? They keep an eclectic inventory, and I'd love to say hello to Joy and Danny. I stopped in there a few months ago and saw tables and chairs that may work. Are you wanting complete sets, or mix and match?"

He pulled onto Route 2. "What do you think? Mix and match might be easier to pull off and may cost less."

"Mixing the style of chairs and tables will add a fun touch, and you could use colorful tablecloths to add personality." Marigold pulled a crochet hook and yarn out of her bag.

"I love your ideas, and I hope you'll help me get the outside space together."

"Sounds fun. Thanks for including me." Her hands worked the yarn with the hook.

Johnny saw a pull-off area and guided the truck to a stop. He turned to her and took the yarn and hook and placed them on the seat, then wrapped his hands around both of hers. "Don't thank me for including you. I want you in all parts of my life. I love you, Marigold."

Her eyes glistened as she blinked to hide tears, and her chin quivered.

With a gentle hand, Johnny wiped a tear from her cheek. "Why the tears?"

She let go of his hands, reached in her bag, pulled out a tissue, and wiped her face and nose. "I don't want to interfere with you and Alexa. I'm afraid I'll keep you from reconnecting, and I don't know what to do about my obsession with finding Dad. For so many years, I've missed opportunities because I've had such a singular focus. Yes, I help my friends, go to church, teach the little ones in Sunday School on occassion, and I appear strong, but in the back of my mind I wonder what happened to him and what I've missed out on." She dabbed at her eyes. "Why would you want to be with a mess like me?"

Johnny moved the yarn and hook and scooted closer to her. He wrapped his arm around her shoulders and pulled her to him. "Why wouldn't I want to be with you? Your heart has ached for a long time, and I want to ease the pain. I want to be part of your life. You are an amazing woman for all you've been through. I love how you have faith in God even as you hurt, and I love how you take care of the people God places in your path. I remember how you helped Sadie and Joel last year. And good grief, you're an entrepreneur with an independent spirit who has taken care of herself for years. I want to help take care of you, ease your burden and love you."

Marigold's eyes rounded. "Oh, Johnny. No one has ever said such kind things to me. I love you, but I've got to let go of the past and move on. I've dug a ditch, and I have to climb out. Pray for me, and I'll pray for you and Alexa."

"Thank you, and by the way, Alexa spoke highly of you. She enjoyed the kayaking and thinks you are an intelligent, lovely woman. She told me, in her words, 'Go for it.'" He raised his hands and cupped her face. "May I kiss you?"

A nod answered him. She closed her eyes, and he touched his lips to hers, not in a hurry. He tasted the strawberry on her lips, then he leaned away. "I love you, and I'll wait for you."

A bare whisper escaped her mouth. "Thank you. I love you, too."

A huge grin crossed Johnny's face, and his heart pounded as he turned the key. "Ready to pick out furniture?"

"Yes, I am." She picked up her crochet and beamed a smile.

~~~~~

Stacked in Jenga style and secured with bungee cords, three wooden tables and six chairs rode in the truck bed as Marigold and Johnny pulled into Netty's. On their way to the ferry in Marblehead, they ordered and dug into Netty's chili dogs loaded with cheese on the bottom, then topped with a hot dog and chili sauce. Between bites, they slurped on thick blackberry shakes.

Marigold slid the straw from the cup and licked the ice cream treat off. "We could eat these with a spoon."

With a smile, Johnny agreed. "This is one of my favorite treats when I come to the mainland."

The rare indulgence left Marigold and Johnny full and satisfied on their ferry ride.

As Johnny drove the truck onto Abbott Island and traveled to his restaurant, Marigold assessed the furniture through the rear window. Not one chair matched another, and the round wooden tables from a now-closed cafe had been a steal. With muscle and soap, they planned to scrub them clean, then paint them in shades of blue, and various tans and white, to reflect the national colors of Greece. At the craft store, Marigold had picked out blue, white, and yellow flowered fabric with a vintage look for the tablecloths she planned to sew. With Henry's help, they'd paint the chairs in a few days.

As though summoned by her thoughts, Henry sat on the bench in front of the restaurant. Johnny pulled to the curb and hurried around the truck to open Marigold's door.

Henry bounded across the sidewalk. "You found a bunch of treasures."

Johnny unhooked the cords around the furniture. "We sure did. I think these will make the patio welcoming to our guests."

Marigold lifted a ladder-back chair from the truck bed and carried it into the dining area. Thankful she had the strength to help, she hiked to the truck and hoisted two smaller chairs from the truck bed, while Johnny unhooked the other bungee cords.

Henry pulled a table out. "Perfect size for the patio."

Marigold tucked a chair under each arm and trekked to the door. "Glad you think so. You'll have to help Johnny paint them. Plus, he said he has a few in the backroom he wants to restore." She settled the chairs against the wall and faced Henry.

"He's the boss." He wiggled his eyebrows. "I'd do anything for him. He saved me from myself."

Not sure how to respond, Marigold nodded. Johnny's sous chef had lived on the island for a few years, but she had never heard his story. If memory served her, Johnny brought him into the business not long after he had rented a cabin on the edge of town. No doubt Johnny helped the young man. With a heart for others, his kindness touched many folks — one more thing she loved about him. His concern for others reminded her of her dad.

During her childhood, her dad had brought home a co-worker who had no place to live. He had lost his home due to medical bills from an illness that took his wife. His name was Joe, and he'd stayed in their basement for a couple of months until he found work. Dad told her he wanted to help others because someone had assisted him when he needed help. Maybe someone took care of him after the accident, if they found him out there, lost. She had considered so many scenarios. Were his bones sunk into the muck of the woods? Did he wander to another community? Had he lost his memory? Anything might have happened. Several times she had driven to the site of the accident and considered the events of the stormy night, but the peace of understanding the truth slipped through her hands like water in a fountain.

Help me let go, God. If I never find the truth, I at least want to live the rest of my life content.

"Mari, can you grab this chair, and I'll go back for the last table." Johnny's voice broke into her thoughts.

"Sure, I've got it."

The chairs and tables lined one side of the dining area, where fresh paint graced the walls. The cleaning crew Johnny hired would scrub the floors tomorrow. Afterward, Johnny and Henry planned to restore the order of things and restock the kitchen.

"Do you have a signature dish selected for the reopening?" Marigold sat in one of the ladder-back chairs and crossed her legs.

Johnny lowered himself to sit beside her. "I have a couple in mind. Want to come for dinner tomorrow and have a tasting? I'll ask Joel, Sadie, and Lucy, and of course, Henry."

"Sounds fun. Mind if I bring Charlotte?"

"Please do. Bring Levi, too, if he's not working." Johnny stood and offered Marigold his hand. "In the meantime, I'm off to get a few more things together before the day ends. Let me take you home, then I'll come back and finish."

A few minutes later, Johnny parked in Marigold's driveway. "I want to walk you to the door, beautiful lady."

At his sweet words, her face warmed. "You don't have to."

"How do I get my goodnight kiss if I don't?" He eased out of the cab and went to open her door.

"You're something else." As they walked to the door, he wrapped an arm around her waist, and she held on to him.

"Thank you for your help today. I appreciate your eye for style and your creative energy." He tucked a strand of hair behind her ear.

"I do what I do. I'm happy you were pleased with what we found."

"What I'm pleased with is you. I enjoyed today and hope we have many more." He leaned in, lifted a hand to the side of her face, and pressed his lips on hers. "Goodnight."

From the porch, she watched his taillights fade down the road. She lifted her fingers to her mouth and relished his kiss. A sense of peace shrouded her aching heart.

Inside the house, Marigold sat in her recliner, tugged off her shoes, and flipped the footrest out. Days like today left her thankful for the people in her life. Johnny's patience was golden. Joy welled inside her at the touch of his tender kiss. For the first time, her life felt complete, but did her emotions deceive her? Emotions never served her well, since they left her empty after her mom died and her dad disappeared. Hurt encircled her when she lived with her grandmother and her harsh ways. Although happiness filled many of her days on the island, she found it as fleeting as Lake Erie's waves as they ebbed and flowed.

The joy in her life stemmed from God's love. Thank goodness, He never changed. Perhaps if she allowed herself to be loved by Johnny, peace and contentment might follow, but how could she know for sure? Marigold's faith in God stayed strong, but her faith in people not so much.

Cassatt loped across the head of the chair and hugged Marigold's neck.

"Ahh, my furry friend, I can always count on you for comfort." She leaned back, closed her eyes, and thanked God for a perfect day. Her love for Johnny bloomed, like the bud of a rose—something beautiful, yet fragile.

CHAPTER TWENTY-ONE

Laughter flooded Johnny's tiny house on Tuesday evening, as his friends set up folding chairs and tables for the tasting feast. The fragrant air, spiced with oregano, roasted vegetables, and seared meats, tempted the taste buds. Henry and Johnny loaded the kitchen counter with fresh Greek dishes and plates of dessert.

"Ladies and gentlemen, after I say grace, please use the fine china, aka, disposable plates, and fill them."

After Johnny blessed the food, Marigold reached for his hand before she gathered her plate. "This smells amazing, and I love all the colorful veggies. You guys have outdone yourselves."

Johnny bowed to her. "Please fill your plate and tell me what you think. I've prepared a few tried-and-true dishes, and a couple of different ones I'm considering for the grand reopening."

"I'm sure whatever you've prepared will be perfect."

He leaned in and kissed her cheek. "The most perfect thing here is you."

A blush colored her cheeks. "Not even close." She swatted his shoulder. "I'll go fill my plate now."

His face split into a grin as he turned to speak to his guests. "Joel, I hope you try the souvlaki beef shish kebabs. They're marinated in a garlic, lemon, olive oil marinade and threaded on the skewer with red peppers, onions, and zucchini."

With two of the kebabs on his plate, Joel added lemon roasted baby potatoes. "Can't wait to dig in."

Sadie lifted a bite of the orzo pasta salad to her mouth and tasted it. "Oh my goodness, this is so good."

Johnny nodded. "Thank you. Do you like the lemony vinaigrette?"

"It's delicious and perfect for a light summer dinner." She closed her eyes and savored the taste.

"Henry's specialty. He mixes the perfect balance of ingredients."

The young man stood beside Johnny and beamed.

~~~~~

Charlotte and Lucy filled their plates and joined Marigold at a table in the corner.

"Does Johnny cook for you all the time, Mari?" Lucy bit into a Greek-style spinach and feta turkey burger. "Mmm...this is a winner."

"No. He cooks on occasion, but I enjoy fixing him a meal once in a while. I figure he's tired by the end of the day and can use a break."

"Man, it must be daunting to cook for a chef." She wiped tzatziki sauce from the corner of her mouth.

"I don't give it much thought. I fix what I learned how to cook and he eats, with great appreciation." Was Johnny being nice when he told her he loved her food? He devoured the hamburgers with Worcestershire sauce and the homemade potato salad. Nothing fancy, she called it country comfort food. *Okay, enough with the doubts. Johnny loves me and my food.*

Johnny's voice rose above the conversations. "Don't forget to try the desserts. We have honey orange-blossom baklava, and I made a white chocolate filo tart and Henry baked kourabiethes, an almond shortbread. Make sure to lick the powdered sugar from your fingers. Then we'll know they were good." Laughter traveled through the room.

Plates filled with one of each tasty treat, the ladies returned to their table. Lucy tapped Marigold on the arm. "Are you okay? You've been quiet."

Marigold laid her fork on the table. "I've been wrestling with a decision." She stood, lifted her water glass and fork and clicked the utensil to the glass. The room quieted as Marigold's breath quickened. She closed her eyes and forced herself to calm. Eyes open, her gaze met Johnny's. "First, I want to say, all the food is delicious, and I'm praying the re-opening is successful. Second..." She cleared her throat. "I need your help. This is hard for me since I tend to be rather independent." A low chuckle rumbled through the room. "Okay, I'm very independent." Her friends nodded. "As most of you know, I've spent many years wondering what happened to my dad. He's been missing for forty years, and it's time I let go and accept he's not coming back." A sob caught in her throat. "I've decided to stop searching and give the whole mess to God. It's time I move ahead and let go of the past. I've lived there long enough."

Johnny moved to her and pulled her into a hug. "I'm proud of you."

"Thank you. I want to be held accountable and not descend into a rabbit hole again."

"You got it, and we can all help you." He turned to their friends. "Let's gather around Marigold and pray for her."

Her friends circled her. As she listened to Johnny speak encouraging words and seek help from the Father, her heart lightened. She planned to celebrate fifty-five instead of mourning one more year without her dad. She'd consider Johnny's proposal, if he asked her again, or at least decide if marriage was for her. Either way, she would celebrate and invite her friends to cheer on one more year.

~~~~~

Wednesday afternoon, Ivy, Violet, and Poppy sipped Lady Grey tea from delicate china cups at the local tea house. The lemon and orange hint of flavor with the bergamot soothed Ivy's nerves. She reached for a blackberry scone, placed it on a flowered plate, and added clotted cream.

"I haven't eaten here in a while. They make the best scones. Have you tried the cinnamon ones with the brown sugar glaze? They're amazing. They're seasonal in the fall."

Babbling was Ivy's go-to when she didn't want to approach a subject. Certain Violet would object, she planned to tell her without backing down, she and Poppy planned to stalk the lady on Abbott Island. Not stalk, watch — no, observe. Yes, observe.

Soft instrumental music drifted from ceiling speakers as the sisters nibbled on their scones and sipped tea. "It's nice to have the morning off. I haven't taken a vacation day in months." Ivy plucked a scone crumb from her skirt.

Poppy tipped the cream pitcher and splashed milk into her tea. "With most of my classes in the evening, I'm free most mornings. Violet, what keeps you busy these days?"

"Keeping up with Joseph and the kids. He took on the school duties this morning so I could meet you. I haven't had a minute to myself in a long time. This is nice." She picked at her scone.

"It's on me. I wanted to treat you both, and I'm thankful you're here." Ivy stirred a second sugar cube into her tea. The sweetness overrode the tea's subtle flavor, but stirring gave her something to do while she figured out how to tell Violet their plan to visit Abbott Island.

Poppy leaned away from the table and flipped her hand in the air. "Ivy and I are going to go find this Marigold chick this weekend. We figure she's still on Abbott Island. You said you don't want us to go, but we've already decided."

So much for easing into the discussion. Ivy gripped the handle on her cup and tipped the drink into her mouth. Here came Violet's diatribe on why they should let it go and not search for their half-sister. Of course, Violet's concern for Dad influenced her decisions, but they could ease him into the situation or not tell him. Then again, he'd want to see his oldest daughter. Mom had left them with a mess.

"So you're going after all. Anytime soon?" Violet's question lacked the judgmental attitude Ivy expected from her.

Ivy straightened her back and faced her sister. "We plan to arrive on the island Friday evening and stay through Sunday to check things out. More or less a perusal of the island and catching a glimpse of this woman. From Mom's photo, we saw she had long white hair, or at least she did a few years ago. She may run a business on a beach, and she dresses like a flower child who got stuck in the seventies."

"I'm going with you." Violet dabbed her lips with her napkin. "After you all left the other night, I decided you were right. We have to figure this out. It's not fair to Dad or the island lady. If our dad is her dad, she must be wondering what ever happened to him. Dad is wise, and he'll deal with it as best he can."

Poppy's mouth gaped and Ivy's eyes widened. "Sure. We'd love to have you, but you said your kids had a swim meet."

"Joseph's mom and dad will be happy to take them. I can miss one meet for something this important. What time are you picking me up?"

"I'll be around to get you about four o'clock Friday evening, to get us on the ferry by seven. By the way, I was searching the island's website and saw a Greek American restaurant is reopening after a fire. The menu looks tempting, so I want to stop there for lunch on Saturday, if it's okay." Ivy folded her napkin and placed it on her plate.

"Sounds good. Thanks for organizing the trip." She raised her hand in the air. "A girl's day out with a purpose."

Her sisters shook their heads, and Poppy touched Violet's hand. "You always have to have a purpose, don't you?"

~~~~~

The sky showed off an array of pink, yellow, and blue with a few cirrus clouds as Marigold delighted in the sunrise on Thursday morning. Cassatt rubbed her fur on her owner's legs, then curled into a ball. Bible in hand, Marigold settled on the porch swing. Her coffee steamed beside the toast she'd allowed to get cold. Her stomach knotted as she read Psalm 55:22. "Cast your cares on the Lord and he will sustain you; he will never let the righteous be shaken." *This is a huge care, God, and I'm handing it to You.*

Cassatt jumped to the swing and rubbed her face against Marigold's arm as if to comfort her. "You sweet girl. You'll help me do this." She petted the cat. Brushing her hand over the soft fur calmed her nerves. She lifted her pet to her lap and embraced the quiet morning.

By ten o'clock, Marigold unlocked the kayaks and set out the sandwich board to announce prices and hours. Charlotte had applied her artistic skills and chalked a water scene across the bottom with people in boats, in hopes of attracting more people. She had discovered folks neglected to read the sign on her building, where the lettering had faded from bright blue to a pale shadow of itself. With the new board, she could add specials and holiday pricing. Satisfied with the placement in the sandy grass, she stacked the paddles against the side of the shack and settled in her macrame swing chair with a copy of a Deborah Raney book. With so much on her mind of late, she missed reading. Before tourists and islanders descended on the beach, she embraced the quiet.

Charlotte stowed her beach bag in the building. "Good morning, Miss Mari."

Marigold closed her book and slid out of the chair. "Hi. Hope you've had a good morning. I've been here about an hour and sent one couple into the water. Otherwise, the morning has been quiet. How are you today?"

The women stood behind the kayaks. "I'm great. I took a walk along the boardwalk trail this morning. The hair on my neck prickled, as if someone was watching me. When I turned, a deer stood behind a tree and stared at me. She was so pretty. Later, I spotted a frog and beautiful dragonflies and damselflies. Makes me wish I lived here all year round."

"The island is a unique place to live. The winters can be hard, but the other seasons are incredible. Have you checked with our school to see if they are hiring? The student to teacher ratio is small and might be inviting."

Charlotte unfolded her lawn chair and nudged it into the sandy soil. "I'm not sure I'm ready, since I've been teaching at my school for two years. I want to establish myself and stay there for a while. Maybe someday I could move here."

Back in her swing, Marigold nodded. "I understand."

"By the way, what you said last night about letting go and giving our stuff to God got me thinking. I've had issues with my brother, and I should give the situation to God and ask Him to help me reconcile. When I consider what you've been through, my problems seem petty. Thanks for including me in your circle of friends. I hope this summer is one where I'll grow in my faith. I'm a new believer, and I want to learn as much as I can from you."

Marigold reached for the young woman and took her hand. "I'm so grateful you're in my friends circle, too. You've been a great help to me already. I'd love to pray for you or with you, whatever you want. Please pray for me, too. I've held onto this hope for so long, and I'm not sure how to let go, except for a day and a prayer at a time." She let go of Charlotte's hand, then twisted her braid around her hand. "We have customers."

As Charlotte helped a family with children figure out who would paddle with whom, Marigold settled in her chair. *Dad's out there somewhere, and I may never see him again. Give me peace, God.*

CHAPTER TWENTY-TWO

The fragrance of lavender, thyme, and rosemary tickled Marigold's nose. She and Johnny had met at the restaurant early Friday morning and placed the tables and chairs in the patio area. A few days ago, Henry had painted the chairs in shades of blue and had given the tables a whitewash over gray. Johnny maneuvered large pots of herbs with a dolly and arranged them in groups near the entry and in two of the corners.

With the furniture in place, Marigold stacked stones around the herbs to create a small rock garden. "The herbs complement the space and they're useful." She rubbed the rosemary stem between her fingers. "This smells heavenly."

Johnny stood back and admired their work. "Those were the only plants I could get on short notice. I had the containers at home. Hope they're okay."

"They're perfect and smell wonderful. When your customers pass them on the way to their seats, they'll get a delicious whiff." She reached for his hand and held on. "You've made great headway considering what happened. I'm so glad you can open again."

With her hand in his, he lifted it to his lips and kissed her knuckles. "Thank you for your help, sweet lady. I couldn't have accomplished all this without you and Henry and our friends."

"You're so welcome. I'm glad Charlotte worked at the kayak rental today, so I was free to be with you." Staying busy kept her mind occupied and off her dad. Being near Johnny all day was an added bonus. "What else can we accomplish inside?"

She trailed him into the kitchen. By the stove, Henry chopped vegetables and prepped for the next day's business. "How's it looking out there?"

"Amazing." Johnny snatched a carrot. "I'm going to give Mari a few finishing tasks, then I'll be back to help."

The sous chef nodded. "No worries. I've got it under control."

"I'm sure you do." Johnny laughed. "Mari, let me get you set up with the artwork for the sandwich board and windows. I appreciate you offering your artistic expertise. If we make the windows colorful and post about the outdoor dining, we'll draw in more people. Joel and Sadie are coming by to string the fairy lights, and Lucy is bringing over candles for the tables. The inside looks great, except for a few finishing touches."

In the dining room, he led her to a booth. "I bought the supplies you asked for to paint the windows, decorate the outdoor board, and add the menu to the indoor chalkboard. I better go and help Henry, even though I'd prefer to stay with you." With a gentle touch, he placed a hand on each side of her face and kissed her forehead. In response, she lifted her face to his and met his lips with hers.

He twined his arms around her. "Keep it up, and I'll never get to the kitchen."

Marigold pulled away and shooed him with her hands. "Get going and cook the food for tomorrow." Her heart pattered as he walked away.

With broad strokes and tempera paint, Marigold painted a Greek flag flying from a pole across the picture window. Not wanting to make the painting permanent, she used a light hand for a transparent look. Under the flag, she lettered, "Grand Reopening. Free dessert with any meal." At the base of the flagpole, she sketched in a few daisies and tufts of grass.

"You're a talented artist." Johnny's voice startled her, and she plopped into a chair. "I'm sorry."

Hand on her heart, she stood. "I was so focused on painting that I didn't hear you come in."

He hugged her to him. "It's been over an hour, so I thought I'd check on you."

"Thank you, I think." She raised an eyebrow, then her face split into a smile as her arms circled his neck. This man with those beautiful brown eyes had stolen her heart. She raised on her toes and kissed his cheek. "If you want me to finish, you've got to stop distracting me."

"I know, I know. Is there something I can do to help you?" Even as he spoke, he kept his arms around her waist.

"Please set the sandwich board in front of this chair, then I can sit here and chalk the information on it. Also, I'll have to have a ladder to reach the menu board."

"Yes, ma'am." He leaned in for one more kiss, then scurried to move the items.

She flipped the page on the sketchbook she had referred to when she painted the window. "Do you like this lettering? I copied the Greek letters for *agape*, the love God gives us. I'm painting it in the middle in a heart, then I'll add outside seating and free dessert at the top or bottom."

"Nothing better than reopening this place with a focus on love. This is perfect, and so are you."

"Hardly, but I'm glad you like the design." She penciled a border around the edge.

Johnny took the pencil and pad away and laid them on a nearby table, then grasped her hands. "You're right. No one is perfect, but you are perfect for me." He planted a kiss on her cheek.

The sound of a throat clearing pushed them apart. "Sorry to

interrupt," Henry said, "but the recipe for the souvlaki shish kebab marinade has disappeared."

A sigh escaped Johnny. "I'll be right there."

Chalk in hand, Marigold leaned into the board and let her hand take over. With a flourish, she drew the letters along with curved lines and curlicues to create an eye-catching design.

By five o'clock, Marigold's back ached. After her artsy afternoon, she had scrubbed dust from tables and booths until they shone. Once she wrung out the sponge, emptied the dirty water, and stowed the bucket, she stepped into the kitchen. "Hey, guys. Anything else I can do?"

Johnny stepped behind her and placed a hand on each of her shoulders. She closed her eyes and let her breathing slow as he kneaded her tired muscles. When he dropped his hands away, she turned to him.

"Thank you."

"No. Thank you. You've earned a shoulder rub, for sure."

The front door banged open and voices floated to the kitchen. Joel, Sadie, and Lucy peered around the kitchen door.

"Hello." Lucy wiggled her fingers.

"Hi. I've got the lights ready for you to hang. They're in the dining room in a box." Johnny placed his hand on Marigold and guided her into the large room. He retrieved a box from a back table and handed it to Joel. "Let's drape them around the fence and spread a few strands of the solar lights around the herb planters. The solar part can be stuck in the ground beside the pots. I also bought a small canopy for each table. They'll make the space cozy and be cooler in the daytime."

Lucy fingered a strand of lights. "These are pretty. The little star shapes will twinkle. Won't they?"

"I'm not sure. They were on sale, so Mari and I grabbed them."

Joel toted the box through the door to the patio and his friends followed.

Johnny pulled a bag of clips from a toolbox. "I bought these to attach the lights to the fence. Okay?"

"Great idea." Marigold picked one up and held it against the fence. "You even matched the color."

"Let's get started." The group strung lights, erected the canopies, and placed a candle on each table. When they finished, Johnny flipped a switch and lit the place.

"What a magical and romantic place for a proposal." Lucy's eyes snapped from Johnny to Marigold.

"Lucy, let's go. Johnny has a big day tomorrow." Sadie tugged on her arm. "What time do you open?"

"We're open eleven to nine for tomorrow. Then we'll be open eleven to seven Sunday through Thursday and eleven to nine on Friday and

Saturday for the summer. You are all coming tomorrow, right?"

"You bet. I've heard you're serving great food." Joel laughed.

"You should know—you tasted all of it."

The crew moved to the front door and spilled onto the sidewalk. "Thanks again for coming and helping. I couldn't have done it without you. Henry and I will close and get rested for tomorrow. See you then." He grabbed Marigold's hand as their friends walked away and Henry went inside.

"I can't say thank you enough for all of your help. You are an amazing lady. I never dreamed I'd meet someone like you."

"I can say the same about you. I've enjoyed helping, and I'm excited you're reopening so soon."

He clasped both of her hands. "I've got to get inside. Do you want me to take you home when I'm finished? It'll be about half an hour."

"No. I rode my bicycle, and it's a beautiful evening to ride home." She gave his hands a gentle squeeze. "I'll be in tomorrow. Charlotte and I are splitting the day, so we can both come here to eat."

"Great. Goodnight, Mari. Sweet dreams." He leaned in and snatched a kiss.

Kitchen spices clung to him and embraced her in comfort. "You, too."

He stepped back inside. Marigold pulled her bike from the rack and dropped her purse into the basket. She mounted the seat and placed a foot on the peddle. Across the street, three women stood on the sidewalk and pointed at Johnny's Place. Maybe they planned to eat there. She peddled to the curb they occupied and stopped in front of them.

"Johnny's opens tomorrow at eleven."

The three could be sisters, but one had red hair, while the others were blonds. They all had blue eyes, similar to her own. She'd not noticed many people with the blue she saw in the mirror every morning. The redhead opened her eyes wide as if she'd seen a ghost. The blond-haired woman, with a stylish cut, nodded.

"Thank you. We're food bloggers, and we heard the restaurant had a fire and may be opening again tomorrow. We're anxious to taste the cuisine."

"I'm sure Johnny will be happy to serve you and excited you want to blog about the restaurant. Can I help you with anything else?"

"No," they answered in sync.

"Okay. Take care." Marigold placed her feet on the pedals and rolled away. *That was odd.*

~~~~~

Violet shook her head at Ivy. "Food bloggers? Seriously? How can we pull off food blogging without a blog? Won't this Johnny guy want to see what we write about his restaurant?" The streetlights flicked on as

130

darkness filled the sky, and the waves knocked against the docks.

Ivy pushed her hand through her hair. "Let's head to the place we're staying and get some sleep. I'm worn out."

The sisters ambled along the walkway to the bed-and-breakfast. "She caught me off guard, like I'd done something illegal." Ivy waved her hands in the air.

"I get it, but we were walking by the restaurant we want to eat at tomorrow, so we'd know where it was. Nothing else." Violet heaved a sigh.

Ivy stopped and put a hand on each hip. "I've never stalked anyone before, and I'm nervous, okay? If you want to instruct me on how to do this better, please do. Otherwise, I want some sleep." She turned and stomped along the sidewalk. A couple on the other side of the street grabbed their children's hands and hurried them along. "Oh great, now I'm scaring people.

Violet jog-walked to catch her sister. "You did say the word *stalked* a bit too loud. Now they think we're crazies who follow people."

Poppy caught her sisters, passed them, and held out her hand for them to halt. "You two stop bickering. We are here for one reason, to find the person who may be our half-sister. We won't get anywhere acting like children."

"Poppy is right. We're acting silly. I'm sorry, Vi."

"Yeah, me too. When I get out of the house, away from the kids, I've got to act more mature." The three walked by a beautiful white, two-story home scrolled with gingerbread. "What a gorgeous house. I could live there."

"Me, too." Ivy snapped a photo with her phone. "How about you, Poppy?"

"I can imagine the second floor as an art studio. I bet it gets amazing natural light through those Gothic windows." She stared at the house, then turned to her sisters.

"Something about the lady we talked to has been bugging me. I'm sure you noticed the long white braid like the mystery woman in our photo. She wore jeans and a t-shirt instead of the hippie clothes, but she seemed about the size of photo lady, but the body type isn't what got my attention." She tapped her lips with her finger.

Ivy tilted her head and stared at her sister. "Well, go on."

"Did either of you notice her eyes? I know it was getting dark, but there was enough light from the shop windows to see her eye color." She paused again.

"Good grief, spit it out." Violet huffed.

"They were the same vivid blue as ours—and Dad's."

CHAPTER TWENTY-THREE

At 8:30 Saturday morning, Johnny cruised his truck downtown. The Greek food truck he had lost sleep over had disappeared last week. Town folks had shared that the owner thought he might make more money in Sandusky, something about supply issues. Odd, since they had less competition with his place closed. A grin crossed his face. One less complication for Johnny.

Across the street, Lucy climbed the steps of the General Store as Johnny parked along the street beside the restaurant. He got out of the vehicle and waved. "Morning, Lucy."

"Hey, Johnny. Ready for today?" She adjusted the strap of the over-sized leather bag she carried.

He lifted a couple of boxes from the truck bed. "I sure hope so. If I'm not, I'm in trouble." With his knee, he nudged the patio gate open. "Thanks again for all your help."

"You're welcome. I'm going to tell all my customers to stop by." She unlocked her door. "Later."

Johnny toted the boxes into the kitchen. A few last-minute purchases for the restaurant had arrived yesterday. He and Henry never had enough dish towels or mixing spoons. He glanced around the well-equipped room and let out a happy sigh. "I can't wait to get started."

"Hey, boss. I'm excited too." Henry stood in the doorway between the kitchen and dining room with his hands on his hips.

"You're early. I wasn't expecting you for another half an hour." He lifted the new towels from the box. "I washed these last night to get the sizing out, like my momma always did. Figured they'd be more absorbent."

The sous chef caught the one he tossed to him. Henry held the fabric close to his nose and laughed. "Smells springtime fresh."

"Funny, aren't you? Let's get these put away, then start cooking. I can't wait to get into our routine." Beads of sweat popped on his forehead. He turned the thermostat for the kitchen down a notch. "Good thing we can control the kitchen's temperature apart from the dining area."

"Yeah. We'd freeze people out." Henry tied an apron over his clothes. "I'll put on my jacket when it gets closer to opening time."

Johnny repositioned the skull cap he preferred to wear while cooking. Although he owned a toque blanche, the tall white hat many chefs wore, he preferred the cap and encouraged Henry to wear his. The laid-back island life dictated a less formal attire. "Sounds good to me. If we're comfortable, we'll work better." He glanced at the clock. "We have two hours until show time."

The men chopped, seared, and prepped dishes of Greek food and American fare. Garlic and herbs filled the kitchen with the perfume a chef loved. In an hour, Johnny expected the serving staff and the kitchen help. He anticipated smiling faces and people pleased to be at work. About fifteen minutes before ten, a knock pulled him away from the stove.

"Someone is early." He wiped his hands on a towel and moved to the front door. On the other side, he glimpsed a face he had hoped to see today.

With a click, he unfastened the lock and opened the door. "Alexa, you made it." He swept his daughter into a hug, then stepped back. "You are beautiful, as always."

"Aw, Dad, you're making me blush." She looked past him at the remodeled room. "Wow, you've been busy."

"You've heard the song about getting by with help from friends? I couldn't have done this alone. Henry has been amazing, and of course, Marigold and my island friends. The staff helped, too. I can't wait for you to see the patio." He led her to the door. "Check this out."

She stepped into the open area. "This is gorgeous. The mismatched chairs are fun and the little herb gardens smell amazing."

Johnny beamed. "We added fairy lights, too. Well, Joel and Sadie did."

"Oh, romantic. I bet you'll sit out here with your lady friend." She winked at her dad.

His cheeks warmed. "Maybe. What am I saying? Of course I will." He turned and walked into the building.

She followed him in. "You two are so cute. I'm happy you've found someone. By the way, is Henry here?"

Johnny made an abrupt turn and faced his daughter. "He is. Why do you ask?"

She backed away a step.

The young man stepped out of the kitchen. "Did I hear my name?"

A grin spread across Alexa's face. "Hi, Henry. I thought you'd be here cooking your heart out."

Johnny stepped between them. "We'd better get to work if we want to be ready to open."

Alexa tugged on her dad's sleeve. "Is there anything I can do to help?"

Henry cleared his throat. "She could finish rolling the silverware into the napkins and make sure the menus are ready."

"Good idea." Johnny led his daughter to the servers' station. "This way, the waitstaff won't have to worry about it. Thank you."

Alexa lowered her voice. "What's up with you not wanting me to talk to Henry?" She stacked a knife, fork, and spoon on the napkin, folded the corner, and rolled it closed.

Johnny rubbed his cheek. "Nothing. Henry is my right-hand guy, but I know what dating or marrying a chef entails, and I don't want you hurt because he may not have time to give you."

"Don't be silly. Just because things didn't work out for you and Mom doesn't mean the same would happen to me. I think Henry is cute and could be a friend. Nothing more. I'd like to make friends on the island if I'm going to visit or stay for a while." She rolled another set of utensils.

"You're right. You're an adult. Here I am thinking of marrying Marigold, and I'm after you to be careful." He grabbed a napkin and dabbed his forehead.

Alexa's mouth opened, and she stared at her dad. "Did you say you're getting married?"

"What? No. I mean, I've asked Mari, but she isn't ready. I was going to talk to you about it, but I haven't had a chance. I hope you aren't mad."

"Mad? I'm happy for you. I pray she says yes. Marigold is awesome." She wrapped Johnny in a hug.

"I'm so glad to hear you approve." He hugged his daughter, then let go. "We'll talk more later. I've got to get cooking."

Johnny hummed as he layered a pan of pastitsio, a Greek-style lasagna. *Alexa approves, now if only Marigold would say yes.*

~~~~~

Waves rolled in and reflected the blue sky, while children's laughter drifted on the soft breeze. Families crowded the public beach beside the kayak stand. A young lady with bobbed blond hair swung in a chair tied to a tree. Saturday morning on the island buzzed with activity. Ivy pulled her sedan into a parking spot at the top of the hill, a great place to spy on the lady they hoped to find.

Poppy lowered the backseat window before Ivy turned off the engine. "Are we sitting in the car, or are we going to talk to someone? The girl by the kayaks might know where to find hippie lady."

The oldest sister tapped on the steering wheel. "I'm not sure. I want to scope out the situation. What do you think, Violet?"

With a pair of small binoculars, Violet peered out her window. "I don't see anyone who fits the description of the lady Mom called Marigold, do you?"

"You brought binoculars? A bit much, don't you think?" Ivy shook her head.

Violet snatched a bag of chips from her huge purse. "I brought snacks, too. Isn't this a stakeout, you know, like on television?"

"You need to get out more." Ivy closed her eyes and leaned her head

135

on the seat's rest, then lifted her head and looked at her sister. "Let's walk to the beach and scope out possibilities."

All three sisters opened the doors and exited the car. Together, they ambled to the sand.

Poppy held her hand to the side of her mouth and stage whispered, "Are we going to talk to the blond?"

Ivy stopped and bumped into Poppy. "I'm not sure. Let's play it by ear."

As they approached the kayak stand, the blond woman hopped out of the swing and turned to them. "Hello, ladies. Can I help you?"

Violet moved ahead of the others. "Good morning. We're visiting the island and checking out the possibilities of things to do." She tripped over a piece of driftwood, then righted herself. "Are you the owner of the kayaks?"

She scrunched her brow. "Um, no. I'm Charlotte. Marigold is the owner. Why do you ask?"

Ivy pushed her way past Violet. "Just curious. You know, you're young to have your own business. We're trying to encourage our youngest sister to start a business and hoped you might have pointers." *Could my answer be more lame?*

Poppy's eyes widened, and Violet bumped her with her elbow.

Charlotte nodded. "Sorry to disappoint. Marigold won't be here until later, or I'm sure she'd be happy to help you. While you're on the island you should try out Johnny's Place They're reopening today after a fire, and I know they are fixing delicious food."

"Thank you. We might be back to kayak tomorrow or another time we visit." The three of them turned and scurried to the car.

With seat belts buckled, Ivy sped out of the lot. "Awkward. Sorry I threw you out there, Poppy, I had to say something."

They motored away from the beach to the road that looped around the island. The water splashed against docks on one side while they gawked at homes on the other. "I'd love to have a house on this island to bring the kids to in the summer. We'd have so much fun." Violet pointed out the window. "Check out the adorable cabins. I bet we could rent one of those. *Sadie's Place.* Cute name. I wonder if she's the owner." She jotted the name and phone number on a pad from her purse. "We could start by renting, then buy a place. I want to call my hubby."

Ivy glared at her sister.

"Not now, I'll call later." She tucked the notepad in her bag.

"I'm sorry, Violet. I'm nervous about finding out if our mother kept this woman from knowing Dad. My heart aches for her, but even more for Dad and for us. To find out Mom was capable of hiding the truth all these years makes me sick."

With her hand on Ivy's arm, Violet bowed her head. "Lord, provide guidance and wisdom. Please show us how we can glorify You in this mess."

"Thank you. I should pray more often." Ivy pulled the car into a spot near the downtown. "What do you say we get lunch at Johnny's?"

"I'm ready to eat, but there's a line." Poppy stepped out of the car and closed the door. "We better put our names in."

Inside the restaurant, a young woman with a pixie cut and big brown eyes greeted Ivy. "Welcome to Johnny's. How many?"

"How long is the wait?" She lifted her sunglasses from her face.

"About thirty minutes. While you wait, check out one of the shops across the street. The beeper I'll give you will alert you it's time to be seated."

"Great. Table for three, please."

The young woman handed her the beeper. "Here you go."

Ivy pushed out the door to where her sisters waited. "We have about thirty minutes and a beeper will alert us. She said we can go across the street to the shops if we want."

"Cool, there's a cute t-shirt store to check out." Poppy led the way across the street.

Inside they perused the shirts and trinkets. A tie-dyed one had an outline of the island with Abbott Island in script. "I think I'll buy this one. I love all the colors." Poppy held the shirt to her chest.

"Definitely your style." Violet twirled a clear tube filled with sparkles and stars. "I'm getting these for the kids."

"Fun." Ivy held a candle called island breeze. "This smells amazing, like you expect vacation to smell at the beach."

As they paid for their purchases, the beeper sounded.

"Good timing."

At the restaurant, a different hostess led them to their seats. "We have a table outside and one in here. Which do you prefer?"

Ivy spoke over the hubbub. "Outside, please. The weather is beautiful."

Seated at an outdoor table, Poppy checked out the area. "This is nice. I love the mismatched chairs and the rosemary planted in the pots. I overheard someone say this is a recent addition. What a smart use of space. I'd love to paint on the fencing. I can imagine island life murals. Maybe they'd hire me?"

Ivy sighed. "I love how the two of you get side-tracked." Her cell phone dinged. "Ugh."

"What's wrong?" Violet laid her hand on Ivy's arm.

"A text message from Christopher Downey. He wants to know if I've figured anything out yet." She clicked a button, and the screen turned black. "I'm not dealing with him right now, and I'm getting hungry. What looks good?"

"Everything." Poppy stared at the menu. "I'm going to try this turkey burger with feta, and the seasoned potatoes. My mouth is watering."

The server stopped by their table and offered a plate of pita bread and red pepper humus. "Compliments of the chef." He rested the plate in the center of the table. "Are you ready to order?" His red hair shone like copper in the sunlight and his blue eyes reflected a happy soul.

Violet ordered the Greek chicken salad, Ivy the pastitsio and Poppy the burger.

"Thank the chef for the hummus. It looks yummy." Poppy flashed her brilliant smile.

When the waiter left, the sisters dipped the pita into the hummus.

"Wow, this is amazing." Ivy licked her lips.

"It is." Violet coughed as if she choked on the bread.

Ivy patted her back. "Are you okay?"

"Yes. I sucked in a breath because I think I see who we're looking for." Violet's hand covered her mouth. Ivy and Poppy followed Violet's gaze to a woman with a long white braid, dressed in a flowery, loose-fitting dress.

CHAPTER TWENTY-FOUR

The oak trees bent over the wooden fence and shaded the outdoor dining area at Johnny's. With temperatures in the eighties, the feathered limbs provided a comfortable canopy on Saturday afternoon. Patrons at all four tables chatted and tasted Johnny's cuisine. Seated with Joel, Sadie, and Lucy, Marigold glanced around the green space. She admired the hard work each person at her table had contributed. When Johnny had showed her the area the night of the fire, she envisioned young couples dining in the evening by fairy light. Perhaps first dates or proposals might occur.

Proposals. She had not answered Johnny's question. Would she, or wouldn't she marry him? Today, committing to him seemed frivolous, because he deserved someone committed to a future filled with hope. If her friends heard her thoughts, they'd argue with her.

What about Alexa? What if his daughter wanted this time to build a relationship with her dad? The young lady had greeted her at the door and said she was filling in for the hostess. She had hugged her and appeared happy to see her, yet Marigold couldn't shake her doubts.

In the early morning, Marigold had begged God to help her let go of her search for her dad. Her heart wanted to move on, but she'd have to discipline herself to change her mindset. After forty years of hoping, she had prayed for focus on Johnny and to have a relationship with a real person instead of imagining how life would have turned out if her dad had come home.

Marigold lifted her fork to her mouth. "Ouch." A foot connected with her shin. "Lucy, why did you kick me?"

"You were daydreaming, and I wanted your attention."

"Why not say my name instead of kicking me?" She rubbed her shin.

"I didn't mean to do it so hard. I'm sorry, but did you notice the three women over there?" She turned her head to peer at a nearby table. Marigold, Joel, and Sadie craned to see, too.

"Yes, I saw Elliot seat them." Marigold sipped her water. "I spoke to them yesterday, and they mentioned they were food bloggers interested in tasting Johnny's cuisine." Her brow furrowed. "Does something about them bother you?"

Lucy leaned in and quieted her voice. "They keep ogling us. Are they trying to figure out who we are?"

"I probably seem familiar because I spoke to them yesterday." She turned to them and met the gaze of the redhead. With a nod and smile, she acknowledged her and turned to her friends. "One thing I noticed about them the other day was the color of their eyes. All three of them have the same bright blue as mine. I don't see my color often, unless the person wears contacts. This may sound funny, but the redhead seems familiar, but I can't pinpoint it."

Sadie pushed her plate away. "Have they been here before and rented kayaks from you?"

"Could be. I cater to a lot of folks in the summer." Marigold folded her napkin and dropped the cotton cloth on her plate. "I'm stuffed. Johnny is such a talented chef, Henry too. If I marry Johnny, I'll gain twenty pounds the first month."

Lucy jumped from her seat, hurried around her chair, and wrapped Marigold in a tight hug. "You're getting married?" Her voice rose an octave.

"Lucy, sit. No, I'm not getting married, at least not right now. I shouldn't have mentioned it. I've not made a decision, yet. Please don't tell people I'm getting married." Her cheeks burned with embarrassment. When she garnered the courage to look around the seating area, she caught the stares of the people at the tables. "I'm sorry folks, there was a misunderstanding." As her gaze moved to the door of the restaurant, she saw Johnny turn and retreat to the kitchen. He had heard her. "I have to go talk to Johnny." She rose from her chair and dashed to the kitchen.

Johnny stood over the stove, stirring sauteed vegetables. A whiff of peppers and onions drifted across the room.

"Johnny, do you have a minute?" Marigold pleaded with her eyes.

~~~~~

Even with the air conditioning on, the kitchen heat caused Johnny to perspire. He pushed the skull cap back to allow air to his bald head. Marigold stood in the doorway seeking his attention, but pressed for time, he continued to work with the food. Her reaction to Lucy told him one thing. She had no intention of getting married. The last few days had filled him with hope she would let go of her search for her dad and live in the moment, instead of the past. What a dolt he had been to think his love changed her heart. After Alexa gave her blessing, he had planned to pop the question one more time, and soon, around Marigold's birthday, but not now. Not after witnessing her words to Lucy.

He wiped his hands on one of the new towels and stepped to the woman he loved. "I can't talk right now. I'm pretty busy."

She stepped closer to him. "I'm so sorry. I hope you don't think I'll never marry you. Lucy caught me off guard."

"No worries, Mari. I've got to get to work." He stalked to the stove.

~~~~~

The patio space closed in on Marigold as she trekked to the table to tell her friends goodbye. The smell of the Greek food she had savored moments ago nauseated her. She lifted her bag from the chair as her friends stood to join her.

"I've got to go check on Charlotte and give her time to come here and eat."

Lucy took her by the elbow and guided her to the restaurant's register. They paid for their meals and moved to the sidewalk outside. "I'm sorry, Mari. I caused this with my over-exuberance." She patted her friend on the back. "Did you get to talk to Johnny?"

Sadie and Joel huddled near Marigold and Lucy. Sadie touched Marigold's arm. "Is there anything you want us to pray about?"

Marigold ran her hands over her white braid. "Yes. Please pray I can talk to Johnny, and he will understand me. I've been trying so hard to move beyond the past, but I've got to work harder and seek God's guidance and the wisdom He has for me. Fifty-four isn't the end of the road, but I know I'm getting on in years."

"Of course not. You're still young, with things to do." Lucy hugged her. "We love you and want the best for you. If I can do or say anything to help, let me know."

"Don't you think you've said enough, Luce?" Joel ribbed his sister.

"Not funny. Isn't it time for you to go to work?"

He tipped his cap, kissed Sadie on the cheek, and walked to the police station behind the General Store.

Sadie sidled up to Marigold. "Come over this evening, and I'll make dinner. You can play with Rosie. She always brings you joy."

"Can I come, too?" Lucy chimed in.

"Of course. I'll see you both at 6:30. Dinner will be light since we stuffed ourselves at lunch, and I'm going back in to buy dessert. We have to sweeten ourselves, right?"

Marigold chuckled at Sadie's joke. "Thank you. A few hours with you two will be a blessing."

~~~~~

As soon as the three sisters paid the woman at the register, they scuttled out of the restaurant. A fishy odor rode the breeze that blew in from the lake.

"What on earth happened? Sounds like Marigold has never married and might now." Ivy squinted in the bright sun.

The three moved away from the entrance to the eatery.

"There are picnic tables in the town square. Let's sit for a minute." Violet led them across the way to a grassy area decorated with a replica of a lighthouse.

They gathered around the table and piled their purses and bags in the middle. "I think the chef has a thing for Marigold, and so what if she's never married, Ivy, neither have we." Poppy tilted her head and gave a quizzical look at her oldest sister.

"She's quite a bit older than us, and by the way, we don't know if she is our sister. Her eye color matches ours, and some of her mannerisms remind me of Dad, but we have zero proof. I'm not sure whether to pursue this." Ivy pulled a tissue from her purse and blew her nose. "Excuse me. I must be allergic to something on this island."

"The kids are dealing with allergies. It's the time of year when the nasty yellow stuff is everywhere." Violet picked at her fingernails. "What time are we going home tomorrow?"

"Let's leave early afternoon." Ivy stood and hiked to the nearest trashcan to toss her tissue. At the table again, she lowered herself to the bench. "I wonder if Marigold went to the kayak rentals. Let's take a couple out and one of us can sit near her and make conversation. Chat with her about who she is. Casually, of course."

"I can chat her up. I'd rather sit on the beach than be out on the water." Violet lifted her purse from the table and slung it over her shoulder. "Let's go." Her sisters followed her to the car and loaded in.

Ivy pulled the car onto the street. "Let's swing by the bed-and-breakfast and change clothes. I don't want to kayak in a sundress or go without sunscreen."

Clothes changed and windows down, they headed back to the beach. Ivy snugged into a parking spot and turned off the engine. "I love the scent of the beach, the cocoa butter, and the fresh air. It reminds me of when Mom and Dad took us to the lake to swim. We have great memories, don't we?"

Violet and Poppy remained quiet.

"Why aren't you saying anything?" Ivy looked from one to the other.

Poppy nodded to the lake and Marigold's rentals. "We have wonderful memories, but does she? Has she spent her life wondering what happened to her dad? Or did she move on? Makes me sad for her. We got her dad, and she got left out."

In the backseat, Violet unbuckled her seatbelt. "I agree, but we're here to make amends and set what we can right. We've got to figure out if this is our sister."

~~~~~

The sun's bright light sprayed across the lake like sparkling diamonds. A slight breeze blew in from the water as a great blue heron sailed across the sky. Two kayaks leaned against the building, dripping water from the last excursion.

"You've been busy, Charlotte," Marigold said.

The young woman jumped. "I didn't hear you come behind me." She hung a towel on a clothesline her boss had strung. "It's been nonstop, which I love." The pretty young woman's face lit with joy. "You're early. I thought I worked until two today."

"After I ate, I went home and changed. Johnny's is crazy busy, and I didn't want to stay at a table when others were waiting." Marigold refused to mention her embarrassment and humiliation when her best friend and true love overheard her denying marriage. To be so adamant about not getting married must have hurt him. What if he broke off their—what? Friendship? Her mistake might cost her a beautiful future with an amazing man. Time to stop focusing on the bad and focus on the good. She helped her friends and gave them sound advice, yet she failed to help herself.

A serene smile crossed Charlotte's face as she placed a hand on Marigold's shoulder. "You seem troubled. Is everything okay?"

"Nothing a few hours on this beach won't help. Now, you go on and get yourself ready to go to Johnny's with Levi. I know you say it's not a date, but it's nice for the two of you to spend time together. I'll pay you for the full day, so no worries there." She moved her hand as if to shoo Charlotte away."

"You are so kind. Thank you." She scurried to the shed and grabbed her bag. "I'll see you tomorrow." Charlotte waved and walked across the sand.

Marigold kicked off her flip-flops and walked to the edge of the water. The gentle waves washed over her feet. Something about the steady rhythm of the ebb and flow reminded her of God's neverending love for her. *Lord, help me make things right with Johnny. I love him so much. I don't want to lose him, too.*

CHAPTER TWENTY-FIVE

Voices of people playing on the beach floated to Ivy as she and her sisters neared the kayak stand. A few feet away, the person they believed to be Marigold faced the water.

Violet rifled through her bag and retrieved the photo of the woman they had found in their mom's box. "Look."

Ivy and Poppy paused and stared at the picture. From the back, the lady on the beach resembled the woman in the photo. Same long braid, similar size, flowing, flowery sundress. If the lady wasn't her, she had a twin.

"She has to be the same person." Ivy studied the woman as she turned from the water and ambled to the rental area. "She's a beautiful woman. Her eyes are the same color as ours and Dad's, she's tall like Dad and Violet, and her hair is Dad's shade of white."

Violet pushed the photo into her bag. "You two get on the water and let me chat with her. I'll spread my blanket near her and strike up a conversation."

The faint smell of hot dogs roasting drifted to the beach from the campground on the hill as the sisters approached the kayak stand.

"Good afternoon, ladies. Welcome to Abbott Island beach." Recognition flitted across the rental owner's face.

Ivy pushed her sunglasses up the bridge of her nose. "Um, we'd like to rent a couple of kayaks."

"You've come to the right place. How many?" She waved her hand to the boats.

Poppy winced at Ivy's stiffness. "Two, please. Violet's going to hang out on the beach."

"Great, let me get them ready." Marigold moved to the plastic vessels and wiped sand and water from the seats. "Have you kayaked before?"

"She has, but I haven't." Ivy pointed to Poppy.

"By the way, I'm Marigold." She handed the sisters life jackets and a piece of paper and pen. "You must wear these at all times while you're on the water, and please sign this waiver for me." They signed and returned the paper and pen. "Aren't you the food bloggers I met yesterday? I saw you at Johnny's earlier today."

Violet squashed her blanket to her chest. "Yes. I'm Violet and these are my sisters, Ivy and Poppy."

Marigold handed them paddles. "We have something in common."

Ivy's heart fluttered. Did she know who they were? "What?" Her voice shook.

"Our names are all flowers. My Dad loved anything to do with plants." A sadness shadowed Marigold's eyes as she cleared her throat. "And by the way, I hope the little misunderstanding about Johnny and me won't color what you write about his restaurant. He is an amazing chef and a kind-hearted man." Marigold pushed a loose strand of hair behind her ear. "Forgive me for the confusion I caused."

Poppy patted Marigold's arm. "No worries. The food was delicious and the service excellent."

"I'd love to read your review. Can you give me the website?" She dragged the kayaks to the water.

Poppy glanced at Ivy as they trotted to catch up. "We're still new at this, and we haven't finished the site yet, but when we do, we'll be in touch."

Marigold raised her eyebrows. "Okay."

Ivy's stomach ached as if beach glass tumbled inside. The woman didn't believe them, or at least doubted them. What if Violet jabbered too much and created more questions than answers?

"Let me demonstrate how to get in and out of the kayak without tipping." She turned and sat on the seat, then lifted her legs to rest on top of the vessel. "For the paddle to work effectively, turn the blade this way and draw it through the water."

Poppy went through the steps, too. "I'll help her once we get on the lake."

Ivy settled on her kayak as Marigold waved. "Have fun."

~~~~~

The kayaks bobbed in the water as Ivy and Poppy paddled away. A plastic bottle floated near the shore, and Marigold waded across and captured the debris. She shook the excess water off and carried it to the recycle bin beside her shed. Violet had spread a blanket out beside the tree where Marigold's macrame swing hung. Curious why she chose a spot close to the kayaks, Marigold sashayed across the sand and stood in front of her.

"Violet, you can go farther along the beach."

She slathered on sunscreen, then lifted her sunglasses to rest on top of her head. With the sun shining on her, the blue of her eyes popped. "This spot will work. There are so many people on the beach and quiet sounds perfect. I have three kids, and I seldom have a moment to myself."

"I can see where the noise level would keep you from joining the craziness of all the kids running around." A laugh escaped Marigold. After she had hurt Johnny today, sadness had swept through her and made itself at home. A good chuckle eased her soul and lifted the burden of guilt. After dinner with Sadie and Lucy tonight, she'd try to call Johnny and ask if they could talk.

The young lady in front of her leaned on her elbows and stretched in the sun. "Do you work here every day?"

Marigold moved to her swing chair and slid in. "Most days. This is the first year I've hired help. I find as I get older, I can't do what I did when I was twenty." She swayed the swing in a gentle rhythm.

Violet interrupted Marigold's peaceful moment. "Have you always lived on the island?"

"Since I was eighteen." Not keen on sharing her life story, Marigold chose her words with care. Violet acted nice enough, but she had not met these sisters until last night.

She sat upright and wrapped her arms around her knees. "You're what, fifty?"

This lady asked too many questions. "Thereabouts, yes." Marigold's shoulders tightened and her stomach clenched. "I'm going to sort a few things in the shed, if you'll excuse me." She scooted from the swing and entered her building. Inside, she hung the life jackets in size order, sorted the paddles into matching sets, and reorganized her cleaning supplies, all tasks she usually finished at the end of the day. Half an hour later, Ivy and Poppy paddled to shore.

Marigold scurried to them and stepped into the shallow water. "I hope you enjoyed the lake."

"We did. It was relaxing." Ivy put her feet in the water, stood, then rolled her shoulders. "I'm not used to too much physical activity, but I'd do this again."

Poppy climbed out of her vessel and gave her sister a light punch on the arm. "You loved it, didn't you?"

Ivy rubbed her arm. "Okay. I admit, you were right."

"Most people find the water calming." With tow ropes in hand, Marigold pulled the boats to the shed, then took the life jackets and paddles. "You were out an hour. It's nineteen dollars each, but since it's your first time on the island, I'm asking nineteen for both of you."

Ivy and Poppy trekked to the blanket and nudged their middle sister's foot. The only one who brought her purse, Violet stood, pulled out a twenty, and carried it to Marigold. "Here you go. Keep the change. I appreciate you letting me camp out by you." Violet shook sand out of the blanket, folded it, and followed her sisters to the car.

"Thank you, and no problem. I hope you had time to relax." Something about the three of them niggled at Marigold. If they were food bloggers, why not share their website or at least talk about their passion for food? Plus, Violet asked a lot of questions for a mom who wanted a few minutes of peace and quiet.

~~~~~

Maple trees shadowed Sadie's porch as the back-and-forth motion of rockers tapped the wooden floor. Lucy, Marigold, and Sadie watched Rosie chase a rabbit across the yard, then dash up and down the steps. After a few minutes, the golden retriever flopped on the floor, tail wagging.

Marigold leaned over and ran her hand along the dog's back. "Oh, to lead a dog's life. Sure would be less complicated." She straightened in the chair. "Thank you for the sandwich and fruit and the company."

Sadie sipped her lemonade, then placed the glass dotted with beads of condensation on the table between them. "You've been quiet tonight. Are you okay?"

"It's been a strange day. First I insulted Johnny, more like hurt his feelings." Her hand covered her heart. "Then this afternoon, those three ladies who said they were food bloggers stopped by to kayak. Something seemed off with them."

Lucy moved from the rocker and sat cross-legged on the floor. "Sorry, I couldn't see you from over there. This is better. What do you mean by off?"

"They didn't act enthusiastic about food or blogging and the taller one asked me a lot of questions." Marigold yawned. "Sorry, I'm tired this evening."

The floor squeaked under Lucy. "I didn't talk to them, but I noticed they had intense blue eyes, like yours. I've not seen the color on anyone else."

Sadie nodded and chuckled. "Maybe they're distant cousins you didn't know you had."

"I doubt it. I don't have cousins. Mom and Dad had no siblings, and Grandmother never spoke of any relatives. Doesn't matter, they're leaving tomorrow. I hope they enjoyed their stay and say good things about the island."

With her head against the railing, Lucy petted Rosie. "Are you going to talk to Johnny? He loves you and still wants to marry you."

"How do you know?" Marigold lifted her hands palms up.

"Remember when Sadie said she didn't want anything to do with Joel?" Lucy smirked at her sister-in-law.

Tilting her head, Sadie widened her eyes. "Why are you dragging me into this?"

"I'm reminding Marigold of how your and Joel's story turned out. You two are lovebirds now. Married lovebirds who are going to make me an aunt." A grin spread across Lucy's face.

A deep sigh escaped Marigold's lips. "Yes, I'm going to talk to him. I'm not sure when, but I will. I want to make this right."

~~~~~

Dusk colored the evening with shadows as Johnny climbed out of his truck. Home after a long day, he carried a tote of laundry to the house. Alexa waited on the porch.

"Hey, sweet girl, I'm so happy you're here."

She held the door open for him. "I'm happy to be here."

With the load of soiled linens stowed in the utility room, Johnny plopped on the couch. "My bones are weary, but what a great reopening. I loved seeing all the customers enjoying the food and the patio."

In a chair opposite her dad, Alexa crossed her legs. "The entire island came. I'm impressed at how the people here love and support you. I can see why you live here."

He nodded and unbuttoned his chef jacket. "I'm blessed, for sure."

Alexa studied her dad.

"What? Why are you looking at me as if you don't believe me?" He leaned against the blue and white striped couch cushions.

She uncrossed her legs and leaned his way. "I believe you, but I'm wondering what happened with you and your lady. When Marigold left, I saw she tried to talk to you and you blew her off."

"Not good." He sank into the cushions and closed his eyes.

"Dad, what happened?"

He sat straight and shook his head. "I overheard her say she wasn't going to marry me, or at least I think she said she wasn't. I may have not heard the whole conversation. I'm sure I overreacted." Elbows on his knees, he put his head in his hands.

"You can fix it." His daughter left the chair and perched on the seat beside him. She wrapped her arm around his shoulders. "Talk to her."

The hug from his little girl poured comfort over his weary being. Thankful they'd found their way to a good relationship, Johnny cherished his time with her and respected her counsel.

"You're right. I'm not sure what was said, and I need to find out and make amends. I'm not sure I want to stay on the island if I don't have Mari in my life." He squeezed his daughter's hand. "I love her so much. Seems odd telling you, but it's true. I have to find time to sort this out. I'm not sure when, but I will. In the meantime, I've got to get sleep before we do this all over again tomorrow."

They stood and hugged.

"You'll figure it out. She's a special lady, and don't feel weird telling me. I'm glad you see me as a grown-up." She chuckled.

"Goodnight, sweet girl."

"'Night, Dad."

CHAPTER TWENTY-SIX

Wednesday morning dawned with red streaks in the sky. An old saying, "red skies in the morning, sailors take warning," pestered Marigold. At seven o'clock, the tinted skies held no threat of a storm. The weather radio mentioned no rain on the horizon, but the skies prompted her to be aware. Regardless, she hoped for another prosperous day with tourists, as long as the weather held.

Her cat, Cassatt, yowled for her food and wove in and out of her owner's legs.

"You wait your turn. I'm reading my Bible, then I'll feed you." The cat's persistence wore her down, and she walked to the kitchen and poured a bowl of kibble. "Happy now?" The fur ball yowled again.

"What?" Marigold shook her head and sauntered to the living room. In her recliner, she lifted the foot, rested her legs on it, and opened her Bible in her lap. Other than a brief text thanking her again for her help on Saturday, she hadn't seen or heard from Johnny. Of course, the restaurant kept him busy, but she missed him. With the reopening, he had no time, yet she had hoped to explain herself. Lucy's reminder of Joel and Sadie's story urged her to find Johnny and apologize and explain. The hurt expression on his face had wounded her heart. Why had she let words she didn't mean fly out of her mouth?

She read through the passage where she left off before Cassatt interrupted her, and embraced the words of Romans 15:13, "May the God of hope fill you with all joy and peace as you trust in Him, so that you may overflow with hope by the power of the Holy Spirit."

Hope, one of the most positive words in the Bible. Her soul longed for the joy and peace God's hope offered. She vowed to let go of the past and move to the future with Johnny by her side. Determined to find him today and talk to him, she closed the book. Head bowed, she prayed for words and wisdom, then headed to the kitchen to eat breakfast before she left for work.

Later, on the beach, Marigold found Charlotte unlocking the kayaks and prepping the area for the day. "Aren't you taking the day off?"

"I was, but Levi had to work, so we didn't go to the mainland. He had planned to go with me to check on my apartment and grab dinner." The young woman carried towels to the table beside the shed.

Marigold pulled the vessels apart and laid two on the sand. "Do you want a different day off?"

"Maybe Friday. Can I let you know?"

"Yes, and since you're here I may leave early today. I have something I want to do."

"Sounds good."

By three in the afternoon, several families had rented kayaks for one-hour excursions and returned from the water. A group of teens had sailed out about 2:30 and planned to return by four. The trees along the campground waved as the wind whipped. Waves rolled in to the shore, higher each time.

"The way the water is acting tells me a storm is brewing. Did you see the red sky this morning?"

Charlotte's brow bowed into a frown. "I didn't notice. You think a storm is coming?"

"Could be. Let's secure the kayaks so they don't blow away."

The wind surged over the beach and blew sand in their faces.

Marigold shoved her hair from her face. "Let's get this stuff put away, then you go home."

"Okay, but I don't want to leave you." Charlotte toted the towels to the building.

Marigold untied her swing from the tree. "I'll be fine. I have to wait for the kids who went out. Hopefully, they have the sense to come in or at least paddle to shore. I'll call the Coast Guard and alert them."

"Okay."

They stowed the paddles and closed the doors on the shed.

"Go on home now." Marigold made a shooing motion with her hands.

Charlotte secured her backpack. "Be careful and let me know you got home, okay?"

"Sure."

~~~~~

Tourists and regulars devoured Johnny's special of the day, the feta burger. He thanked God for the plane and pilot who carried his deliveries of food products to the island once a week. The freezer held much of the food he ordered. Most weeks the ferry carried produce to him, along with spices from one of the local markets. Island living took resourceful fortitude, but he loved it.

One of the summer waitstaff tapped Johnny on the shoulder. "The folks who were sitting on the patio carried their food and drinks in. They said the wind picked up, and they couldn't eat outside." The waiter's face told him they had to find a place for the patrons to eat.

Johnny checked the dining room. The community table, a space for folks who didn't mind sitting with people they might not know, was open, but not clean.

"Let's get this ready for them."

Within a few minutes, Johnny cleared the table, and the waiter wiped it. Grateful, the customers gathered and chatted with one another.

"Problem solved." Until the lights flashed. "Oh no." Johnny opened the door as thunder rumbled. Moments later, the lights went out. "No worries, folks. We have a generator and candles."

The waitstaff lit candles on each table.

In the kitchen, Johnny turned the gas off on the stove, then kicked on the generator. "We'll have to close for the rest of the day. The generator will keep the freezer and refrigerator running, but I don't want to use the stove. We've been through this before. Right, Henry?"

"Sure have."

Johnny entered the dining area. "Thank you for coming in today. We'll be closing for the rest of the day. Finish your meals at your leisure. There will be no charge."

The diners clapped for Johnny. He took a bow and exited to the kitchen.

"Let's clean as best we can." Johnny rinsed pans in the sink. "Did everyone who ordered get their food?"

"We sent out the last meals about five minutes ago." Henry bagged salad fixings and stored them in the refrigerator, then washed the container from the greens.

Johnny stopped and bent over the sink. Marigold's face flashed through his mind. Was she on the beach or safe at home?

Henry dried a bowl. "What's wrong?"

"I'm worried about Marigold. I haven't talked to her since Saturday, and I'm guessing she's working at the beach."

Henry patted his back. "Why don't you go over there, make sure she's okay?"

"Can you finish here? We don't have much more to do and the waitstaff has the dining area covered. I'll be back as soon as I can. If you don't see me by the time you close, go home."

"You got it, boss."

~~~~~

The waves crashed and thunder roared across the sky. Raindrops hurtled from the clouds in rapid succession. Marigold stood inside her building with the door cracked open and waited for a call from the Coast Guard. The rain pounded on the metal top, louder than a rock concert. In the past, a few kayakers had been stranded, but the shore patrol found and rescued them and the kayaks. She prayed the same happened today. The four boys signed the paper stating they were eighteen or older and one said they had been on the water several times, but they had hesitated to wear their life jackets. She prayed they had left them on.

Wind whipped the door from her grasp, then slammed it against the side. With a towel over her head, she grasped the handle and yanked the metal door closed, except for a sliver to let light inside. With her other hand, she pressed the button to awaken her cell phone. No calls or alerts. With the noise of the storm, she hoped she had missed a call, but no one had contacted her. The signal might have failed again.

Huddled in the shed, she tied the doors together with a bungee cord and hoped the rubber held them in place, then she uncovered a step stool she kept on hand. A chill shivered along her spine, and goosebumps freckled her arms as her stomach growled. She had stashed snacks in the basket of the golf cart this morning. They had no doubt blown away or were drenched by now.

While she waited, she peered at her phone again. A text alert flashed from Johnny.

Where are you?

After she tapped in an answer, a phone message appeared. *Message not delivered.* The storm had knocked out her cell service. No messages from the Coast Guard now. No matter what, she planned to hold tight. If a call failed, they would send someone to tell her. At least she had shoved her water bottles in her bag this morning. She uncapped one and took a sip, then she rose from the stool and peeked out the crack between the doors. The lake agitated like a washer and sent high waves close to the building. With eyes on the storm, she jumped when a knock slammed against the side of the shed, and an eye peered in at her.

"Mari?" a voice shouted above the roar.

"Johnny?" Marigold shouted through the crack. "I'll unhook the cord. Keep hold of the door so it won't fly out."

He grabbed the door with both hands, backed into the building, and hooked the bungee around the handles.

Marigold threw her arms around his neck.

He brushed her damp hair away from her face. "I had to find you." His forehead rested on hers as he encircled her waist with his arms and pulled her to him.

She rested her head on his shoulder for a moment, then pulled away and looked at him. "Why'd you come?"

He let go and held her hands in his and recounted what happened at the restaurant and his fear of her being in the storm. "After our misunderstanding on Saturday, I had to make sure you were okay."

Tears stung her eyes, and relief flooded her soul. "I've missed you."

Johnny raised his voice above the din. "I've missed you, too." A frown crossed his face. "Why are you hiding in your shed? I drove by your house first, then I drove by here and saw your golf cart."

"Four young men took out kayaks and haven't returned. I'm waiting on the Coast Guard to let me know if they found them. I can't go home until I hear from them." She sighed. "The storm rolled in in record time. I'm worried about them, and of course cell service is down."

"Mine too." He yanked a bag of homemade rolls from his jacket pocket. "I wasn't sure where I'd find you, so I grabbed these on the way out of the restaurant."

"Thank you. I left my food in the cart, and I'm starved." With a grateful heart, she broke off a piece of the buttery bread and savored the bite. "Delicious."

"Eat as much as you want." The roar from the wind quieted to a hum. "I think the worst part might be over."

Marigold unhooked the cord on the doors and opened them. The sun shone as the rain cleared and a rainbow curved over the water. "The rainbow God promised Noah. I'm always astounded by God's artwork."

Before either one said another word, a patrol car approached. Joel stepped out in full rain gear.

"Hey Mari, you'll be happy to hear we got a call from the CG and they rescued the kayakers. They recovered two of your kayaks. The men rowed onto a private beach and waited. Paramedics checked them out, and they're fine. The Coast Guard will return your boats."

"Praise God! I was afraid the young men didn't get to shore in time. Thank you for coming by to tell me." She hugged her friend.

"I've got to check on damage to the island. Take care and be careful going home."

Johnny shook Joel's hand. "I'll get her home, no worries."

The officer pulled away, and Johnny turned to Marigold. "What can I help you with?"

She walked behind the shed. "The boats I had tied survived with no damage, and everything else was in the building. The cart is okay, so I'm driving it home."

"I can put it in the bed of the truck. I've got a board to use for a ramp." He released the tailgate and dragged a thick, wet board out. "Let's see if it'll start." He turned the key and a low hum sounded. "If you'll drive it, I'll make sure it stays on the ramp."

A few minutes later, Johnny secured the cart, then helped Marigold from the truck and into the cab.

From behind the steering wheel, he held her hand and prayed a prayer of thanksgiving for her safety and for the kayakers.

"Thank you, Johnny. I'm so grateful you came today. I admit, I was getting nervous about the guys out on the water, and I wasn't thrilled to be stuck in the shed."

His hands touched each side of her face and drew her to him. The kiss he shared with her replaced her goosebumps with waves of warmth.

"I'd do anything for you, Mari. Including apologize for not listening to you on Saturday. I'm so sorry."

"I'm sorry, too. My pride tends to take me on the wrong path. How about we talk tomorrow? Waiting out the storm wiped me out."

"Sounds good. I hope you realize how much I care about you."

"I do." She wrapped her hand around his. "Thank you for loving me despite my faults."

CHAPTER TWENTY-SEVEN

Ivy's favorite cafe bustled with people as the sun shined through the plate-glass window on Thursday. Tired after the weekend trip to Abbott Island, she sipped her Earl Grey tea from a paper cup and waited for her sisters. The corrugated wrapper protected her hand from the heat, but nothing could keep her heart from hurting over what her mother had done. How had she lived with herself? The idea their childhood was based on a lie sent chills along her spine. No doubt Mom loved them, but what kind of mind turned a man into someone she wanted him to be, then married him and raised a family, knowing he had a daughter who missed him?

"Excuse me, Ivy." Christopher Downey towered over her. "Can we talk?"

Ivy waved to the chair across from her, upholstered with a striped aqua and pink fabric. "Have a seat." *What now?*

He sank into the cushy chair and set his cup on the table between them. "I'm sorry to bother you, but I saw you through the window and wanted to chat a minute."

His politeness piqued her curiosity. The other times she had encountered him, his terseness set her on edge. "I have a few minutes before my sisters get here. What do you want to talk about?"

He folded his hands in his lap. "First, I'm sorry I accosted you in front of your dad's house and harassed you with my phone calls. I should have asked you what you knew. I never considered you might be unaware of the circumstances."

Ivy eyed his crisp white shirt and Brooks Brothers satin tie. Exquisite taste covered him. "My sisters and I had no idea our mother gave our father another identity. After she passed away, we found a box of information regarding what happened to Dad. It's a long and complicated story, and I'm sorry she stole your grandfather's identity. I can assure you my dad knows nothing about it. We haven't talked to him yet. He's in an assisted living facility and is ill."

"I'm sorry about your mom, and I won't bother your dad, but I need the details of what happened." He lifted his cup and drank.

Ivy surveyed the cafe for her sisters. Still not here. "I'd be happy to share what happened, but we haven't put all the pieces together. I can assure you my dad's life left no black marks on your grandfather's legacy. He never applied for social security or Medicare. Mom had other monies and insurance set up for him. She knew what she was doing. I'm sad to say it is an embarrassment to me and my sisters. Dad is an upstanding man who worked hard to provide for us. If you can be patient, I will fill you in, but not yet."

"Sounds fair. You have my phone number. Call me when you're ready to talk." Christopher rose from the chair and retrieved his cup. "Thanks for your time." He stalked away.

Ivy's head hit the back of the chair, identical to the one Christopher had occupied. Life had flipped upside down in a matter of days. Positive the woman they met on the beach was the Marigold they had searched for, Ivy had executed a thorough internet search and only found the website connected to the kayak business. This woman had stayed off the grid.

"Hey, Sis." Poppy flopped into the chair Christopher had vacated and Violet eased into one beside her. "This is a great place to meet. I love the pop art on the walls and the exposed ceiling with the air ducts painted black. Pretty cool."

Ivy nodded. "Did you see the guy in the white shirt and purple tie, with blond hair and green eyes?"

"Got your eye on someone?" Poppy pointed out the window. "The guy talking to a man in a suit?"

Ivy glanced outside, then turned to her sisters. "Yep, Christopher Downey, and he came in to chat with me. I told him I'd talk to him more after we put all the pieces of this ridiculous puzzle together, and I assured him Dad was a good man and left no negative marks on his grandfather's name."

"Was he rude again?" Violet stared at him.

"No. He apologized for his behavior."

"Good." Violet handed Ivy and Poppy each something wrapped in a white paper bag and a paper plate.

"What's this?" Ivy asked.

"An orange scone. I wanted to try theirs, so I bought you both one too." She bit into hers. "Umm... so good."

"Thank you. Smells delicious."

Ivy nibbled a corner of the pastry. "Yum." She set the plate on the table. "We talked about Marigold on the way home Sunday, but have you thought any more about what we should do? Most important, do you think Marigold is our half-sister?"

Violet folded her arms across her chest. "While I talked to her on the beach, her movements reminded me of myself, the way she went about things. When she dragged the kayaks she did a little tug, then walked with it. I tug, then walk when I pull the kids' wagon. Most people pull the wagon or whatever and walk at the same time. Her eyes match ours and

Dad's and her smile mirrors Dad's. I'm not saying for sure, but I'd say she's the woman we're looking for."

Poppy folded her legs under herself and tucked into the chair. "I agree with you. When we guided the kayaks to the beach, she waved at us like Dad. He bends his fingers up and down, like a kid, instead of a full-on wave. She's nice enough, and she has Dad's work ethic."

With the buzz of customers behind her, Violet tapped her fingers against the chair's arm. "Speaking of Dad, how are we going to tell him what Mom did?" She broke off a piece of scone and waited.

"Good question," Ivy said. "Do we rip off the bandage, so to speak, or ease him into it?"

"I say, ease him in. Dad is too old for too much shock at one time. Take him to dinner and break the news." Poppy pushed her red curls away from her face.

"No," her sisters replied in unison.

"Okay. What do you want to do?"

"Sorry, Poppy." Ivy sipped her tea. "We need to tell him at home, for the sake of privacy. With no clue how he'll react, I'm afraid the shock might affect his heart."

"You're right." The youngest sister fingered a curl. "Do we tell him first or Marigold? Will they want a paternity test?"

Violet gave a slight gasp. "Good question. Should we talk to a lawyer? Dad has one."

Ivy gathered up the paper plates. "Not yet. Let's plan to return to the island and talk to Marigold. She may knock all of our speculation down."

"Good idea." Poppy gathered empty cardboard cups and tossed them in the trash.

Violet lifted her phone from her bag and checked the calendar. "I can go a week from this Saturday." All three agreed on a time and prayed the lady they wanted to talk to would be available.

~~~~~

At two o'clock, Thursday afternoon, clear skies replaced the storms from the day before. Robin's egg blue filled the sky while white puffy clouds floated high. Johnny stepped out of the restaurant, climbed in his truck, and drove to Marigold's house.

When he pulled into her driveway, he parked and made his way to the porch. He rubbed a hand over his bald head and wiped away beads of sweat. Seeing Marigold had never made him perspire before. His stomach knotted as he knocked on the door. What if she decided not to date him anymore, or at the least chose not to marry him? His heart ached at the possibility of losing her. He had never met a woman like her, who took care of herself and cared for others the way she did. A believer, a kind heart, and a volunteer in the church and community, he longed to keep

159

her in his life.

The aqua door swung open. "Hi. Come in." Marigold motioned to the living room.

Johnny trooped in and waited for her to sit before he perched beside her on the couch. "How are you today? Did you get some rest after the storm?"

She stilled, hands in her lap, then nodded and fluffed her skirt. "I'm good. After a warm shower last night, I had the best night of sleep I've had in a while. I think the whole incident exhausted me." She patted his knee. "I'm glad we have time to talk. Charlotte has the rental covered, and Henry has your place under control."

Johnny laughed. "Yes. I left Henry in charge of dinner prep. I'll head back by 3:45." He wrapped his hand around hers.

Her eyes sparkled with unshed tears. "I am so sorry. Can you forgive me for making a scene at your reopening and for airing our relationship with strangers? Sometimes my pridefulness causes problems. I've fought it for a while, and I pray and ask God to help me, then I turn around and put my foot in my mouth again. I didn't mean to hurt you." Her eyes begged for forgiveness.

"First off, I'm a grown man, and I should have controlled my response and listened. I'm not making excuses, well maybe I am, but I was distracted. The restaurant was packed, and I had work to do. Even so, I should have taken a moment." He closed his eyes and bowed his head, then lifted his face to hers. "Did Lucy try to embarrass you?"

"No. I embarrassed myself. I made the comment, if I married you, I'd gain twenty pounds because you're an excellent cook. Lucy thought I said I was getting married, and she ran around the table, congratulated me, and made a ridiculous scene. Then you came out and heard me declare I wasn't getting married. It was all a huge misunderstanding. I'm sorry for hurting you."

She grasped his hand with both of hers. "You are an amazing man. I love your heart for people and your desire to serve God." Cassatt climbed on to Johnny's lap. "Even the cat loves you." Her lips curved into a smile. "I'm struggling to let go of finding Dad. I should have a long time ago. I've lived my life hanging on to the hope I'd find him. Now it's time to leave the past behind and live for today. I do love you, you know."

How could he not realize? This gorgeous woman friended him when he had no one. If not for her, he might have given up on island life and the restaurant. The first nine years he lived there, Marigold encouraged him in his endeavors, and this last year she shined her light of love on him.

"I know you love me, and I love you. I can't imagine my life without you, and I never dreamed I'd fall in love in my fifties. Our love isn't young love, or puppy love. I think we both understand life at this age and understand when a person comes along who fills the empty space in our hearts, we should explore the possibilities. Someday soon I'll ask the question again, and I hope you'll say yes. Until then, pray about us, and I will too."

He stood and lifted her by the hands from the couch. "You're my best friend, Mari, and I want you by my side, always."

She encircled his waist with her arms and rested her head on his chest. His arms tightened around her and they shared a promise and a hug.

~~~~~

The clock on the mantle ticked off the minutes as Marigold, wrapped in Johnny's arms, listened to the beat of his heart—a security she had not found since her mom died and her dad disappeared. Time to let go of the past and move into the present. She loosened her hug and stepped away. Face tipped to Johnny's, she studied his handsome, tanned features. His deep brown eyes held love for her. Never had she imagined a man could care for her with so much kindness and compassion. "I promise I'll pray over my decision. You've no idea how much I appreciate your patience. I'm not an easy woman to love, and my independent streak runs deep."

The corner of his mouth lifted into a grin. "I appreciate you can take care of yourself, even though I'd want to help you along the way."

Her hand rested on his chest. "I'll do the best I can to receive your help with a joyful attitude." She chuckled. "I sound like a Bible verse."

"You sound like Marigold." His mouth covered hers with a softness she longed for and an acceptance she never imagined. This man smoothed her rough edges and filled her with joy.

CHAPTER TWENTY-EIGHT

From the screened-in back porch, Marigold delighted in the goldfinches and house finches as they nipped nettle seeds from the feeder. The little birds added shades of yellow and red to the foggy morning. Seven o'clock on Friday morning, her Bible on her lap, she asked God to affirm what her heart understood. Light filtered through the fog and lifted it from the trees along the fence. A doe and her baby munched on grass and two bunnies hopped across the flower bed. The stillness of morning carried a peace Marigold cherished as she read through Psalms.

Without warning, Lucy bounced up the steps and popped open the screen door. "Hello."

The peace Marigold treasured disappeared with the fog. "Good morning, Lucy. You're out early."

Her friend slid into one of the metal tulip-back chairs. "I wanted to stop by before work and see what you're doing tomorrow. Are you working all day?"

Marigold placed her Bible and notepad on the round metal table. "Charlotte will be working. She missed hours this week, and I told her if she wanted to make her money back, she could take the Saturday shift."

Lucy rubbed her hands together like a child eager for her favorite snack. "Cool. I want to redeem myself for my faux pas at Johnny's." She took a quick breath. "I want to take you and Sadie to Harmony Spa in Vermilion tomorrow, for a girls' day, as an apology for opening my big mouth. Will you go?"

"Sweet girl, of course I'll go." Marigold's face split into a smile as she stood, then pulled Lucy into a hug. She let go of her friend and stepped away. "I believe the three of us need something fun. I've been in such a mood."

"You? No." Lucy covered her mouth with her hands. "There I go again. I think sarcasm is my second language."

"Or maybe your first."

Ringing laughter echoed from the porch to the yard.

"I think we woke the rest of the creatures in my yard. Do you have time for coffee? I have your favorite creamer, almond sweet cream."

"No, I want to do paperwork before the store opens so I can go tomorrow." Lucy stood and walked to the door. "I think Sadie is going to drive her mini-Cooper. She loves her Coop. We'll pick you up at ten tomorrow morning."

"See you." Marigold waved, then carried her Bible into the house. Cassatt meowed for food. "I'm coming, my spoiled princess."

In the kitchen, she French pressed coffee, then added creamer and the dark, hot liquid to her cup. She opened a tin and took out a cranberry muffin Sadie had made for her. The young woman, who had taken over her grandmother's business, carried on the same kindness she had learned from her Grammy Julia. Marigold's heart ached from missing her dear friend, who had passed. Grateful for Sadie and the continued connection to Julia, she buttered the muffin and prayed a prayer of thanks.

By ten o'clock, Marigold drove her golf cart to the beach. Along the road, Charlotte ambled in capris and a short-sleeved tank. She swatted her hand through the air in front of her.

"Morning, Charlotte. Are the mayflies attacking? Hop in."

She climbed in and sat beside her boss. "These bugs are crazy. Do they do this every year?" She waved away another one.

"They do. Believe it or not, having large droves of them is a good thing for the lake. At night they swarm the streetlights, and the next morning we find them piled on the ground."

Marigold parked the cart, and she and Charlotte toted their bags to the shed. "One thing I learned from the storm the other night. I'm putting my lunch and snacks in here instead of leaving them in the cart's basket."

With the kayaks set up and ready for business, the ladies cleared debris washed in from the lake. As Marigold walked the shore, she spotted a piece of a ceramic plate or bowl the size of her palm. A blue and white pattern swirled under the glazed finish and the edges shone smooth as glass. Treasures from the lake filled the shelves of her screened porch. She loved the found trinkets, but she planned to gift this one to Johnny. She would fashion something special for him from this piece decorated in Greek colors. A three-dimensional collage, with other ephemera she had gathered, clicked in her head like the light of a bulb. Her heart lightened as she planned a gift for her love.

~~~~~

A horn honked in front of Marigold's home on Saturday morning as she scurried to slip on her shoes and find her purse. Outside, Lucy slid out of the front seat of the Mini Cooper and motioned for Marigold to sit beside Sadie while she scooted into the back.

"Good morning, ladies. This is a treat. I didn't know how much I needed this until you asked." Marigold buckled her seatbelt.

Lucy poked her head between the front seats. "First stop is the new bakery, Bluebird's Baked Goods. Fresh coffee and amazing donuts, according to Levi."

"He'd know. He loves his pastries." Marigold chuckled.

Sadie nodded. "He can down at least three of my jumbo muffins in one sitting." She glanced at Marigold. "Is anything going on between Levi and Charlotte?"

Marigold raised her eyebrows. "You know I'm not a fan of gossip. She hasn't said anything, but he stops and talks to her once in a while and they eat together sometimes. Of course, he says he's patrolling when he stops." A snicker skittered from the back seat.

By eleven, they sat on benches near Vermilion's beach and munched on donuts and sipped coffee.

"This cake donut with vanilla icing and coconut tastes like summer." Lucy licked her lips, then sipped her steaming coffee.

"I picked the Danish with cream cheese and cherries. The young lady who waited on me told me the topping was made from fresh cherries from a nearby farm." A crumb stuck to Marigold's shirt.

Sadie licked her fingers. "The eclair filled with maple-vanilla pudding and drizzled with brown sugar icing is—all gone. My goodness, it was tasty." They shook with laughter.

Lucy brushed her hands together to dust off crumbs. "Our appointment is at one. What do you want to do until then?"

"I'd love to go to the artist boutique and see what's new, and I'm hoping to buy a shadow box." Marigold tossed her cup in the garbage.

Sadie followed her. "What are you making?"

The three of them walked along the sidewalk to the middle of town and crossed the street to the local art store.

"I found a pretty piece of pottery on the beach the other day, and I'd like to make something for Johnny. The piece is blue and white, so I plan to create a tribute to his Greek heritage. I've been reading about Greek culture and discovered how interesting the country is. I never wear them, but there are places around the ancient ruins where high heels are forbidden. The authorities are afraid they'll damage the ancient ruins."

Lucy stopped and lifted her tennis shoe. "Wow. I don't wear heels much either, but what a hoot. Although I understand what they mean."

Watercolor paintings featuring lighthouses and sailboats graced the display window, along with ceramic pitchers in shades of aqua and green. Beach glass strung into wind chimes dangled from pieces of driftwood.

"I love the chimes. They'd be pretty on the porch." Sadie held her hand above her eyes and peered in the window. "Let's go in."

The scent of summer tickled their noses when they walked in the door.

"It smells like a fresh breeze." Lucy closed her eyes and inhaled.

On a table centered in the entryway, Marigold examined a replica of a small sailboat, a reminder of the one she had sailed on with her parents. For her tenth birthday, they traveled to Geneva-on-the-Lake and stayed with friends who owned a sailboat. The family soaked in the sun, and

Marigold fell in love with the water.

She cringed at the tug on her emotions and moved through the store to find something to distract her from the memories. Sunlight shone through a glass vase displayed in the window. The pinks and reds caught the light and gleamed. Perfect for cut flowers. She checked the price. Despite the steep price, she deemed the vase a symbol of new life, a reminder to speak to God when discouragement plagued her. Not an idol, instead the vase served as a nudge, to help her remember her promise to God to live in the present and embrace life.

Lucy sidled to Marigold. "Find something pretty?" She eyed the vase. "The colors are gorgeous, and you found a shadowbox."

"I'm going to splurge today. I haven't bought anything for myself for a long time." Not wanting to share the reason she selected the colorful piece, she trooped to the counter to pay before she changed her mind.

Sadie stood behind her with the beach glass chimes, and Lucy purchased a cotton summer shawl.

Lucy ran her hand over a wool-felted sheep displayed near the counter. "It would be easy to spend all my money in this store."

"Me, too." Sadie dangled the chimes in front of her. "Good thing I didn't come here when I decorated the cabins. I'd have blown my budget."

Paid and ready to go, Marigold and her friends strolled out to the sidewalk. "Your cabins are lovely. Don't change a thing. You may want to come back and buy artwork for the nursery."

"I have ideas." A squeal escaped her, and she clapped a hand over her mouth. "Oh, didn't mean to be loud."

Lucy hugged her sister-in-law. "You can be as excited as you want."

They stashed their packages in the car and made their way to Harmony Spa.

Lucy opened the door and held it for her friends. "I'm excited, and I want to squeal now."

In a massage chair, Marigold rested her eyes and let the masseuse knead her shoulders and back muscles. Never in her life had she experienced a massage—this lady had the hands of an angel. Thank goodness Lucy had chosen the massage where she could sit face forward in a chair and remained dressed, instead of lying on a bed under a sheet.

At her age, she dreaded anyone seeing her without clothes. As the woman's fingers kneaded her neck, tension released. Most of the time, stress traveled straight to her neck and shoulders, but the tension from letting go of her dad's mystery and the decision whether to marry Johnny or not tightened her muscles.

The masseuse patted Marigold's back. "You're all finished. Did you ladies sign in for a facial?"

Lucy piped up with her face planted in the circle pillow of the chair with a muffled yes.

"There's your answer." Marigold followed the masseuse to meet the esthetician.

"This is Allie. She'll be applying your facial. Enjoy." With a finger wave, she left.

"Have a seat and relax, and I'll take care of the rest. Have you had a facial before?"

Marigold brought her braid to the front of her blouse, then settled into the chair. "No, I haven't."

"First, I'll cleanse your skin, which looks great, by the way. You must use sunscreen." She applied a fruity-smelling lotion and rubbed it in, then used a warm cloth to remove the lather.

Marigold nodded. "I'm outside most of the day, so I try to be careful."

Would marrying Johnny mean she might close the kayak business? At fifty-four, changing jobs might not be so bad. What was she thinking? She loved the beach and helping people enjoy the island, and Johnny wanted her to be happy. *Stop over-thinking.*

An hour later, the three friends crossed the street to a fifties-style restaurant.

By the entrance, Lucy stopped. "Want to eat a late lunch?"

"Yes, I'm starved. I ate the snack they offered at the spa, but this baby is hungry all the time." Sadie patted her belly.

Lucy led the others into the diner. "We better feed you."

After they ordered, they checked out the vintage signs and collectibles.

"Some of this stuff must have been around since the sixties."

"Watch it, Lucy." Marigold laughed.

"You never seem as old as you are. I heard the esthetician tell you how good your skin looks. I bet Johnny tells you all the time how beautiful you are."

Marigold gave Lucy a mom stare. "You're incorrigible."

"You're right, I am, and I'm sorry I caused trouble for you and Johnny at the restaurant the other day. I get excited when it comes to romance."

Sadie eyed her sister-in-law. "If you're so thrilled about romance, why aren't you dating?"

"Have you seen the men on the island? I haven't met anyone I'm interested in, so I live vicariously through my friends."

Sadie tapped her mouth with her finger. "What about Owen Bently, the cute farmer on the other side of the island? I've seen him hang around the store until he can talk to you."

"He's a nice guy, but all we've done is chat about vegetables and weed killer." Lucy rolled her eyes.

"If I can find a man at my age, your fellow is out there, and he'll come around soon." Marigold patted her hand.

"Speaking of Johnny..."

The waitress served burgers dripping with American cheese, salads, and water. "Anything else, ladies?"

"No, we're good. Thanks." Sadie smiled.

As soon as the waitress left, Marigold leaned toward her friends. "Can I ask the two of you to pray for me? I'm trying to resolve my issues with my dad's disappearance by letting go, then I'll focus on Johnny. I'm struggling and need your support." She folded her napkin over her lap. "I'm finding it hard to imagine sharing a home with a man. I've been alone for so long, and I'm set in my ways. If I married him, I'd want to live in my house. I've established my gardens and have things the way I like them."

Sadie grasped Marigold's hand. "I can tell you from experience, living with a man is amazing, but you'll have to make room for him. I tried to give Joel whatever space he needed, and it's worked."

"One thing is for sure, I'll be happy to give Johnny the kitchen. If I never had to cook again, I'd be thrilled." She patted Sadie's hand. "You two pray for me, please?"

"Of course," they answered in unison, then bit into their burgers.

CHAPTER TWENTY-NINE

Open books lay scattered across Violet's dining room table. Ivy had invaded her sister's house, determined to research their dad's memory loss. As Ivy scribbled on a notepad, Violet spoke into her cell phone.

With a click, Violet ended the call.

"Is she coming?" Irritation saturated Ivy's voice.

"She's on her way. She mumbled something about missing art supplies."

The air conditioner kicked on and blasted cool air into the room.

"Good. We can all search these medical texts and try to understand what happened to Dad. I mean, how does one lose his entire life up to the point of an accident? This manual reports at least three or four major types of memory loss. Retrograde comes the closest to what Dad may have experienced, but this says it's rare for all memories to leave and not return, but possible." *Unless Mom convinced him he was Edward Downey, and Dad chose not to question her.* Ivy drummed her fingers on the table.

Iced tea slid down Violet's throat as she thumbed through a book.

"Maybe he had retrograde and dissociative. A person who suffers emotional trauma may suffer from dissociative amnesia. If he witnessed his first wife's death, he may have blocked everything out."

Ivy rubbed her temples. "We may never know. I doubt he's able to tell us much about it now. Forty years is a long time to live as someone else. Plus, it's unwise for us to diagnose him when we lack a medical background."

The front door slammed and footsteps sounded in the hallway. Poppy tromped in to join her sisters.

"What a day. Half of my art supplies disappeared. I think I know who took them. Another teacher had a class in my room yesterday. When I checked on my workspace this morning, a bunch of stuff had gone missing. I had to track down paint and brushes this afternoon, so I skipped lunch." She released a sigh.

Violet lifted a plate of cookies for Poppy. "Eat a couple of these and you'll be fine."

"Um, thanks." She slung her backpack to the floor and flopped into a chair. "What's all this?"

"We're trying to figure out what happened to Dad. Ivy brought the books from the library."

"These books look heavy."

"They're medical texts about memory loss. If we understand what happened, the information might help us talk to Dad." The smart watch on Ivy's wrist alerted her to a message. With a glance, she clicked off the notification. "I wish he'd stop."

"Who?" The sisters sounded like a pair of owls.

"Christopher Downey. I told him I'd tell him when I knew something."

Poppy pointed to Ivy's wrist. "Block him."

Ignoring her sisters, Ivy moved on. "Mom must have thought the way to help him was to take care of him herself. From what she wrote in the journal, he stayed with her a few weeks before she gave him a new identity. We may never know what happened, but I'd like to understand better before we talk to him."

"We're talking to him?" Poppy's red curls bounced when she turned to Ivy.

Her sister jotted another note on the paper. "If we want him to meet his other daughter, we've got to share what we found. As much as I want to hide this from him, it's wrong. Mom may have been okay with fooling Dad, but I'm not."

"Gotcha. So, what are we looking at?"

For the next two hours, they gathered information and tried to make sense of the medical terminology.

"Who wants to go with me Wednesday and talk to Dad?" Ivy's red-rimmed eyes watered.

"We'll both go, right, Poppy?" Violet said. "Ivy shouldn't go alone."

Poppy pushed her curls away from her face, stood, and paced to the sliding glass doors. "What time?"

Ivy closed one of the books. "Can you meet me for dinner at 5:00? Then we'll go see Dad before 7:00. I don't want to wait too late or he'll be sleepy."

"Sounds good." Poppy opened the glass door. "Mind if I sit out here a while, Violet? I want time to think."

"Sure."

Cookie plate in hand, Poppy stepped out onto the patio.

~~~~~

The boardwalk creaked under her feet as Marigold trekked along the raised walkway through the woods. Dragonflies and damselflies swirled around the bridge where she stopped and enjoyed the red-winged blackbirds playing on cattails. On this hot July Fourth, she longed for solitude before the evening festivities. At eight o'clock on Monday morning, no one else hiked across the marshy wetland to the embayment pond. Unique to the island, the pond rose and fell with the lake's tides. Marigold followed the walkway to a secluded beach. With a stick, she stirred the sand and searched for beach glass and pretty rocks to add to her collection.

A glint of blue sparkled in the morning sun. She plucked the glass gem from the sand and held it to the light. In that moment, Marigold's shoulders relaxed, as if the burden she carried so long released and floated away. She dropped to her knees and bowed her head.

"Thank You, Lord, for Your answer to my prayer."

At peace, she rose, tucked the beach glass in her pocket, closed her eyes, and listened to the waves brush the shore. Joy filled her heart, and realization dawned. She no longer clung to doubts about letting go of the search for her dad or her answer to Johnny's proposal, if he asked again.

~~~~~

Tourists and locals crowded the beach, as a festive vibe echoed across the sand for the July Fourth evening celebration. All the kayaks Marigold had rented floated in the bay and waited as the sky turned from baby blue to inky black.

"Hello, beautiful lady." Johnny approached from behind her and placed his hands on Marigold's shoulders. "I'm guessing you rented all your boats."

She rested a hand on his. "We did. Thank goodness for Charlotte. Everyone descended on us at once." She leaned her head against his chest. Comfortable with this wonderful man, joy danced inside her like the children who twirled across the sand and waved sparklers. "They're all floating in the water, waiting for the show."

"Hey, guys." Joel, Sadie, and Lucy approached, carrying lawn chairs. "Mind if we join you?"

Marigold waved to a spot nearby. "We saved you a section. Not easy with this crowd."

The group set their chairs on the grassy area to the side of Marigold's business, and all five of them settled in for the show.

"This is perfect. Thanks for saving us a spot." Joel kicked off his flip-flops.

Johnny turned to him. "Not on patrol tonight?"

"Levi is in uniform." He pointed to the young man who stood near Charlotte. "I'm unofficially on duty, in case someone gets crazy."

"Here's hoping the crowd stays calm." Johnny tipped his ball cap.

A whirring sound streamed through the night as bursts of dazzling color sprayed across the sky. The fireworks lit the dark, one after another. Pinks and greens danced as red and white sparkled.

Marigold leaned her head against Johnny. "This brings back memories on this island. I moved here in June and sat on this beach in July with Sadie's mom and her friends. So much has changed, but I'm so grateful to be here with you. This is, what, our fifth year we've celebrated together?"

With his arm snugged around her shoulders, he kissed her temple. "Pretty sure it's year five. The first few years I lived here, I watched from the campground. My buddy used to come and camp, but he moved to Montana. This was one of the first things we attended together. I'm not sure why it took us so long to date, but I'm glad we figured it out."

"Me too." She pointed to the sky. "The finale is starting." The glimmering fireworks painted sparkle after sparkle against the black night, with a magnificent display of red, white, and blue. "I love this part."

Cheers rose from the beach when the last light fizzled.

Sadie handed her folded chair to Joel. "I love how the island closes most of the shops and gathers here for the celebration. It's so much fun." She readjusted her messy bun.

Lucy bagged her chair and hefted the strap to her shoulder. "We've never missed one, have we, Joel?"

"Been to every one since we were born. It's a great way to spend a summer evening." He waved at Levi. "We're going to start a fire in our pit if anyone wants hot dogs or marshmallows."

Johnny turned to Marigold. "We'll pass, but thanks for the offer. You kids enjoy yourselves."

Marigold smiled when Lucy called out an invitation to Levi and Charlotte as she and Johnny walked to the kayak shed. "Thanks for saying no. Once all the kayakers come in, and we put them away, I'll be ready to go home and put my feet up."

"I was thinking the same thing, but can we sit on your swing before I head home? We haven't had much time for the two of us."

A smile parted her lips. "I baked peanut butter chip cookies and made lemonade."

"Sounds perfect."

~~~~~

An hour later, Johnny and Marigold appreciated the breeze from the lake as it cooled the July heat. Lightning bugs flickered like tiny sparks of fireworks and crickets serenaded. The couple munched on cookies and let the swing sway them.

"The fire department did a fantastic show this year." Marigold sipped the lemony drink.

"Has the volunteer fire department always set off the fireworks?" Johnny brushed crumbs off his denim shorts.

"I believe so. A built-in safety if something goes wrong." With a flick of her wrist, she tossed her braid behind her back.

Johnny placed his hand on hers. "Have I told you how much I love you?"

Her face warmed from his words instead of the night's heat. "You've told me a time or two." She ducked her head, then looked up and her eyes met his. "I love you, too."

He raised her hand to his lips and kissed her work-worn knuckles. "You are the most amazing woman I've ever met. You've lived with loss, yet paved a way for yourself. Your faith has held when things were bleak, and you make the best cookies ever."

A flutter moved from Marigold's head to her toes and returned to her heart. "You are the kindest, most patient man I've met, and your baklava melts in my mouth." She rested her head on his shoulder. Johnny kissed her hair, then lifted her face to his. Their eyes met, and he touched his lips to hers and lingered there for a few moments.

Marigold relaxed and kissed the man she loved with her whole self, releasing the emotions she had buried for so long. When they parted, she rested her forehead on his, then lifted her face and reveled in letting go of the past and seeing the future in Johnny's brown eyes.

"You've given me hope I've never had and a reason to leave the past behind and build a life with you. I may be in my fifties, but you make me feel young and loved. Thank you."

"I'm enamored with your giving spirit and the way you care for others." He held both of her hands. "You've changed my life, Mari. You understand. When I came to the island, I struggled with depression, even though I was trying my best to start over. Meeting you and knowing what you had done as a single woman inspired me. Your friendship has encouraged me. Now, your love makes me whole. I want to care for you and give you whatever you need."

"I'm overwhelmed." She sniffed tears of joy. "I love you, Johnny."

"I love you, too."

She tucked her arm in his and soaked in the distant sound of waves washing the shore in time with the sway of the swing.

CHAPTER THIRTY

Humidity and heat pressed in on Ivy on Wednesday afternoon. Perspiration dripped in her eyes as she hurried to meet her sisters at Dante's restaurant. Inside, she lifted her face to the air conditioning duct. Relief from the wretched high temperatures revived her spirit. At the hostess desk, she signed in for a table for three. Her sisters promised to meet with her, then visit their dad together. Nausea rose in her stomach at the idea of revealing Dad's past to him. After much discussion, Violet and Poppy had agreed to tell Dad what Mom had done. Still reeling from the truth, Ivy's heart ached for herself, her sisters, and her dad.

"Right this way." Ivy followed the hostess to a booth with high wooden seats. *Good, some privacy.* "I'll seat your sisters as soon as they arrive."

"Thank you." Ivy lifted the menu and flipped it open. The choices were too rich for her quivering stomach. Broccoli cheese soup sounded good.

"Hey, sis." Poppy's voice bounced like the curls she had tamed into a ponytail. She slid into the seat across from Ivy, with Violet right behind her. "Who decided to eat at Dante's on the hottest day of the year?"

Ivy dropped the menu to the laminated table. "Hey, you two."

A waiter approached. "Can I take your drink orders?"

Poppy tilted her head and squinted at him. "We need a minute."

After he walked away, Poppy took Ivy's hand. "You're pale, are you okay? I mean, none of us are all right, but your color is off."

"My stomach hurts. It's nerves, but I'll be okay. I want to get this over with. After we talk to Dad, we have to meet Marigold. If she'll listen to us, then who knows what?" Ivy pressed her head into her hands.

Violet reached for her sisters' hands. "How about I pray right now for God's guidance and calm?" She thanked God for her sisters, then sought help and wisdom. "Amen."

By the time Violet's prayer ended, the waiter returned.

"I think we're ready now."

Each one ordered their drink and meal choice.

Ivy breathed a deep breath. "Thanks, Violet. Your faith amazes me."

"It's not me, it's God. He loves me, and I do my best to be faithful."

Ivy spread her napkin on her lap. "I'd like to go to church with you. I haven't been in a while, and I think it's time to renew my faith."

"I'd love for you to come. You too, Poppy." She eyed her younger

175

sister.

Poppy stared at a spot on the wall, then turned to Violet. "I will. I've been going to the little church in my neighborhood, but it would be nice to visit where you go."

Ivy cleared her throat. "Let's figure out the best approach with Dad. Should we blurt it out, give hints or clues to his past? What do you think?"

Violet fingered the diamond necklace she wore every day. The one Joseph gave her for their tenth anniversary. "At eighty-four, a gentle approach is best. He's had one stroke, and we don't want to cause another one. The doctor says he's doing well, but I don't want to jeopardize his health. I'm thankful the coughing was from allergies."

The waiter carried a tray filled with food and drinks and delivered the soup and salads to their table.

"Thank you." Violet smiled at him.

With her spoon midway to her bread bowl, Ivy's eyes misted. "I'm afraid Dad will never forgive Mom."

Poppy poked her fork into the lettuce and chicken in her salad, then dipped it in dressing. "The decision is Dad's. All we can do is deliver the information and do our best to help him through this mess. I'm having trouble forgiving her myself. When she stuck all the papers and her journal in the box, she knew we'd have to sort it all and figure out what to do. I hate this for Marigold, too. At first, I resented her and the fact she would take Dad's attention once he realized who she was and what happened. Now, I pray she accepts the truth and doesn't hate us." She bit into her dinner.

Quiet hovered over the table except for the sound of soft jazz music, silverware clicking, and the sisters chewing their food.

"Anyone else hate to hear other people chew their food, or is it me?"

"It's you, Poppy." Violet stabbed a tomato.

Poppy ignored her and rolled her eyes. "Am I the only one who has anything to say about what we're about to do?"

With sorrow in her heart, Ivy shook her head. "No, you aren't. I've been sorting through the scenarios, and if we start with mentioning the box of items Mom left us and go from there, he may be more open and take it better than we think, but if he gets upset, we'll stop and then decide what to do." She sipped a spoonful of soup. "When do we talk to Marigold? I hope she's willing to visit Dad. We don't know her, although she seemed like a decent human."

"That crossed my mind, too." Violet swigged her tea. "Sorry, the salty dressing makes me thirsty. We talk to Dad and see if he remembers anything at all. From the journal entries Mom wrote early on, she worked hard to keep him from remembering anything about his past. I still find it hard to wrap my head around the fact she didn't take him to the hospital.

As an EMT, she must have assumed she could take care of him. Funny thing, she left the EMT job about a year later and worked as a waitress." She took another drink. "Mom loved us, but she did act squirrely at times. Remember when she helped Dad dye his hair? His roots were blond, but she wanted him to be a brunette. He let her, too. Weird."

"You're right. She was afraid someone might recognize him." Poppy covered her salad with her napkin. "I'm full, and it's about time to go talk to Dad."

"Me, too." Ivy pulled out her wallet. "Dinner is on me."

"Thanks, sis." Violet smiled. "We'll do the best we can with this. Trust God to see us through."

~~~~~

The air conditioner hummed, while Cassatt curled into a ball and slept on the kitchen floor. Marigold stacked ham, co-jack cheese, and tomato on wheat bread, then added mayo and sliced the sandwich in half. She added baked chips to her plate and carried the food and a glass of water to the living room. The cat stretched and followed her. "Too hot to eat on the porch, Cassatt."

For a Wednesday, business had been busy. So many tourists visited the island the week of July Fourth, the locals hunkered down at home and avoided the eateries and shops.

After the last bite of sandwich, her mom's trunk tempted her curiosity. She had read a few of the letters but left the rest to sit untouched. She carried her dishes to the sink, then headed to the living room and opened the chest. A war inside her tangled the progress she had made toward putting her worries about Dad to rest, competing with her desire to immerse herself in their story. Her yearning to learn their love story won out.

> Dear Louise,
> I'll be at the soda shop at 4:00. Not going Dutch. I want to pay
> for my girl's soda. I can call you my girl, right? See you Saturday.
> Yours,
> Nick

Dad sounded so plucky. He teased Mom when she tried to be frugal like Grandmother. From what Marigold remembered, she had never wanted for anything until she lived with her grandmother. The woman had invented recycling, with each morsel of wax paper and foil reused until it fell apart. Some of the frugality stuck with her as she made her own life. Grandmother's ways frustrated her at times, but she had taught her to survive on a dime.

In the trunk, another peach envelope stuck out from beneath the others.

> *Dear Nick,*
>
> *Mother suspects I'm meeting a boy. One of her gossipy friends told her she saw me downtown in the presence of a boy. I couldn't lie, so I told her I'd met you at the fair, and we did indeed meet for a soda. She shook her head and tried to shame me, but I didn't let her. I asked if she'd meet you, and she said yes. Perhaps to tell you to behave yourself, or to get lost.*
>
> *I'm hoping you can charm her like you have me. Come by on Saturday at five o'clock for dinner and pray all goes well.*
>
> *See you soon,*
> *Louise*

Mom must have loved Dad early for her to have him meet Grandmother. She hoped the next letter revealed whether she accepted him or told him to go away.

> *My Dearest Nick,*
>
> *I'm so glad you and Mother got on okay at dinner. It was sweet of you to compliment her cooking. She was pleased you enjoyed her apple cake so much. After you left, she said you were nice enough. Which is more than she's said about anyone else I've dated, which is all of two boys. Ha-ha. Looking forward to seeing you again on Saturday.*
>
> *Your best girl,*
> *Louise*

After Marigold finished reading the letters, she discovered a small journal buried under her parents' marriage certificate and her birth certificate. Mom penned an entry about their small wedding in the chapel and the tears Grandmother shed. On the wedding night, they moved Dad into Grandmother's house and she allowed them to live with her for six months. Grateful they moved before she was born, Marigold closed the pages and stored the memories in the trunk.

Mom must have inherited her playful spirit from her father, the man Grandmother loathed. Marigold might never know what happened in her grandparents' home, but at least true love had lived in her parents' marriage. She and Johnny might be late to the party, but she sensed their marriage, if he proposed again, would pass the test of time. What was it Sadie's Grammy said? Better late than never.

Fifty-four sounded old to Marigold's ears, even though age depended more on a person's attitude than actual years. Outdoor activities kept her younger than her age. Johnny's outlook of living life to the fullest shined a light of vitality on hers. Perhaps a marriage in the fifties, accented by the wisdom of experience, equaled two people ready to meet life with a balance of excitement and quiet peace.

Cassatt wove herself between Marigold's legs.

"What do you think about a man living in our house?"

The fur ball purred, waved her tail, and curled on the ottoman.

"Is your tail wag a sign of surrender? Or a sign you don't care?"

By eight o'clock in the evening, the heat cooled to a tolerable eighty degrees. Marigold unrolled the outdoor water hose and dragged the green rubber snake across the yard to the front flower beds. She sprayed a cool mist over the memorial bed for her parents. Eyes on the future, she carried the hose to the beds beside her porch and thanked God for His creation and for bringing Johnny into her life. The black-eyed Susans shone in the evening light as their golden petals circled the flat brown centers. Bees buzzed around the purple lavender and deep red bee balm. She admired the busy bees collecting pollen from their favorite plants.

In the back yard, she sprayed the cilantro, tomato, and pepper plants. Soon she'd stir salsa on the stove and can it for herself and her friends. Dad had taught her how to plant tomatoes and her tastebuds thanked him. She and Johnny could plant a garden and use the vegetables for the restaurant. Peace settled over her as she dreamed of a new chapter in her life.

CHAPTER THIRTY-ONE

The odor of bleach in the assisted living facility stung Ivy's nose and alerted her someone had been cleaning. Later than they intended, the sisters trekked to their dad's room about 6:30. A young man, dressed in blue scrubs, stood in Dad's doorway and cracked jokes with him, while he held a dinner tray of half-eaten food. Ivy cleared her throat to get the man's attention.

"Good evening, we're here to see Dad."

"Hello. I love sharing jokes with your dad. He's a hoot." The young man waved at Dad and made his way along the hall.

Dad's laughter met them at the door.

"Glad you're having fun." Poppy bounced into the room and wreathed her arms around his neck. "It's so good to see you." She planted a kiss on his comb-over, then stepped away so her sisters could greet him.

"I brought you your favorite no-bake cookies. The kids and I made them this afternoon. I left out the chocolate, because I know you prefer peanut butter without chocolate." Violet placed a tin on the table next to his chair. "You might want to ration them out."

"You know me too well. I love those cookies and could eat the whole batch in an afternoon." He rubbed his tummy. "Hi, Ivy. What brings all three of you at the same time?"

His oldest daughter deposited the cardboard box from their mom's closet on a simple wooden coffee table, hugged him, then settled on the couch. "We wanted to visit, and we've got a couple of things to talk to you about."

How to begin?

Poppy jumped in. "Dad, do you think you ever had any other children besides us? You know, before you met Mom?"

He blinked and wrinkled his brow. "Can't say for sure. You know I lost all the memories I had before I met Renee. I do have dreams and flashes of what I think might be the past where a girl waves at me. She's on a porch, and I'm leaving, I suppose for work. Her smile stays with me for a long time, after the dream. She wears her hair in a long blond braid." His gaze held on a photo of a lake he had framed years ago. "I'm not sure if she's a real person. I've lost so much." Tears glistened behind his tortoise shell glasses. "Why are you asking me now?"

Violet glanced at Ivy, then at her father. "Dad, we found something we need to show you. We were cleaning out Mom's office and found this box in her closet. She meant for us to discover it after she passed. There are things in it you may not be aware of or want to hear."

He rubbed his hand over the stubble on his chin. "At my age, you might as well rip the Band-aid off, as they say. What's got you girls all in a flutter?"

Soft jazz music floated from his radio and filled the silence. With a handkerchief, he dabbed at the corner of his mouth.

Ivy lowered her head and prayed a quick prayer for wisdom, then moved a footstool near her dad's chair. She lifted his hand in hers and held on for strength. "Do you recall anything about the night or weeks after Mom found you?"

With his free hand he tugged at the neck of his Cleveland Browns t-shirt. "I do. Somehow, I landed on Renee's porch. My head hurt, and I had cuts and bruises on my arms and torso. I'm not sure, but I always believed I'd been in an accident and got lost in the woods." His eyes closed, then fluttered open. "Renee nursed me. The first week I drifted in and out. She said I was dehydrated and worn out. When I recovered, I aimed to leave, but she said, 'No.' She was mighty persuasive. Before long, a couple months had passed, and we grew to love each other. She had found my billfold on me and helped me get a job. A year later, we married."

Ivy released his hand. "Didn't you wonder what your life was before the accident?"

"Sure, but I had no memories. Your mom took me to a doctor, and he was baffled. Said most people remember something, but I didn't. Renee encouraged me to let it go and move on." He scratched his head. "So I did. I worked for a local landscaper, made enough money, since Renee had inherited the house, and we were blessed with you three beauties." A flash of satisfaction crossed his face. "Why all the questions, and what's in the box?"

At the table, Violet lifted the journal, clippings, and a few photos.

"Where did this one come from?" She darted a puzzled glance at Ivy. "Is it a yearbook photo?"

Ivy jumped from the stool and grabbed the clipped picture. "I did some digging and found this in an archive file of a school north of here. Check out the name."

Marigold Hayes.

She returned the other items to the box. "Maybe you should do this, then." Hands on hips, she stepped behind her sister.

"Dad, do you know this girl?" Ivy's hand trembled as she held the photo for him.

~~~~~

Seven o'clock in the evening and people milled along the street. Mini-golf drew a crowd with the weather a few degrees cooler. Johnny locked the door on the restaurant, grateful Wednesday proved to be a shorter day. Most of the tourists had stopped in for lunch and played in the evening. Made sense to enjoy the air conditioning if they didn't partake in the water sports.

"Hi, Dad."

"Alexa, what are you doing here? In the middle of the week?" Before he turned a full one-eighty to her, she flung herself into his arms. Through sobs, she babbled.

Off balance, he righted himself and wrapped her in a hug where she curled against him. "I can't understand you."

Without words, his lips touched her hair, much like he did when her goldfish had died when she was six. A few minutes passed and her body calmed. She stepped away and hung her head.

Johnny pocketed his keys and gestured to a bench across the street. "Want to sit?"

"Sure."

They crossed the street, then trekked through the grass to a public landing. There she huddled beside him on the wooden seat. Waves splashed along a nearby dock and a boat's motor moaned in the distance.

"What's going on? Did a young man break your heart?" He dabbed the sweat on his face with a handkerchief.

"No. I don't have a boyfriend." She blew her nose on a tissue. "It's my job. I hate it."

Johnny leaned his arms on his knees and folded his hands in front of him. "What happened? You were happy last time you were here." He searched her face for any clue to help him understand.

She dabbed her eyes. "I was, because I got to work outside while I was here. At the museum, I spend so much time at a desk. I want to be more involved with the activities, teaching children, and the director passed over me and gave those responsibilities to one of the newer employees. I didn't get a degree in geology to sit in a building all day. I want to be out researching and discovering." She sat straighter. "I loved teaching the kids about the glacier rocks. I think I want to get a job with the park services and do outdoor programming. I have my master's degree in environmental studies, which helps, and I'd love to live here on the island."

Johnny's heart raced and dropped at the same time. Excited to have his daughter near, but hesitant because of his intentions to marry Marigold. Alexa enjoyed Marigold's company, she had told him so, but would she find it awkward for her dad to marry again while she had no love life? As a young woman and his daughter, he longed for her to find happiness in all she pursued. She could work for him until she landed a new job, if she wanted. Even live with him, until she established herself.

"Have you already quit your job?"

Her eyes widened. "No. I'm not stupid." A frown drew a crease across her forehead. "I took a few days off. Can I stay with you until Sunday? I want to search for a job and figure out my next step." Her eyes begged him to agree.

~~~~~

The air conditioner kicked on and drowned the jazz music from Edward's radio. His hand shook as he accepted the photo from Ivy.

"Dad, do you recognize the girl in the photo?" She returned to the stool beside him and studied his face for any change in expression.

A bare whisper pushed through his lips. "Marigold."

"What did you say, Dad?" Poppy knelt beside the chair, and Violet hovered over his shoulder.

He slid back and rested his head on the chair. Eyes closed, he held the picture with both hands. "I've seen her. This is the girl in my dreams. When her mother and I left for a short trip, she stayed with her grandmother and stood on the porch and waved goodbye." A tear trickled from his eye. "I can't remember her mother, but I think I buried the memories because I had you and your mom." He opened his eyes and turned his face to each of his daughters in turn. "I wanted to live in peace and not cause any strife. Your mom dealt with depression and mood swings, and no one talked about those sorts of things then. Thank goodness she found help when she got older." He stared at the wall. "She was so good to me, to us, most of the time, and I wanted to keep the peace." He dropped his head into his hands.

Ivy's heart ripped in two, as she grasped her throat with her hand. Violet bowed her head and moved her mouth, most likely praying. Poppy rubbed her dad's back and whispered in his ear. The three sisters huddled around their dad, the rock of their childhood. Any time their mom had one of her spells and went to bed for a few hours or days, he took them fishing or to the park. He taught them to love their mom by his steadfast example.

In the recliner, he sat straight and rested his arms on the chair. "Why do you have this photo?"

Ivy scooted the coffee table closer to him. "When we went through the box Mom left, we found her journal and newspaper clippings. A few of the news articles were about an accident and some were honor roll lists and school events that listed Marigold Hayes." She lifted the journal from the container. "From the stories Mom wrote in her journal, we believe you were Nick Hayes, and you were married to a woman named Louise who died in a car accident. Her obituary says she left behind a daughter, Marigold, and her husband was not found."

Dad's coloring paled to a grayish cast. "How did I not remember?"

He rubbed his eyes. "Louise sounds familiar. Do you have a photo of her?"

"I didn't think to print one of her, let me see if I can find one on my phone." Ivy scrolled through a list of pictures. "I believe this one is her. She was in the newspaper archives for winning a pie baking contest."

"She made the best blueberry pies." He licked his lips. "I can about taste them."

Poppy patted his knee. "You don't like blueberries."

"You're right. Your mom detested them. I guess I just went along."

Ivy turned her phone to him. He grasped the cell phone and stared at the picture. "Louise. Do you see a likeness between her and Marigold?"

The sisters passed the phone to each other and nodded. Violet returned it to Ivy, who stared at the resemblance. "They do appear similar, about as much as me and Mom, but she resembles you too, Dad."

Edward slapped his hand on the chair arm. "Is Marigold still alive? Is she around?"

Poppy searched her dad's face, then pushed out the words. "We know where she is."

"Have you talked to her?"

Poppy paced across the room. "Sort of. She lives on Abbott Island and runs a kayak rental business. We visited the island to find out if she was your daughter. I know you say she resembles her mom, but she has your eyes, our eyes, the same bright blue. We don't have the most common color."

"What did your mom's journal say? If I was Nick Hayes, how did I become Edward Downey?"

Ivy explained how her mom had help creating a new identification and I.D.s for him, and how she found him and nursed him to health.

"We can leave the box here for you to dig through, or take it if you don't want to.

Edward rose from his seat. "You can leave the box, but I want you to come here, and let me hug all of you."

They gathered in front of him. "I hope this hasn't caused too much pain. It must be hard for you to wrap your heads around. I'm not sure why your mom hid all this." He went one by one and embraced each daughter. "I need to meet this woman you believe is Marigold and find out if she remembers me, but I won't if it will hurt you."

They gave him a group hug. Violet's arm snaked around his shoulders. "We've prayed about it, Dad, and we want you to talk to her. Yes, it's hard, but we don't want you to miss out on seeing your first child again."

A sob rumbled from his chest. The girls encircled him and hugged until he calmed. After they pulled away and he eased into his chair, Ivy lowered to the stool and held his hand.

"We plan to go on Saturday and talk to her again and find out if she's willing to come and visit you. We'd take you, but a trip to the island may wear you out too much."

"Probably true. I sure hope she'll come." He kissed Ivy on the cheek.

CHAPTER THIRTY-TWO

Thursday morning, the smell of coffee enticed Johnny out of bed. "Morning, Sunshine."

At the kitchen table, Alexa clinked a spoon in her mug as she poured in creamer. Through squinted eyes, she glared at her dad. "Morning."

"You're awake early. Couldn't sleep?" He shuffled across the floor in his slippers. From the cupboard, he collected an over-sized mug, then poured black liquid from the pot. He reached in the freezer for an ice cube, then plunked it into his coffee. "Enough to cool it a bit. Glad I had creamer left from your last visit. The almond keeps a long time."

She raised her mug to him. "Thanks, Dad."

At the table, he poured a bowl of oat cereal and milk, then sliced a banana on top. He lifted the spoon to his mouth as Alexa stared out the window at the woods. Was she making plans to stay with him, maybe a tiny house in the back lot? No, she promised she'd keep her job until she found a new one.

"So, what are your plans for the day?"

She sipped her drink. "I'm going to rent a kayak and relax on the water for a while. Then can I help you at the restaurant? You know, hang out with Henry in the kitchen."

Johnny spit a bite of cereal on the table.

"I was kidding, Dad. Chill." She twirled the spoon between her fingers. "What's so bad about Henry?" A glimpse of mischief twinkled in her eyes.

"Nothing is wrong with Henry, he's an awesome guy. I'm not sure I want my little girl dating a chef. We've talked about this before."

"I don't want to marry him, but I'd like to make friends on the island." She rinsed her cup in the sink. "I'm going to do some job searching on my computer this morning, and then go see Marigold. I'll stop by the restaurant later."

"You're serious about changing jobs?"

Hands on her hips, she stood in front of the sink. "Yes, I am. Since I know I can stay with you, I have time to work out the details."

He dropped his spoon on the table with a clink. "You do realize I live on an island, right? It costs a lot of money to ferry to and from the island. Can you afford the fare?"

She breathed in as if to gather her courage. "I know you live on an island. An amazing island. I've saved a good bit of my paycheck each time.

187

I don't have college payments, I went on scholarship, remember? My car is paid for, thanks to the money Grandpa left me. So, I have little to no debt." She picked up a dishcloth and wiped the table clean. "I want the chance to explore and discover what the possibilities are, unless I'll be in your way."

"I get it, and you've thought this through. You're welcome to stay as long as you want." He rinsed his dishes in the sink. Nothing left to say, except he supported her and loved her. "I have to leave in about a half an hour. If you need me, call. Love you, kiddo."

With a peck on her dad's cheek, she sashayed out of the kitchen and retreated to the extra bedroom. If she lived with him, he would adjust, but the small space might get crowded fast.

~~~~~

A bright blue sky met Marigold and Charlotte on Thursday morning. Sun shined through cotton candy clouds and warmed the sand under their feet. With a bucket of suds and sponges, the two women scrubbed the kayaks from one end to the other. Seagulls wandered nearby in hopes of a lost snack or fish treat.

With a sprayer, Marigold washed away the environmentally friendly soap and rinsed the area. She turned off the spigot and coiled the hose on the holder attached to the building. "Thanks for helping me this morning."

The young woman beamed. "I love this job. It's a nice break from teaching."

"You've been a blessing, for sure. My back can only do so much of the lifting and cleaning anymore. The beginnings of aging, I guess." They worked together to prepare for the tourists. "Thursday often brings in the folks who want to spend a long weekend."

"I'm happy to help however I can." Charlotte carried a pen and clipboard with the papers customers signed before embarking on a trip, and placed them on the table. In her red-and-white-striped tank top and denim shorts, she could pass for a natural islander.

Before Marigold finished wiping off the last boat, Alexa strolled across the sand.

The older woman placed a hand on her lower back and eased into a straighter stance. "Morning."

The young woman, dressed in a bathing suit and shorts, hugged a towel in her arms. "Did Dad tell you I was here? I got in last night."

"No, I haven't heard from Johnny since earlier yesterday. What brings you back?"

"My job."

"Are you doing another tour of the glacial grooves?"

The young woman laughed. "No. I took time to get away from the museum and figure out what to do. I'm tired of being chained to a desk. I loved being outside, teaching." She spun in a circle, hands out. "The students were so much fun. Now I hope to find a way to work in a natural setting all the time."

"You should talk to Charlotte. She teaches full time at a school on the mainland, she can clue you in about working with children all day."

"I wanted to talk to you first." Alexa tightened the hold on her towel.

"Want to walk along the beach before it gets crowded?" Marigold took a step to the edge of the water. "What did you want to talk about?"

Alexa stared at her feet as she ambled along the surf, then raised her face to meet Marigold's. "I plan to move to the island and live with Dad for a while, so I can figure out what I want to do. I've spent my whole life learning. Don't get me wrong, I enjoy finding out about new things and discovering what I'm passionate about, but I'm tired. I think my brain needs a break. Mom had me in so many activities as a kid, then college, and now work. I missed out on getting to know Dad, and I want to take the time to be with him." She took a breath. "I know you two are dating and I don't want to interfere, but do you mind if I spend time here?"

Marigold stopped, turned to Alexa, and gathered her hands in hers. "I won't ever stop you from spending time with your dad. For now, rest and take in the beauty of the island." The young woman batted her eyelashes as tears shimmered. "I will move aside for you. Your dad loves you so much and needs to know how much you love him."

Alexa squeezed Marigold's hands. "Oh, no. I don't want you to move aside. I want you to be part of the circle. Dad loves you, and I do too."

The corners of her mouth curled up and her eyes crinkled. "Are you sure?"

"Positive."

"I'd be happy to spend time with both of you. You have a gracious and kind heart."

An impish grin made her mouth switch. "I learned from the best."

"You sure did."

Alexa stepped away and eyed the beach. "I think I'll camp out here and catch some sun, then I may kayak later."

"Sounds good. Do you have sunscreen?"

"In my pocket, but thanks." She situated her towel on the sand.

"Back to work, for me." Marigold waved and sauntered to the shed. It had been forty years since she belonged to a family unit. Could she embrace the idea of sharing Johnny with his daughter? Of being a step-mom?

Lord, help me.

~~~~~

After a successful day at the beach, Marigold carried a glass of sweet tea to the screened-in porch. She set the drink on the small, round side table, then unfolded a full-length, cushioned lawn chair and curled into the comfortable seat. A sigh escaped her as a goldfinch and a red-headed house finch danced around the feeder. The life of a bird seemed so easy. For a moment she leaned into the headrest and closed her eyes. In her mind, she imagined a life with Johnny and the changes she would make to accommodate him and Alexa. What if he sold his house and they both moved in with her? She wanted to ask him what his plans were for his house, but she couldn't.

"I know, God, I have to trust You. You've given me peace with Dad's disappearance. You'll give me peace in this situation, too."

The jangle of her phone jerked her out of her daydream. Her heart revved as she stepped into the kitchen. Let it go to voicemail or answer? Her curiosity won.

"Hello." She pushed her braid behind her and sank into a wooden chair.

A woman's voice shot through the phone. "I'm trying to reach Marigold Hayes. Is this her?"

"This is Marigold." Her mind wandered to the kayakers she had served today. Did someone have a problem? Her number was posted on the side of the building in case anyone wanted to reach her, but customers seldom called.

"My name is Ivy. My sisters and I met you when we rented kayaks. Violet sat on the beach, while Poppy and I went out on the lake. You might remember Poppy's wild red hair."

She pursed her lips and pictured the sisters. "I remember. How can I help you?"

"Um. We're coming to Abbott Island on Saturday and hoped you might have time to chat with us. We have a few questions for you."

"About the business?" She tugged her braid in front of her and wrapped the silver strands around her hand. "Saturdays are busy."

"I understand, and no, not about the business. We may have a connection. Curious, you know."

"Sure. I can't meet until afternoon when my employee can take over." She scrunched her forehead. "Where do you want to meet? There is a park in the middle of town, or a picnic area near the glacial grooves."

"The area near the grooves works. It's near the beach, right?"

"Yes. That's convenient for me." She stood and paced across the floor. "I'll see you then."

"Great. Thank you so much."

The phone clicked off.

What now? Ivy sounded mysterious about the whole thing. Was she a cousin she didn't know about, or maybe she knew them from school? No, too young. Whatever they wanted, she would find out Saturday. In the meantime, she planned to talk to Johnny about Alexa.

~~~~~

Friday morning, dew dotted the spiderwebs in Marigold's gardens. With shears, she deadheaded the daisies and zinnias to encourage more blooms. The flowers in the garden that she had planted to honor her parents grew with gusto this year. Lots of sun and rain helped, plus fertilizer. As she snipped the dead blooms, she clipped and placed fresh ones in a bucket for arrangements. Her friends might enjoy a bouquet, so she'd drop them off on the way to work. Beside the house she cut black-eyed Susans and lavender. Her nose delighted in the fragrant herb.

After she added more flowers to her batch, a *thump, thump* on the road pulled her away from her work. She shaded her eyes and searched the road.

"Johnny." With a thud, her tool and bucket hit the ground, and she hiked across the yard to meet him. "Out running again?"

He stopped and bent over with his hands on his knees. After taking a breath, he stood to his full height and nodded. "Yes. I do my best thinking on the road."

"Do you have time for tea? Cold or hot."

"Yes, and time for my best girl." He winked, then followed her to the house.

"Let me grab my stuff, since I was about finished." The bucket with colorful blooms landed in the kitchen sink and the shears on the counter. After she scrubbed her hands, she poured two glasses of iced tea. "Here you go."

He tipped the glass and poured the sweet liquid down his throat. Ice cubes clinked in the empty glass as he set it aside. "Thank you."

"More?" She held out the pitcher.

"Sure."

She poured the tea. "You were running and thinking, huh? Perhaps about Alexa?"

His brows scrunched and forehead wrinkled. "How did you know?"

In the seat across from him, she ran a finger through the condensation on the glass. "She stopped to talk to me yesterday, said she wanted to move to the island and find a different job." She raised her hand to her mouth, then lowered it. "I hope she told you already."

He lay his hand over hers. "Yes, she told me. No worries." With his other hand he wiped perspiration from his head with a handkerchief. "I don't know what to tell her. She has a great job, but I get the appeal of working outside." His eyes held hers. "Most of all, I don't want her being here to change our relationship."

Marigold ducked her head and studied her flip-flops, then lifted her face to meet his. "I admit, I have concerns, too. I don't want to interfere

191

with the two of you growing your relationship. I can get out of the way and give you both more time to spend with each other." The quiver in her voice showed disharmony between her words and her emotions.

"No. I don't want you to get out of the way, as you put it. I want to marry you."

Tears pricked her eyes. "I know."

"I'm not asking today, but I will ask again soon, so please don't let Alexa's presence change anything for us." He lifted her hand to his mouth and kissed her fingers. "Alexa loves you, too, and I have no doubt she's happy for us." He stood with his hands on Marigold's and lifted her from the chair. "If we do marry, I'd like to move in here and let Lexi live in my house. You never know, it might be a win-win."

"Something to consider." Peace flooded her.

With a hand on either side of her face, his lips met hers with a good morning kiss. Or was it an I-want-to-kiss-you-every-day-for-the-rest-of-my-life kiss?

CHAPTER THIRTY-THREE

The bright morning sun cast rays through Marigold's kitchen window and bathed Johnny and her in soft light. He hugged her to him and appreciated the fragrance of the lavender she carried on her from the morning cuttings. His hands moved to her shoulders, and he leaned back.

"You're so beautiful." He dropped his hands to his side and rested his head on hers. "We can work with whatever Alexa needs, can't we?" His heart hoped she said yes.

Her hands wrapped around his. "Of course. I'm not sure what I was worried about. She's a delightful young woman, and she told me how much she wanted you and me to be together." Her lips branded his cheek with a kiss. "I'll do whatever I can to help her and you."

A sigh of relief pushed out of Johnny. "Thank you."

"Sit with me on the porch for a minute. I want to tell you about a strange phone call I got last night." She walked him to the front porch and they sat on the swing. "Remember the three sisters who came to your restaurant? One had curly red hair, one appeared polished, and the other one was tall like me?"

"I think so. Were they there when I misunderstood what happened with you and Lucy?"

"Yes. Later in the day, they came and kayaked." A wrinkle formed between her eyes. "One of them called me and asked if I'd meet with them this Saturday at four. I have no idea why. She said it wasn't business-related."

He reached his arm across the top of the swing. "Do you have any family you don't know about?"

She leaned into him. "I don't think so, but I'm not sure. I never met many of my dad's people." She fingered the ends of her hair. "Did you notice the sisters' eyes are the same color as mine?"

He turned her face to look at her eyes. "The brightest blue I've ever seen."

She blinked at him. "Exactly."

"Do you want me to be there with you?"

"No. I wanted you to know, though. In case I disappear." A nervous laugh flew from her mouth.

"I'd search to the ends of the earth for you." His lips touched her forehead.

"Thank you."

He checked the time on his watch. "I have to go home, take a shower, and get to work."

"Me, too. Thanks for the chat. Hope you have a good day."

After a quick hug, he bounded down the steps and jogged away.

~~~~~

Saturday morning, Cassatt curled herself on Marigold's pillow.

"You're as fidgety as my stomach this morning." With a yawn, Marigold rose from her bed and shuffled across the room. The clock on the nightstand flashed nine o'clock. She'd slept late for a Saturday morning. A dream of her being chased by the three women she planned to meet today startled her awake when they ran her into the lake. Silly dream.

In the bathroom, Marigold studied her face in the mirror. Smile lines, as Sadie called them, creased out from her eyes. A frown line split between her eyes. Those blue eyes she and her dad shared, and now three women she didn't know, stared at her. Maybe they wanted to know about life on an island. Lots of people asked her questions about how they survived in the winter. *Whatever they want, I pray God gives me wisdom and discernment.* In the meantime, off to work.

By 3:45, Charlotte and Marigold had served twenty-five customers and still had five out on the water. Marigold chuckled to herself for her worries at the beginning of summer. At this rate she would exceed her predicted income for the season.

An alarm dinged on her cell phone to remind her of her meeting.

Charlotte lifted her sunglasses. "Do you need to go?"

"Yes, but I'll be back to help close." With her bag slung over her shoulder, she waved to Charlotte as she walked away.

"No worries. I'll close if you're not here."

"Thank you."

Marigold trudged along the path to the picnic tables. When she rounded the curve, she spotted the three sisters. A box rested on the table, along with a basket.

As she approached, her stomach lurched. Something did not feel right. After a quick prayer for calm, Marigold held her head straight and tightened the grip on her boho bag.

"Hello, ladies. Nice to see you again."

Ivy, the one with the stylish hair and classic shorts and top, stood to greet her. She gestured to the bench. "Please join us. You remember Violet and Poppy?"

"I do." She scooted onto the seat and let her bag rest next to her.

Ivy offered her the basket. "Violet made cookies and we have water. Want one?"

What if they poisoned the cookies? Or the drink?

Why am I thinking like a mystery novel?

"Sure, I'd love one. What kind?"

Violet held up the one she was eating. "Oatmeal chocolate chip. My kids and I made them. They love to bake."

"My friend Sadie makes those, and they're one of my favorites. Thank you." She broke off a piece of cookie and savored the sweetness. "Delicious. How many children do you have?"

"Three. They keep my husband, Joseph, and me on the go."

A sip from the water bottle cooled Marigold's throat. "I'm sure they do." She focused on Ivy, who appeared to be the leader of the sisters. "How can I help you today?"

The redhead, Poppy, elbowed Ivy in the side. The woman cleared her throat and removed a book from the box, perhaps a journal.

"I'm not sure how to start this conversation, so I'm going to be blunt. We think you are our half-sister."

If a rock landed on her head, Marigold couldn't be more stunned. "Your half-sister? What are you talking about?"

Ivy handed the book to Marigold. "This is our mother's journal. We found it after she died, when we were cleaning out her office. The box has evidence you may be our sister."

Marigold closed her eyes and allowed the information to fill her brain. Dad must be alive, or had been for many years. She opened her eyes and pierced Ivy with a stare. "What about my dad? Is he alive?"

Violet, who sat on the same side of the table, touched Marigold's hand. "Yes. He's alive and in his eighties. He lives in an assisted living facility. Health issues, typical for an older man, require extra care."

"Does he know?"

Ivy's mauve fingernail poked at a chocolate chip in the cookie. "He does. We talked to him before we contacted you. When I showed him your yearbook photo, he whispered your name and his eyes lit with excitement. We left the box with him for a few days, then picked it up to bring to you."

Poppy lifted photos and newspaper clippings from the box and spread them on the table.

"He recognized your mom's photo, too. I'd found one online of a newspaper article where she won a pie contest." Ivy tapped a photo. "We know this must be a shock, but we wanted you to know."

Marigold ran her finger over the picture of her mom. "What happened? I don't understand where Dad has been for forty years. I've searched in every way possible, but found nothing."

Poppy stood and walked around the table to sit by Marigold. "In the journal, Mom explains everything. Dad lost his memory from before the accident, as well as the wreck where your mom died." She cleared her throat. "Mom found him in her woods, behind her house. He must have wandered across a ravine and wound his way through the forest behind Mom's cabin. She was a volunteer EMT at the time and knew what to do."

Ivy interrupted. "Mom was a good person, but she had mental health issues left undiagnosed. She had what Dad called spells. Most of the time, she was great. We think he felt sorry for her and fell in love with her while she helped him recover. They did go to the doctor for his memory issues, but the doctor couldn't help him."

Violet shuffled through the box and found the IDs her mother had made. "Mom gave him a new identity with the help of a friend. Dad didn't know. She slipped them in his wallet and told him he was Edward Downey."

Marigold's hand covered her mouth and tears trickled down her cheeks. Her shoulders shook as she sobbed. "I've waited so long to find him. I can't believe this."

In an instant, all three sisters huddled around her. "We're so sorry for what our mother did." Ivy sniffed and wiped her eyes. "Our dad is a sweet man."

When Marigold's body calmed, she lifted her face to the women she might share blood with. "I have so many questions."

Poppy tucked her hand into Marigold's elbow. "Of course you do. We want you to take the box home with you and read what you want." She patted Marigold's arm with her free hand. "We plan to stay on the island until tomorrow evening. If, or should I say when, you are ready to talk again, call me." She released her arm and dug in her purse, then handed her a square business card. "This is my cell number."

The card bore art brushes and a palette. The recognition of similarities dawned on Marigold. "You're an artist?"

"I am. I have a show in a gallery and teach classes." A smile crossed Poppy's lips. "Watercolor, mostly."

"I macrame, crochet, and work with fibers, and sell them at craft fairs to supplement the kayak business." She glanced at the card again, then at Poppy. "I also noticed we all have the same eye color, like Dad." With a tissue she wiped her eyes and nose.

Marigold turned, rose from the bench, and faced Ivy and Violet. "I noticed your eyes when you were here before. They're such a vibrant color, I was taken aback by the similarity. Now I know why. Plus, we're all named after plants."

Ivy took both of Marigold's hands in hers. "If you have any doubts, we can do a DNA test, but I think when you see your dad, you'll know. Again, we are so sorry for what Mom did, I hope you can forgive her."

"I'm speechless, but have so many questions." She rubbed her forehead. "What time are you leaving tomorrow?"

"We plan to leave by four in the afternoon," Ivy said, "so we can be home in time to prepare for work on Monday."

Poppy laughed. "What she means is, so she can prepare for work. Violet and I don't go into an office, our work is always with us. Right, Vi?"

Violet gave a half shrug. "Yes."

Marigold lifted the box from the table. "Can we meet here tomorrow afternoon? Sometime after church?"

They all nodded, and Ivy touched Marigold's forearm. "Of course. We'll be here. Can we drop you somewhere with the box? It's heavy."

"No. I'm good. My golf cart is at the bottom of the hill." She moved to the path, then turned to the sisters. "Thank you. I know I'll have questions."

Her heart swirled with confusion, joy, hope, and shock, while her legs trembled. Her eyes focused on the golf cart, as she willed herself to keep walking and not collapse. Had she found her father after all these years? She prayed it was so.

CHAPTER THIRTY-FOUR

Photos, news clips, notes, and ephemera spread across the kitchen table. Her father's life after the accident loomed before her as she puzzled over where to begin. Saturday evening ticked by as Marigold studied the details of her dad's history.

Her mom's obituary, the yearbook photo of Marigold in her red dress her mom had sewn, Dad's new identity, a grainy photo of her dad in the plea she had sent to the newspaper when she was eighteen. Forty years of searching had come to an end, if this was Nick Hayes instead of Edward Downey. Warmth spread across her chest. She had found her dad. His face, in a recent photo the sisters gave her, showed wrinkles and age, but his eyes sparkled the way she remembered and his smile never changed.

By nine o'clock, Marigold snuggled into her recliner and opened the journal. As she turned the pages, her heart surged with anger when Renee confessed she had kept Dad captive, even though she had seen the obituary and an article claiming Nick Hayes had disappeared. The fury subsided as the story changed to a love story of two lost people who loved with an incredible depth. At least Dad was cherished in his second life and had not lived on the street. By the time Marigold closed the journal, her empathy for Renee and her dad included the sisters. Without Renee, her dad might have died in the woods or spent his life lost. Instead, he worked in landscaping, which he loved, and raised three daughters, her half-sisters. Women her heart longed to know better.

At midnight, Marigold donned pajamas and lay in her bed, her mind rolling with *what ifs* and *whys*. Her question *why* to God had stopped long ago, but the *what ifs* filled her mind with doubt.

~~~~~

Sunlight filtered through the window and awakened Marigold on Sunday. Flipped on her back, she batted her eyelids to open and adjusted to the morning light. Cassatt climbed across her and kneaded her paws into Marigold's chest.

"Morning, Missy. I'm getting up."

At 9:30, Marigold, donned a flowered caftan, cinched by a belt, then re-braided her hair. Johnny's truck engine rumbled as he rolled into the driveway. The story she wanted to tell him swirled through her mind like a cyclone. So much truth, revealed in so little time, left her reeling with joy and fear. Before she stepped out the door, she straightened her shoulders and breathed in the fragrance of lavender and lemon thyme.

On the passenger side of the truck, Johnny opened the door for her and helped her to the seat. Behind the wheel, he reached across and pecked her cheek with a kiss. "How is the most beautiful lady on the island this morning?"

From the back cab seat, Alexa leaned to the front. "Thanks, Dad." Then she laughed. "Marigold, I agree with Dad. You are beautiful."

Her face warmed at the compliments. "Thank you both, your kindness overwhelms me." Tears formed in her eyes and brought on a sniff.

"You okay?" Johnny's hand gripped hers.

Uncertain whether to share her visit with her new sisters with Alexa, she squeezed his hand and nodded.

By the time the three of them arrived at church, the lot had filled. They hurried in and found their seats. No time to talk to Johnny about her dad, so she lifted the hymnal from the holder and worshipped.

After church, Marigold caught a ride with Charlotte, and Johnny and Alexa left to work at the restaurant. Without time to talk the situation over with him, Marigold decided to meet with the sisters at two o'clock.

~~~~~

The sound of waves washing on the shore matched the drumming of Marigold's fingers on the wood. The rhythm calmed her as she sat at the picnic table they had shared last night. The box loomed in front of her as a reminder of the life she missed with her dad. One he had shared with Ivy, Violet, and Poppy. Resentment bubbled, but Marigold tamped down the urge to dislike her sisters. Part of her wanted to dismiss them and find her father and protect him, but from all evidence these women loved Dad as much as she did. What their mother did wasn't their fault.

The three walked toward her from the path, their hair fluttering in the wind as they chatted with each other.

Violet slid in next to Marigold, as the others lowered to the opposite bench. "Did you have a chance to go through the box?"

"I did, and I'm not sure what to say." She picked at the sleeve of her caftan. "I read all the clippings, studied all the photos, and read the entire journal. I don't understand your mother, but I'm thankful she saved my dad, our dad. Without her, he could have died."

A mosquito buzzed the table and Ivy swatted it away. "We don't understand her either, but we're glad she did the right thing as far as helping Dad heal. We may never know what went through her head, but I do believe she had good intentions."

Poppy rearranged her mass of curly hair. "We talked to Dad last night and told him we met you. The first thing he asked was if you remembered him."

A gasp escaped Marigold. "I'd never forget him. He hasn't changed as much as I expected. Always humble and kind." Tears flowed down her cheeks. "These are happy tears." She waved her hands in front of her face. "I still can't believe I get to see my dad again." She paused and wiped her eyes with a tissue. "I will, won't I?"

All three answered at once. "Of course."

"I want to talk to him as soon as I can." She jiggled her foot. "Wednesday is my birthday."

Poppy clapped. "Wow. What a birthday present."

From her bag, Ivy snatched a piece of paper. "This is the address for Dad's place. We'll prepare him for the visit. I think I can get off work."

"We'll both be there, too. Okay?" Violet pointed from herself to Poppy.

"I hoped you'd be, then maybe I can have time with him by myself."

Ivy stood from the bench and walked over and hugged Marigold. "We'll make it happen."

~~~~~

Sunday evening, Marigold had dialed Johnny's number and the phone went to voicemail. She had stopped by the restaurant, but people were standing on the sidewalk, waiting in line to get in.

Monday, she paced along the beach and waited for the last kayakers to return. Once she closed her shop, she hoped to catch Johnny and reveal her amazing news.

The sun hung low on the lake when the last tourists handed her the paddles.

"Thanks so much, have a great night."

With the kayaks tucked in for the night, she drove to Johnny's house. A U-Haul parked in the driveway gave her pause. Joel bounded out of the front door with empty boxes.

"Hey, Mari."

With a wave, she greeted him and parked her cart. "What's going on?"

"Didn't Johnny tell you?"

"Tell me what?"

"Alexa moved in today. She gave notice and will work remotely for two weeks. She's going to help her dad until she finds a job with the park service." He broke the cardboard and shoved it into a recycle can.

"I heard she was thinking about it, but I haven't talked to him since church." She chewed her lip and ran her braid through her hands. "I'll leave you to it and catch up later. Thanks."

Before he made an attempt to stop her, she hopped in her cart and drove home.

Two steps into her house, her cell phone chimed. Without glancing at the incoming number, she answered. "Hello. This is Marigold."

Johnny's voice crawled through the line. "Mari? Joel said you stopped by. I'm so sorry I haven't had a chance to talk to you. Alexa left after church on Sunday, rented a small U-Haul, had her friends load her stuff, and here she is. Between getting the house ready and the cooking at the restaurant, I haven't had time to turn around."

His voice soothed her, but his lack of communication threw her off. If he loved her, why didn't he share about Alexa moving while she had tried several times to share her good news? Not sure whether to be angry or happy for him to have his daughter back, she counted to ten before answering.

"I hope everything works out for Alexa, since she's taking a big chance." Not one to discourage a young person's dreams, Marigold's lack of enthusiasm even surprised her. "You sound busy, so how about I talk to you later? Take care." She clicked off the cell, then climbed the steps to her bedroom.

~~~~~

Tuesday at the beach, Charlotte brushed mayflies from the side of the shed and off the kayaks. "These things make such a mess." She tossed a bucket full of them into the garbage. "You're quiet this morning, Mari. You okay?"

The threat of rain hovered over the island. Angry clouds rolled across the horizon as the sun tried to peek through.

"I'm good. I have a lot on my mind."

The young woman unlocked the metal cord holding the boats and pulled it loose. "Okay. If I can help in any way, I'd be happy to."

Once all the equipment was set, a few customers wandered in.

Marigold took a few moments and wandered to the edge of the water, where tourists positioned kayaks with Charlotte's help. A dad and his daughter floated then paddled together.

Ivy promised to call this afternoon and firm up plans for the visit with Dad tomorrow. The fulfillment of her dream of finding her dad alive rushed over her like a tidal wave, as she shivered despite the warm day. In the photo Ivy had given her, his hair had thinned and grayed, the same white as hers. His blue eyes still sparkled, and he appeared smaller than she remembered. The one thing she had memorized from childhood was his beautiful, heart-warming smile.

Without a word to her friends, since she wanted to tell Johnny first, she planned to drive the two hours, visit, then come home. Maybe none of them remembered tomorrow was her birthday.

Johnny had left a message on her machine last night, but she had no desire to explain everything on the phone, and he should spend time helping Alexa get settled. With his daughter here, maybe Marigold and Johnny should let go of their plans and just be friends. Her heart ached, but she had no intention of coming between the two of them, not after the years she had searched for her own father.

The rest of the day sailed by. As they closed the stand, Marigold turned to Charlotte. "I'll be off the island for a while tomorrow, and I'll be home by evening. If you need anything, you have my cell number."

Her smile wide, Charlotte agreed. "Yes. I have your number. I hope whatever you're doing, it's a great day."

Sweet Charlotte carried a kind word for everyone.

"Thank you. Hope all is well here. See you later."

Once Marigold landed at home, she scrambled eggs for dinner and ate, watered her flowers, and packed a day bag for the trip. She turned the ringer off on her phones and retreated to the bedroom.

~~~~~

The alarm chimed at 5:30 and jostled Marigold out of bed. By 7:30, she pulled onto the ferry, ready for the most anticipated day of her life. The workers secured the gate on the big boat, and Marigold stepped out of her car to watch Marblehead Lighthouse draw near. Once the boat docked, she steered the car onto the mainland, set her GPS, and inserted a CD of music from the seventies. The songs drew her to happier times with her parents, when she and her mom cleaned the house with the music blasting. They had danced with the broom and sang into the duster.

So lost in the tunes, she arrived at the assisted living facility in what seemed like minutes. She steered her car into a spot and stared at her dad's building. Her hands trembled against the steering wheel as she bowed her head and sought God's ear for strength and wisdom. Excitement bubbled in her and her hands shook as she opened the door.

A car scooted in next to hers. Ivy, Poppy, and Violet tumbled out and wrapped her in a hug.

Poppy leaned in. "I'm happy you came. Everything will be all right."

"Thank you for being here with me." She grabbed her bag from the car and walked in step with her sisters to the glass door.

Dressed in a floral print swing-style sundress, Ivy patted Marigold's arm. "We're happy to be here. As much as this shocked us, we want to see Dad happy. Plus, we found another sister."

The four of them made their way to Dad's room, and Violet tapped on the door.

"Come on in." His voice squeezed Marigold's heart. She pushed the door open and stepped inside the small, neat apartment. For a moment she froze and stared at the man she remembered as her dad. Thin white hair replaced the thick blond hair, but his eyes still twinkled bright blue. Wrinkles accented his beautiful smile, while tears dribbled down his cheeks.

A bare whisper misted the air. "Dad." Her voice caught on the tears clogging her throat. She dropped her bag and hurried to the man she called father. "I can't believe you're here."

His body wobbled as he grasped the walker and stood. Once he balanced, he held out his arms. "Can I give you a hug?"

"Yes, Daddy, yes." She wrapped her arms around his frail shoulders and let the tears fall. "I've missed you so much." His hug warmed her as the guard around her heart crumbled.

CHAPTER THIRTY-FIVE

On the beach, Johnny wiped his brow with a handkerchief. He trudged through the sand to the kayak stand. Ten 'til eleven in the morning, and Marigold and Charlotte had not opened yet. Low waves kissed the shore, while seagulls snacked. On the way, he had driven down her street and noticed her car missing. He blew air through his lips and headed to the restaurant.

Inside, Alexa rolled silverware and prepared the tables for the day. "Hey, Dad."

"Morning. Thanks for helping out. I'm glad I have enough business for you to work until you figure out what you're doing."

Thank goodness the food truck moved to the mainland.

"Me, too." She cast him a smile and kept rolling.

He sauntered to the kitchen, lifted his jacket from the hook, put it on, and buttoned the front. "We better get cooking."

"You got it, boss." The marinade Henry prepared gave the room a fragrant bouquet. "I gotta say, this smells delicious."

"I'm sure." With his head down, Johnny perused the menu for the day.

Vegetables sizzled as Henry stirred them in olive oil. "You okay?"

"Yeah, wondering where Marigold is. She wasn't at the beach, and I drove by her house, and her car wasn't there." With a sharp knife, he cropped celery.

"Careful you don't cut your finger."

The knife stopped in mid-air when Johnny saw how close he had come to his hand. *Get your mind off Marigold.*

Henry wiped his hands on a towel. "Isn't today Mari's birthday?"

With a jerk, Johnny's head lifted. "You remembered?"

A frown creased Henry's brow. "You asked me to bake her a cake. I started this morning. It's an Italian cream cake with pecans and coconut. Remember?"

"Yeah, I remember. I wanted to surprise her, but I can't unless I know where she is." He rubbed his head.

"I'm sure she'll come around."

"Yeah, I guess. After the lunch crowd, I'll check again." Satisfied with his decision, he got to work.

~~~~~

Ivy and her sisters bustled to their dad's kitchen. "We'll get lunch. Do you want tea or lemonade?"

In unison, Marigold and her dad answered, "Tea, please." They turned to each other and laughed. She perched beside him on the couch and saw the man she had missed for so many years. She wanted to memorize everything about him. Forty years of lost memories squeezed her heart.

His hand shook as he grasped hers. "I can't believe you're here. I'm so grateful." His words wobbled.

"Me too. I've searched for you ever since you disappeared." She leaned her head to his. "I've prayed for this day for so long. I'm so thankful God gave me a chance to hug you again."

She lifted her bag from the floor. "I brought what few pictures I have of us." From an envelope she pulled a stack of photos. "Here's me as a baby on your lap." She flipped to the next one. "Mom and me and you're standing behind us. I think I was three or four."

His eyes brightened. "Your fourth birthday. I remember because you grabbed a handful of your cake and shoved it in your mouth. See the spots on your cheek? You dotted yourself with chocolate." He held the photo and a tear trickled along his cheek. "Your mother was so beautiful."

"She was. I miss her so much."

They rifled through the rest of the photos.

"Oh my, your grandmother. She was a tough lady. She'd had so much heartache before I met her, and she never liked me."

Marigold chuckled. "She never liked anyone." She paused. "Your memory is coming back, isn't it?"

He nodded. "Some of it, yes. The pictures help trigger what's in this little brain of mine." A smile split his face.

"As I recall, you are one of the smartest men I ever knew."

"Maybe you should keep better company." He clapped his hands and laughed.

Soak all of this in today. Tomorrow he might be gone.

In the meantime, Marigold planned to make as many trips as possible to visit this sweet man. Johnny would be busy with Alexa, which freed time for her to do as she pleased. The man loved her and had wanted to marry her, but did he still? Maybe he had changed his mind and planned to use his time helping his daughter and running the restaurant?

Regardless of her future, the wall around Marigold's guarded emotions tumbled down like the walls of Jericho. Love overflowed for her dad, her new sisters, Johnny, Alexa and all her friends. Her heart exploded with joy.

~~~~~

From the truck, Johnny saw Charlotte help a customer with a kayak. He climbed out and approached the young woman. "Afternoon."

She turned to him. "Hi. How are you?"

He lifted his ball cap and rubbed his head. "I'm good. Is Marigold around?"

Charlotte pursed her lips. "I'm not sure where she is. She told me she'd be off the island today. She said she'd be home this evening. I assumed you were taking her somewhere for her birthday."

The water ebbed and flowed along with his thoughts. "I haven't had a chance to talk to her for a few days. Alexa moved in and I've been working. I tried a couple times, but she never answered. I had planned to surprise her with a cake. Any idea when she'll be back?"

Charlotte lifted her hands with an I-don't-know shrug. "Before the last ferry runs."

"Thanks." Head lowered, he trudged to the truck, and checked his cell phone. No signal. At the restaurant he planned to call her phone again. Maybe Joel or Lucy had talked to her.

A few minutes later, he parked on Division Street and tromped up the steps to the General Store. He wove his way through the tourists to Lucy's office. With a tap on the door, he peeked inside.

She raised her head from her work on the computer. "Hi. Can I help you?"

He removed his hat and stepped into the room. "I hope so. Have you seen Marigold?" He fingered his baseball cap.

"Not for a couple of days. I was going to stop by her place later and wish her happy birthday. Sadie and Joel were, too."

"Okay, I won't bother you anymore."

Lucy stood and walked around her desk. "You're never a bother. I hope you find her."

He sighed. "Charlotte said she went off island today, but I can't imagine where."

"Maybe she went to visit her mom's grave. She's done that before on her birthday."

"Makes sense. I'll see you later." He walked out of the store.

~~~~~

Around her dad's round oak table, Marigold soaked in her new reality. Her dad and three sisters passed bowls of noodles, beef Stroganoff, green beans, and a huge basket of homemade rolls. "This smells amazing. Thank you to whoever prepared all the food."

"You're welcome. It was a group effort." Violet buttered a yeasty roll. "Poppy whipped up the Stroganoff and beans, I made the rolls, and Ivy baked a cherry pie for dessert."

"And I'm here to eat." Dad raised his fork.

Family sharing food and chatting around the table injected Marigold with a surreal sense of belonging. Her dreams had led her to hope she'd join her dad for dinner, but part of her never believed she would find him. Now he filled the seat beside her, along with three women she wanted to call sisters. Even with the joy flooding her bones, a twinge of sadness cast a net around her heart. She missed Johnny. In all the hubbub and missed calls, she had not shared her news, and Alexa occupied his time.

Ivy clinked her water glass with her fork. "Marigold?"

Startled by the sound, Marigold lifted her face to meet Ivy's. "I'm sorry, I was thinking about something."

"I'm sure you have a lot to contemplate. In the meantime, let's lift our glasses to family, in whatever way we got here, I'm thankful we can sit together." She touched her glass to Violet's and they continued to toast around the table.

After Violet and Poppy cleared the table, Ivy served pie with ice cream. "Hope cherry with vanilla is okay. It's Dad's favorite."

A smile cut across Marigold's face. "Mine, too. I love anything with cherries."

Her dad leaned his head to hers. "That's my girl."

Marigold pushed back tears of joy. When she opened them, she waved her hand to cool her face. "I'm overwhelmed by your kindness. Thank you. This is the best birthday I could imagine."

After lunch, the group gathered in Dad's living room and passed the photos Marigold brought and the ones they found in their mom's box. Ivy had gathered a few of her and her sisters when they were young.

"Check out this photo of Marigold compared to the one of me." Ivy handed two pictures to Violet, who shared them with Poppy. "That's a strong resemblance."

Violet gave them to Marigold.

"Our features are so similar. I think we took after Dad." Blond hair covered both little girls' heads, their noses turned up a bit, and their lips pouted. "We were pretty cute, eh?"

The group laughed in agreement. Dad perked up. "Well, I know I was."

"You still are," all four said in unison.

About four o'clock, Marigold sensed her dad's energy lagging.

"I better get on the road. I want to make sure I don't miss the ferry."

As much as she longed to stay in the midst of her family, she wanted to get to the island, her safe place, with her friends. They'd be excited for her and want to hear every tidbit about her dad.

Dad took her hand after she hugged him goodbye. "I'm sorry we were apart for so long, but I'm thankful we can spend time together now. I've missed you so much, especially now I know the little girl who visited me in my dreams was you. I recognized her, but struggled to put it together. Also, I'm sorry for what Renee did. I can't change it, and I love all of you girls and will always be thankful for you." Tears streamed down his face as he grinned.

"It's okay, Dad. I'll be back and enjoy getting to know you all, and I plan on calling you often. Thank you for finding me." Marigold hugged each of her sisters, then turned and hurried out the door.

~~~~~

Orange hovered in the sky, preparing for sunset, as the ferry chugged across the lake. Marigold faced Abbott Island as the homes and businesses drew near. A sense of wonder mixed with relief embraced her. Grateful for an amazing birthday, the idea of going home to her cottage and her cat brought peace. God still worked miracles. He had answered her years of prayers, even as she asked for Him to give her clarity about Johnny and her dad and the relationships she wanted. On the drive home, she vowed to have no more "what if" games.

What if her dad died before she saw him again?

What if Johnny didn't have time for her?

What if her sisters resented her in time?

She refused to allow the events of her life to break her faith. From now on, she trusted God and believed in His presence in each aspect of her life.

When the ferry docked, she drove home and parked in the driveway. On the porch, a lone figure sat in her swing.

CHAPTER THIRTY-SIX

Johnny planted his feet on the floor to stop the swing, then he stood. As soon as Marigold stepped on the porch, he wrapped his arms around her and swung her in a circle. He buried his face in her hair and soaked in her sweet honey fragrance. When he steadied himself and set her feet on the floor, he lifted his hands to her face and kissed her.

"Happy birthday, beautiful."

With both hands, she grabbed the back of his neck and pulled him to her for another kiss. The tension he had held in his neck all day washed away with her touch.

"I'm glad you're home."

"Me too." She rested her head against his chest, then moved away. "Want to go inside? I have something to tell you."

"Sure. Let me grab what I need out of the truck and I'll be in." His long legs strode across the drive as Marigold unlocked her door.

Inside, she flipped on lights as Johnny returned and followed her inside. Cassatt sauntered out to greet her, then mewed at her food bowl. Johnny stood by as Mari filled the cat's bowl.

"She looks hungry."

"She's always hungry." Marigold pushed a strand of hair away from her eye and faced Johnny. She saw the domed plate he held in his hands. "What have you there?"

"Italian cream cake. Henry baked it this morning. I helped make the icing. I hope you enjoy it." The cake rested on a glass cake plate with a dome.

"It's beautiful and looks delicious. Let me get plates." She hustled to the kitchen. In a few minutes she carried plates, forks, and a knife. "You want to do the honors while I brew decaf?"

"Sure. Want to sit on the screened-in porch?" He sliced the cake.

"I'd love to."

A bit later, they sat side-by-side with cake and coffee.

Marigold scooped a piece of the coconut, vanilla, pecan cake in her mouth and moaned. "This is amazing, best cake I've ever eaten."

"I'll be sure to tell Henry. I hope you've had a good birthday." He rested his plate and cup on the side table. "I'm sorry I've missed your calls. Alexa pulled a last-minute move on me, and my life started spinning in circles. She's settled in, finishing her time with the museum and working for me for now, but has applied to the park services in hopes of getting a

211

job. Her apartment lease runs out the end of the month. In the meantime, I want to get back to my life and spend time with you." He reached for her hand. "Have you had a good day?"

Tears seeped from her eyes. "I have." She choked on her answer.

He wrinkled his forehead and squeezed her hand. "Are you okay? What's wrong?"

With her free hand, she dabbed her face with a napkin. "I'm great." She sniffed and pursed her lips. "I found my dad. Or I should say his three daughters found me."

Johnny's eyes rounded. "What?"

"I told you I was meeting the three sisters who came to your restaurant on your reopening?"

He let go of her hand and rubbed his head. "You did. One had red hair, right?"

"Yes, Poppy has red curly hair. Violet is tall like me, and Ivy and I resemble each other, except she's still blond instead of white-headed." She shredded the napkin. "They're my half-sisters, and my dad has quite the story. Close to unbelievable, except they have proof."

The tale spilled from her lips as Johnny tried to soak everything in and understand what had occurred.

He stood and paced the porch. "You're telling me this Renee took your dad in, nursed him, fell in love with him, gave him a new identity, then married him and had three daughters?"

She stood and rested her hand on his forearm. "It's hard to believe at first, but it's true. I read the journal and sifted through papers they gave me. And Johnny, they are the nicest people. My dad's older, but the same. He's not in the best health, but he gets along fairly well. I'm hoping he can come to the island soon."

He wrapped an arm around her shoulders and kissed her cheek. "I'm happy for you, Mari. I know you'll want to spend time with him and get to know your sisters."

Her head rested on his shoulder. "I will want to see them as much as I can. I know he'd never move here, but I'm hoping one of the sisters can bring him sometimes. I'm relieved he's alive and has had a good life."

"If you want me to take you to him, I can. I hope to meet him, if you want me to." His heart ached for her to say yes.

"Of course I want you to meet him. I've been wanting to tell you about him for days, but you were busy and I was planning my trip. You've no idea how happy I was to see you on my porch." She leaned into him.

He tightened his hug. "You know I wouldn't miss your birthday. As a matter of fact, I've made plans to take you to dinner Saturday on the mainland. There's a new restaurant in Sandusky overlooking the lake, a great place to share a quiet meal."

"I'd love to." They laced fingers and watched the lightning bugs dance in the night. "I have a confession."

"What?" He moved behind her and laced his arms around her.

She snugged her head against his chest. "I was worried since Alexa moved in with you, you wouldn't have time for me. I don't want to take you away from your time with her."

"Interesting. I was concerned you'd want to spend time with your new family, and I didn't want to interfere."

She lifted her head to face him. "We're both old worry warts, aren't we?"

"We're not too old for this." His lips touched hers with a promise to love her always.

~~~~~

Sadie and Lucy fussed over Marigold on Saturday afternoon. Four dresses draped across Marigold's bed in various shades of blue. Lucy held one in front of her and twirled.

"I love your clothes, but I'm not tall enough to wear the flowing ones. Don't you think this one makes your eyes bluer than blue?"

Sadie picked a more subtle blue with gray swirls. "This one is nice for a fancy restaurant."

Marigold lifted her hands in front of her. "Okay girls, I think I'll wear the one with the teal and green. I have jewelry to match." She tugged the dress off the hanger and went to the bathroom. When she came out, her friends clapped.

"Beautiful. Let me add the necklace." Lucy snapped the clasp in place. "Turn around."

Marigold modeled the dress. "I see the look in your eyes, Lucy. No makeup. I don't wear it and I don't intend to scare Johnny with a clown face."

Both ladies chuckled.

"Your life has sure taken a spin, hasn't it? Reminds me of the craziness I went through before Joel and I got together. Except yours is much calmer." Sadie hung the rest of the dresses in the closet. "I'm happy for you." She hugged her friend.

Tires crunched in the driveway.

"We'll lock the house. You go meet Johnny." Lucy peered out the window.

In the drive, dressed in black slacks, a light green button down, and a checked tie, Johnny held open the door of his truck for Marigold. "You are gorgeous."

Her cheeks warmed. "Thank you. You look great, too."

She might have been too old for fairytales, but Marigold felt like Cinderella riding in the carriage to the ball, except her prince charming drove a truck.

~~~~~

At the restaurant, a valet parked the Ford while the maître d seated them on the outside deck over the water. A full moon shone on the water as stars lit the sky.

"Want to share a shrimp cocktail?" Johnny asked.

"Yes, sounds good." Marigold unfolded her linen napkin and placed it on her lap. After the waiter took their order, a catamaran sailboat scooted across the lake, lit like a Christmas tree. "The night sailors have fancied their boat."

He wrapped his hand over hers. "This night is almost as beautiful as you. I'm still amazed God brought us together." Water lapped along the dock below. "I never dreamed I'd fall in love at my age. You add so much to my life, and I can be myself with you."

A smile spread across Marigold's face. "I feel the same. I was so worried about us, and for no good reason." His deep brown eyes captured hers. "I've never been in love or been loved. You've changed my life. Thank you for your patience as I searched for my dad. You know I was about to give up, I'd turned it over to God and asked Him to help me move past the longing I had to find Dad. And wow, He answered my prayer in a way only He could. You've been beside me the whole time. Thank you."

~~~~~

Satisfied after a dinner of steak and salmon, Johnny paid the waiter. He pulled out Marigold's chair and guided her across the room. Outside, the valet delivered his truck and they drove down the street to a quiet spot along a boardwalk.

"Want to take a walk?"

She patted her stomach. "Yes. We can walk off some of the rich food."

Along the way, Marigold pointed to the lake. "The sailboat I saw earlier is coming closer. Maybe to the dock over there."

With his arm around her waist, they ambled to the water and watched the boat land. A man tied the vessel off and marched their direction.

Marigold turned to Johnny. "Do you know him?"

"I sure do." Johnny extended his hand to the man. "You're right on time. Dave, this is Marigold. Marigold, Dave. If you don't mind, Dave is going to take us for a cruise on his boat."

Her eyes met his with surprise. "I'd love to."

Dave settled them in, then set the boat to sail. "You two relax, I've got this covered."

Once Dave sailed the catamaran to a deeper part of the lake, he dropped anchor and disappeared into the small hold below.

Johnny and Marigold snuggled on the bench seat and listened to the water lap the sides of the boat. She pointed to the lights aligned with the sail.

"How did you do all this?"

"Dave's an old friend from Cleveland. He moved here to start his charter business." He snugged her to him. "I have a confession."

She leaned away from the plastic bench seat and turned to him. "What kind of confession?"

He inhaled. "I spoke to your dad after you told me about him."

"What? How?"

"Your sister, Ivy, left her business card in my jar. The one where I give away a free dinner a month to whoever enters. I drew it out yesterday and called to tell her she won. Of course, I didn't know who she was until we talked a few minutes. As soon as I told her I was Johnny from Abbott Island, she told me who she was in relation to you. We got to talking and I asked for your dad's number, and I called him last night."

"And?"

"You may have to help me up after I do this." He bent in front of her on one knee. "I asked your dad if I could marry you, and he said yes. What do you say? Will you marry me?"

Marigold covered her mouth with her hand, then dropped it to her lap. "You asked my dad?"

"Yes. I had planned all of this, then the opportunity presented itself." He adjusted his knee. "You haven't answered me, and I'm not getting any younger."

"Yes, I'll marry you."

He scooted onto the bench and gathered her in his arms. Then he snagged a box from his pocket and opened the lid. A sparkling ruby, set in a rose gold crisscross pattern, with four small diamonds on each side glimmered in the moonlight.

"I know you aren't traditional, so I picked your birthstone for the ring." He slid the gem onto her finger.

Her eyes sparkled like the jewels on her finger. "I love it. You picked well."

He caressed her face with his hands and drew her into a sweet kiss.

CHAPTER THIRTY-SEVEN

Three weeks later

A light wind stirred the leaves around Marblehead Lighthouse, as waves splashed the rocks. Under the maple trees, Henry and Joel planted a trellis in front of several folding chairs. Alexa, Ivy, Violet, and Poppy tied ribbons and added black-eyed Susans, daisies, and lavender to the arched latticework.

Marigold huddled in the corner of the boat house to stay out of sight. Lucy tucked flowers in the bride's braid, then pressed a ring of daisies on her head. Her dress, a maxi-length cotton voile, dyed in various hues of light blue, draped to a longer curved hem in the back. Around a bouquet of daisies, black-eyed Susans, zinnias, and lavender, Sadie tied a strip of the same fabric Marigold had fashioned her dress from.

"Can I see the bride?" Marigold's dad's voice sounded through the doorway.

A soft smile crossed her face. "In a few minutes." Her dad agreed to take her down the aisle as long as she didn't mind pushing him in a wheelchair. Not strong enough to walk more than a few yards, he opted to stay safe from a fall and sit in the chair.

No matter how he maneuvered the lawn, Marigold loved the idea of her dad and sisters, along with her close friends, attending the wedding. She had considered getting married in the courtyard of his assisted living facility, but he assured her he wanted to make the trip to the lighthouse. In a few moments, at fifty-five years old, she would marry the love of her life. After all the years alone, other than a few close people, her life exploded with family and friends. Her dad, sisters, soon-to-be husband and stepdaughter, and of course her dear friends brought her true joy.

Thank You, Jesus, for Your patience with me and for blessing me in abundance, and praise God Christopher Downey chose not to press charges against Dad for using his grandfather's identity.

Instead, he was in the process of helping her father secure his original social security number and all the things he needed to complete his records as Nick Hayes.

Ivy poked her head in the boat house. "Johnny and the pastor are in place, along with Joel and Henry."

Lucy fussed with her yellow sundress. "We'll be there." She and Sadie, in her lilac dress, walked on the brick path to the trellis and met the men. A moment later, Marigold stepped outside, placed her hands on her dad's wheelchair, and rolled him to the front of the folding chairs between his daughters, and Alexa, Charlotte, and Levi.

The pastor asked, "Who gives this woman?"

Marigold's dad teared up, then said, "I do, along with her momma in heaven."

Tears coursed down Marigold's cheeks as she took her bouquet from Sadie and moved to Johnny's side. Handsome in navy jeans, a pale yellow button down, and a flowered tie. She clung to his hand. The pastor spoke the vows as they turned to a small table at the front with the framed piece of pottery Marigold gifted Johnny. She had painted the Greek word 'eros' and twined it with 'agape', their love and God's love joined in holy matrimony.

When the pastor pronounced them husband and wife, Johnny wrapped his arms around her, dipped her, and kissed her.

"Woo hoo!" A crowd of tourists visiting the lighthouse, along with Johnny and Marigold's guests, cheered the couple.

Through misty eyes, Marigold smiled and clung to Johnny's hand, something she planned to do for the rest of their lives.

God had known her story all along. With joy in her heart, she gazed at her husband and thanked Him for her happy ending.

The End

THANK YOU!

Thank you for reading this book from Mt. Zion Ridge Press.

If you enjoyed the experience, learned something, gained a new perspective, or made new friends through the story, could you do us a favor and write a review on Goodreads or wherever you bought the book?

Thanks! We and our authors appreciate it.

We invite you to visit our website:

www.MtZionRidgePress.com

and explore other titles in fiction and non-fiction. We always have something coming up that's new and off the beaten path.

And please check out our podcast

Books on the Ridge

where we chat with our authors and give them a chance to share what was in their hearts while they wrote their books, as well as fun anecdotes and glimpses into their lives and experiences and the writing process. And we always discuss a very important topic: *Tea!*

You can listen to the podcast on our website or find it at most of the usual places where podcasts are available online. Please subscribe so you don't miss a single episode!

Thanks for reading. We hope to see you again soon!

About the Author

If Penny Frost McGinnis could live in a lighthouse or on an island, she would. Instead, she and her husband are content to live in southwest Ohio and visit Lake Erie every chance they get. She loves God, adores her family and dog, indulges in dark chocolate, creates fiber arts, and enjoys watching baseball. She pens romance with a dash of mystery and the promise of hope. Her life's goal is to encourage and uplift through her writing.

Connect with Penny:
Website: https://www.pennyfrostmcginnis.com/
Facebook Author page:
 https://www.facebook.com/PennyFrostMcGinnisAuthor
Bookbub:
https://www.bookbub.com/profile/penny-frost-mcginnis
Goodreads:
https://www.goodreads.com/author/show/22233131.Penny_Frost_McGinnis
Newsletter:
https://landing.mailerlite.com/webforms/landing/g2z7q2

CPSIA information can be obtained
at www.ICGtesting.com
Printed in the USA
BVHW031113230323
661008BV00017B/730